I0603938

BONITA Y. MCCOY

BILLIONAIRE COWBOY NEXT DOOR

By Bonita Y. McCoy

To my husband, Victor, who taught me home isn't a place.

But store up for yourselves treasures in heaven, where moths and vermin do not destroy, and where thieves do not break in and steal. For where your treasure is, there your heart will be also.

Matthew 6:20-21

Chapter One

"Houston under water? Who would've ever thought?" The realtor shook her head as she offered the clipboard holding the rental agreement to Dan.

Dan Harris Thibodeaux stood on the lawn in front of a yellow house, holding a medium-sized, wooden crate on his hip. He steadied the pen against the clipboard and managed to sign the first sheet of the agreement. "I know. It's hard to believe." He looked up from the contract and surveyed the peeling paint on the house and the missing railing from around the porch.

The small two-bedroom bungalow was the only thing available anywhere near Silver Spur, his ranch. And even then, the town of Orange Blossom sat a good forty minutes east of his land close to the Sine River.

"We've been busy with all the evacuees coming and going through town." The realtor flipped the page for him and pointed to the line with the big yellow x by it. "You were lucky. This was the last of the rental houses my firm manages." She scanned the pages he'd signed before meeting his gaze.

"So, I heard." Dan handed her back the pen.

"Plus, it didn't hurt that you have family connections. I understand you're related to the late Mr. Harris. He was well thought of around our little town." The realtor gave him a friendly smile.

The Harris name carried weight in most corners of Texas. Dan had grown up with the special treatment that came with it. At times, it bothered him. Today, it worked in his favor.

"I'm his grandson. My mother was his only daughter." Dan moved the box from one hip to the other and ran his free hand through his dark brown hair. He didn't want to seem rude, but the wooden crate was getting heavy.

The realtor, Marilyn Kemp, folded the papers flat on the clipboard and initialed the appropriate lines. "Oh, I'm sorry for your loss. Is your father here with you?"

"No, both my parents have passed." He wished the woman would give him the key or open the door for him. "Would you mind?" He jostled the pine crate. "I need to get into the house if I'm going to unload the truck today. Promised the rental guy I'd have it back by five. I didn't want to keep it any longer than necessary since they're in such high demand."

"I know. Everyone's either trying to salvage what's left after Hurricane Harvey, or they're packing up and leaving for good. I'm glad you're staying." The forty-something agent tossed her bottle-blond hair and winked at him.

He frowned, the muscle in his jaw tightening. "It's a little hard to leave when you have a couple of thousand head of cattle scattered throughout the state." Dan shrugged and gave the realtor a complete once over. She was not his type, too unnatural. He could live with the fake blond hair coloring, but the heavy makeup put him off. Besides, she was a little older than the women he dated. Not that he did. Ever.

"Yes, I imagine it is." She hugged the clipboard to her chest with one hand and touched his forearm with the other. "So, you're a real live cowboy—riding the range, sleeping under the stars?"

"A rancher. Yes." Dan stepped back and took the crate in both arms forcing Marilyn to drop her hand. He'd been glad to find the pine crate buried among the rubble that had once been his family home. Like everything else, he'd thought he'd lost it forever.

Marilyn's voice took on a dreamy quality. "A billionaire. Right here in our little town."

"Could I have the key?" Dan's patience was wearing thin.

"Let me go open the door for you." She smiled and dropped the clipboard into her satchel.

"Oh, you don't have to do that. I can get it from here." Dan moved toward her, but she darted forward along the sidewalk leading to the rental.

"Nonsense. It's no problem." Marilyn stepped onto the white front porch that ran the length of the house.

Dan leaned forward to stop her, but she outmaneuvered him. He blamed his cargo.

"It's the least I can do to welcome you to Orange Blossom. I wouldn't want you to think we're not a friendly little town." With a slight tilt of her head, she flashed him a Miss-America smile. Pulling out a large ring of keys from her satchel, she flipped through them until she found the one she needed.

Dan put the box down on the top step. He thought about making a trip to the truck if she took too long, even if it seemed rude. His people skills—his ranch manager, Rod Carson, had told him—left a lot to be desired.

"Here we go." She pushed the door in with a swing of her hip. "It sticks."

"Good to know." Dan lifted the wooden box and carried it inside. He placed it on the floor beside a small table by the door.

"Let me give you a quick tour. Of course, this is the living room." She waved her hand in the general direction of the couch and armchairs centered around a well-worn coffee table. "This house has a bath and a half with two fully furnished bedrooms." She sashayed forward, opening doors as she went. Dan followed behind her.

"This is the half bath for guests. In case, you make friends while you're here." She gave him the once-over.

Dan squelched a groan. Did she just bat her eyelashes?

"This is the guest bedroom. You'll find it has lots of closet space for an older home." Dan stopped to peek inside. The room contained a double bed covered with a floral-patterned quilt and a dresser that looked like it came from the Great Depression era.

"And this is the master suite." A smile flittered across her lips. She swung open the door and proceeded inside.

Dan hesitated.

"Come on in. I won't bite." The realtor's Texas twang hit hard on the last word.

Dan stepped inside the door against his better judgement.

Marilyn moved to the large queen-size bed and tossed her satchel onto the mattress. Sitting on the edge, she made herself comfortable, crossing her long legs and letting her skirt fall right above her knee. "Just want to make sure the mattress is comfortable." She bounced in place, causing the box springs to squeak, then patted the spot next to her. "Come try it out yourself."

"Thanks, but I need to unload the truck." Dan pointed with his thumb over his shoulder toward the front of the house. Turning, he headed back down the short hall and out the door. Hopefully she'd get the hint.

A minute later, he turned to see the realtor emerge through the front door with her satchel slung over her shoulder. She tromped across the porch and down the steps, but her smile never wavered. "I left the keys on the table by the door along with your copy of the contract."

"Thanks." Dan shook his head in disbelief. The woman had made a pass at him, and now, she was all business. A smirk grew on his lips as he watched her from the corner of his eye.

She went straight to her silver SUV and tossed her satchel into the backseat. Hesitating, she pivoted on her high heels and called, "I'll be seeing you around." With a wave, she slipped into the driver's seat, revved the engine, and took off without a backward glance.

Dan chuckled. It never failed to amuse him when a woman thought all it took was a sweet smile and pretty legs to get to his money.

Hours later, boxes sat scattered around the floor in the living room, master bedroom, and kitchen. He'd placed them into the rooms as quickly as he could so he could return the truck by five. Once done, he'd been surprised by how little remained of his life.

Ms. Kemp's attempt at flirting had run him behind schedule. He'd barely made it in time. The customer who had wanted to rent the truck a day early was waiting at the counter when he arrived.

Now, he stood in the kitchen wondering where to start unpacking the few belongings he had. Lifting one of the larger boxes onto the counter, he peeked inside to see what it held. Finding the pots and pans he'd salvaged from the remains of his house, he unloaded them first.

Marge, his cook, had helped him prepare for his stay in the rental home. Loyal to a fault, she'd been right beside him as he worked to dig through the debris from the hurricane, looking for anything he could salvage and helping him search for the wooden box he needed in order to fulfill Lilly's last wish.

But after a few weeks, they hadn't found much. So, she shopped for him, buying what he needed to fill in the gaps. That's what most of the boxes held. A few old things from the past mixed with a whole lot of new.

Now, Marge had moved to be with her daughter in Alabama. She'd taken the retirement she should've taken three years ago but delayed because, as she told him, she didn't want to leave him all alone in that big house. Not after what had happened.

He smiled thinking of her tending to her grandchildren. She'd served his family well for twenty years, and she deserved every ounce of happiness the Good Lord gave her. Dan sighed. Thinking about Marge made him homesick but not for Silver Spur.

His gaze roamed from the pots and pans on the counter to the cardboard box sitting on top of the wooden crate next to the door. He'd placed it there when he unloaded the truck and planned to unpack that box last. But he couldn't wait; he longed to see her face.

Setting the skillet aside and moving across the

small space, he sidestepped the crumpled wads of packing paper and flattened boxes to reach the table beside the front door. Lifting the cardboard box, he walked to the couch and ran his hand across the top of the cushions, flinging paper and wads of tape out of the way.

Tired, he plopped down. The box sat heavy in his lap. Funny, how a lifetime can fit into one cardboard container. That's what had happened. He'd lived a whole lifetime in five short years.

He opened the lid. His sweet Lilly stared back at him. Her brown hair and tender eyes amplified the ache he carried. The years since her death hadn't lessened his love for her. He raised the picture from the box and held it in front of him. "Why'd you have to go and leave me?"

When no answer came, he put the picture on the coffee table and rummaged through the memories. The box contained photos, cards they had exchanged, and the wedding vows they had spoken to each other about their future. Hers written out on a napkin from one of their favorite diners. His printed out with every word spellchecked, every comma in place.

He loved their wedding picture, but the photo at the bottom captured her the way he remembered her, young and vibrant. Her brown hair blowing in the summer breeze as she smiled over her shoulder at him. They were sixteen, and she was all he could think about.

The knock on the door pulled him from his memories. How long had they been knocking? He jumped up, leaving everything strewn across the couch and the marred coffee table. "Coming."

From the ruckus on the other side of the door, he half expected to find a crowd gathered on his lawn. Surely word of his arrival hadn't spread that quickly. But small towns were notorious for their grapevines. And he didn't know enough about Marilyn to know if she participated in the local rumor mill or not.

Flipping on the porch light, he jiggled the door, struggling to open it. "Hold on, I'm coming." When it loosened, he gave it a quick jerk, and it swung wide.

To his surprise, instead of a mob, a tall, slender, blond stood on his porch. The woman held five leashes in one hand tethered to a bunch of misfit dogs of varying sizes and breeds. One of the dogs barked at him, his tail swishing from side to side against the white planks of the porch.

In her other hand, she held a plate covered with foil. His mouth watered at the delicious smell tickling his nose.

The woman smiled, pushing her bow-shaped lips into a sweet welcome.

Dan grinned. "Can I help you?" His curiosity stirred.

"Yes." She beamed.

The dogs pulled at their leashes. How she managed to hold onto the rowdy bunch was a mystery to him. He pressed his lips together to hide his amusement.

"I'm Nikki Davis. I live next door." She tilted her head in the direction of a blue bungalow with a front porch and a fenced-in yard, then yanked on the leashes. "Sit," the woman commanded before holding out the plate to him.

Not a single dog complied. One of them reached his nose toward the plate and took a sniff. She lifted the plate higher.

Dan straightened. "Is this for me?"

"Stop yanking, you guys," she said to the dogs.

The large white one sat. The dark one—so dark he looked indigo—jumped on Dan, his paws hitting Dan's chest. He pushed him down.

"Get down, Blue." The woman named Nikki pulled back on the leashes, sliding the dachshund across the wooden planks, sending his short legs scurrying. She held out the foil-covered plate again. This time Dan took it. "I thought you might need some dinner."

In the glow of the porch light, Dan spotted a yellow tabby sauntering across his lawn in the direction of his side yard.

Without warning, three of the dogs leapt toward the other end of the porch headed for the cat, jerking her away from the doorframe, out of sight.

Dan stepped across the threshold to see if she was still standing, or if all her pets had pulled her off the edge of the porch into the newly planted hedges. He found her stepping over leashes, trying to untangle the motley crew. "That's a lot of dogs."

"They're not all mine." She divided the leashes between both hands and maneuvered the dogs back to the door.

"Do you dogsit?" Dan asked.

She shuffled to the right trying to keep her footing. "No, I'm fostering some of the rescue animals."

The dachshund wound his leash around the legs of the collie causing both to roll. Meanwhile the large white dog decided to make herself at home and lie down.

"Those left homeless by Hurricane Harvey." Tripping, his neighbor fell forward.

Out of reflex, Dan caught her with his free arm while balancing the plate in his other hand. He pulled her to him to keep her from hitting the porch floor.

"Darn it, Snowball," she scolded, her eyes shifting from the pup to Dan's face, her hand planted on his chest.

Dan gave her a cat-that-ate-the-canary grin.

"Sorry, sorry." She stood on her own, pulling away from Dan's embrace.

"No problem." Dan liked how she smelled—fresh like sunshine. "I'm Dan..." He hesitated and didn't supply a last name. After all, he didn't want a repeat of his encounter with the realtor. "It's very nice of you to bring me dinner and all. I'd ask you in, but my place is a mess, and you—" Dan gestured to the band of misfit hounds.

"Oh goodness, no. Maybe some other time." She turned to go but stopped on the top step to wave good-bye to him over her shoulder.

Dan froze. For a split second, he caught traces of Lilly in her movements.

In that moment, the indigo dog yanked free and darted through the open door straight into Dan's living room. Bouncing on the couch, he sprang to the coffee table and skittered across it, his nails clicking against the hard tabletop. Papers and photos flew in every direction, scattering all over the area rug as he bounded back to the floor, dragging his leash behind him.

Dan closed his eyes pushing down the exasperation rising in him. Before he could react, the hound zoomed down the short hallway to the bedroom.

The woman swept past Dan hot on Blue's heels. As she did, she handed Dan the leashes of the other dogs.

"Blue? Blue, where are you? Bad dog. You're a bad dog."

There Dan stood, leashes in one hand and the plate of food in the other. How the tables had gotten turned on him, he didn't have a clue.

"Ahh…ma'am?"

"Nikki," she called from his bedroom.

He could hear her talking to the dog.

"Come on, Blue. Get off the bed."

Chapter Two

Nikki yanked on Blue's collar, but he didn't budge. She could hear her new neighbor trying to corral the rest of her motley gang into the living room. A grin swept across her lips, glad for him to have a go at her wild bunch. He'd realize it wasn't as easy as it looked, keeping this crew in check while balancing a plate of, well, anything.

She stepped onto the bed, and avoiding the ceiling fan, she pushed Blue from behind. He lay down and rolled over onto his back, so she could rub his belly. "Stupid dog." Irritated, she knelt beside him and scooted him across the bed, dragging the covers with him. Once he was close to the edge, she jumped off, grabbing his collar.

He rolled before she yanked, sending her sprawling onto the floor. When she looked up, she discovered her handsome neighbor leaning against the doorjamb with his arms crossed. A mischievous glint shone in his deep dark green eyes.

Blue rolled himself into the depths of the sheets.

"I planned on sleeping in that bed tonight."

Nikki ignored the amusement in his voice. "I'll be glad to make it for you. No problem."

"It's going to take more than making it to get rid of the dog smell."

"I bathed him yesterday. It shouldn't be that bad." Nikki waved off his complaint.

Blue stuck his nose out from the maroon sheets and whimpered.

"Dog, come!" Dan commanded.

Blue sprang off the bed and fell at Dan's feet. His tongue lolled to one side.

"Why didn't you do that in the first place?" Nikki pushed herself off the floor and wiped her hands across the rear of her jeans. "You could've saved me a lot of time." She didn't bother to wait for Dan's explanation but started fluffing the pillows and shaking out the comforter.

Dan walked over and took the comforter from her hands. His fingertips brushed hers. "Don't worry about it. I'll straighten it before I go to bed."

For some reason, Dan's nearness caused her stomach to flutter, and she became keenly aware of his broad shoulders. The urge to reach out and squeeze his bicep like an over ripe melon at the grocery store pulsed through her. Too impulsive for her own good, she clasped her hands behind her back. "I'd better go collect the rest of the crew." Nikki shot past Dan. His footsteps echoed behind her on the hardwood floor, mixed with the clickety-clack of Blue's nails.

When she entered the living room, she found two dogs on the couch, one on the rocker recliner, and one sprawled out on the area rug, all content to remain as they were. Nikki walked around the room, picking up leashes and dragging them one by one to a standing position.

Dan leaned over and scooped up Blue's leash.

Surveying the room, Nikki cringed. The photos and cards looked like confetti from a popper. Mixed in with the boxes and packing paper, the place could pass for a dump site. "Do you want me to come back and help you clean up?"

Dan lifted a palm. "No, I'll straighten after I eat." His words held no energy.

"I don't mind. After all, we did cause all this." Nikki bit her bottom lip, unsure how to make things better.

"What's under the foil?" He pointed to the plate sitting on the table by the door.

"Pardon?" Nikki asked, not following.

"What'd you bring me for supper?" Dan met her gaze.

For a moment, she thought she caught a flash of mischief in his deep green eyes. "Spaghetti. It's one of my four specialties."

"Oh, an Italian girl."

"No, Irish American, but who doesn't love a good

noodle? I'd better let you eat." Nikki weaved her way to the door, careful to step over the pictures and hoping the dogs wouldn't crush anything too important with their paws. Stopping, she faced Dan. "Again, I'm so sorry. I feel terrible."

"It'll be all right. I shouldn't have left everything out. Who knew, right?" He shrugged.

"Well, goodnight." Twisting the knob, she pulled the door, but it held tight. Scowling, she gave it another try.

"It sticks. Let me get that for you." Dan stepped around her and the dogs. Nudging the Chihuahua who sat in the way, he cleared the path with his foot to the door.

Nikki, absorbed in watching Dan and those biceps, didn't pay any attention to her charges until a wet clump of spaghetti noodles plopped onto her sandal. Cutting her eyes toward Blue, she found him licking his nose to dispose of the evidence. Noodles and sauce lay splattered on the hardwood floor.

How he'd gotten to the food without knocking over the plate, she had no idea. But before she could say anything, Dan jerked hard, and the door swung open.

Three of the dogs lunged onto the porch, pulling their leashes taut.

Dan grabbed her by the arm to keep her from tumbling forward over the other two dogs, Snowball and Blue, who stood licking Nikki's toes and the sauce on the floor.

Nikki squealed and laughed and screamed as their rough tongues lapped up every single blot of sauce on her foot.

Dan laughed too, deep, and rich. At least he was laughing.

~

Dan scratched at the red dots on his arm. He'd changed the sheets before falling into bed worn out, but these spots on his arms and legs this morning were probably flea bites. "Crazy dogs," he muttered as he headed out the front door carrying a bundle of cardboard, then he smiled.

The two mutts had taken care of the spaghetti in Nikki's sandal. But hearing her laugh and scream as their tongues washed over her toes had been the highlight of his evening. He chuckled at the thought of her dancing around as the dogs licked and sniffed.

Throwing the dismantled boxes into the back of his truck, he glanced toward the blue bungalow next door. No sign of his animal-loving neighbor. He plodded back into the house to get the next stack of cardboard and the trash bag full of paper and tape. On his way out, he grabbed his keys and cowboy hat. He needed to head over to the ranch to meet Rod. They planned to check the progress of the fencing before going to look at some grazing land for the few hundred head that were still in North Texas, so they could arrange to have the cattle shipped back.

Hurricane Harvey managed to wipe out his family

home and the bunkhouse. Fortunately, his men had been able to move several thousand head of cattle to safety before the storm hit. Overall, his company had fared well. The beef industry wouldn't be as affected as the oil industry, but there would be a recovery period.

When he returned to the driveway, he found Nikki standing on her front lawn with all her dog friends in tow. If it hadn't been for the dogs, he might not have recognized her.

"Morning," she sang out as she spotted him.

"What did you do to your hair?" Dan tossed the cardboard and trash bag into the bed of his truck and walked over to Nikki. "Are you bleeding?"

She scowled at him. "No, I dyed my hair red to bring awareness to the plight of the homeless animals. It'll wash out in a few days."

"It looks like that stuff I use to play with as a kid. Silly String." He reached out to touch it, but she slapped his hand away.

"You're not married, are you?" Nikki stood with her hip cocked, letting the dogs mill around in the grass. Barefoot, she wore a tee-shirt with a picture of Noah's ark on it and a pair of yellow shorts. Mid-September was tame in southern Texas.

"No." Dan shook his head and didn't feel the need to explain further.

"No girlfriend either, I bet."

"No. Why?" He didn't like the direction of her questions. Had she found out about him? "Are you asking because I said your hair looks like Silly String."

"Good, so you can be taught." She lifted her hand and pointed to the hat in his hand, almost strangling the Chihuahua at the end of the leash. "Are you some kind of cowboy or something?"

Dan hesitated. He'd seen how the realtor had acted knowing about his family money. He liked Nikki, carefree and pretty, but he didn't want her hanging around expecting something from him. "I work on a ranch." *Okay, that was true enough.*

"Interesting. Are you new to the area, or did Harvey leave you homeless too?"

"Harvey." He looked at the five dogs and found a new kinship with them. "I hadn't thought of myself as homeless, but I supposed I am." Dan chuckled at the idea of being a homeless billionaire.

"Do you like being a ranch hand?" Nikki leaned over to pick up a pile with a plastic bag. Dan couldn't help looking. She had nice legs, long and shapely.

"Yeah," He looked away as she stood. "I like working for myself and being outside."

"Oh, I thought ranch hands worked for somebody else."

"They do…but even so, there's a lot of freedom about what to do and when to do it. It's like you work for yourself. You spend time out alone."

"With cows?"

"And horses." He added with a smile. Where was this going?

Nikki tilted her head to one side. Dan could almost see the wheels turning. "I bet you're some kind of horse whisperer, aren't you?"

"I do okay with training horses." He didn't want to brag or anything, but he'd won the purse at a rodeo or two.

"In that case, you should help me at the Humane Society to place the abandoned animals. We could use someone who has a firm hand with them. And the way you handled Blue last night—well, that was amazing."

~

Nikki worked to hide her smile as Dan fidgeted with his hat, running his hand along the rim before sticking the hat on his head.

Blue sat at his feet with large, woeful eyes.

She recognized an easy mark when she met one, and she couldn't resist teasing him. *You are a wicked woman, Nikki Marie Davis.* But her inner adult couldn't stop the child in her from pulling Dan's chain. "You'd be a natural since you work with animals all the time. I bet it wouldn't take you any time to find a home for all 126 of my babies." She leaned over and patted the large white dog.

"Do not tell me you have 126 animals holed up in your backyard." He glanced toward the fence that separated the properties.

"No, the birds and cats are in the house." She paused for effect, eyeing him. "In the broom closet."

Dan's smile emerged free and easy. "You almost

had me there."

Nikki laughed. "The shelter does have a substantial number of animals, and some of the workers have taken home the overflow. If you looked, there might be a bird or two and a few cats lingering about." She didn't think it wise to mention Tinkerbelle.

"Isn't there a city ordinance or something about the number of animals a citizen is allowed to keep?"

"It's not like I have a horse in the living room. Though Snowball might count as one." Nikki squatted and ran her fingers over her lush white coat. "Besides, they're making allowances due to the extenuating circumstances. At least, that's what the mayor said in the newspaper last week."

"Were you joking about the number?"

A hint of compassion played in the tall man's face as he looked over the dogs she had on the leashes. Dan walked closer and squatted to pet the Chihuahua. Blue followed him. Dan rubbed his hands along Blue's neck and scratched his ears. Blue closed his eyes, and Nikki grinned knowing Dan had just made a friend.

"No, sorry to say. There are many pets that didn't make the cut in the family vehicle or had run off before the storm and couldn't be found, forcing owners to leave them behind." Nikki stood, realizing she had been talking longer than she intended. She didn't want to be late for work. "What time is it?"

Dan turned his wrist to check the time, flashing his watch.

It looked expensive. Maybe ranching paid better than she thought.

"Nearly nine." Giving Blue one last scratch between the ears, Dan rose. "Well, I'd better go. I need to drive to the ranch to check on some fencing."

"Oh, how are you with construction?" Nikki asked trying not to stare at his upper body. The sleeves of Dan's tee-shirt showed all the ripples of his biceps.

"I can drive a nail and use a saw."

Nikki forced herself to look at his face—that strong jawline and those fabulous eyebrows that shielded mischievous green eyes. "That's awesome. My church is forming a group Saturday to go to the Senior Citizen's Center to do some cleanup and repairs. Can you use a chain saw?"

"Any cowboy worth his salt can handle that grizzly beast—" Dan said doing a poor imitation of John Wayne. He pushed his hat back on his head for effect. "Lil' lady."

Nikki played along. "Aw shucks, sir. Can't you help a maiden in distress by splitting enough wood for the entire winter with your big strong muscles?" Nikki grabbed Dan's arm and squeezed his bicep.

Dan, with an eyebrow cocked, looked down at her hands.

She let go as if she'd touched fire.

At a loss for what to say, Nikki turned on her heels and dragged the five mutts behind her. Over her shoulder, she called, "I hope to see you Saturday with your chain saw." With a wave, she darted for the front porch. The heat rose from her neck to her face with each step, and she thanked the Good Lord above that Dan couldn't see the blush erupting on her cheeks, certain it matched the color of her hair.

Way to make a fool of yourself. She rolled her eyes and shook her head, telling herself not to get involved. *You've lost your heart one too many times. Besides, he's temporary. A few months and he'll be back at the ranch. Home where he belongs.*

Inside the safety of her front porch, she glanced through the screen for one last look.

She'd been right though about those biceps—solid.

Chapter Three

The receptionist area of the Cowboy Community Church of Orange Blossom radiated conformity. The light gray of the walls complemented the sky-blue carpet hugging the baseboards. The L-shaped counter sported a darker gray coloring with speckles in the Formica that bore several deep scratches from use over the years.

Nikki combatted the dullness of her surroundings by decorating her desk with assorted colors. Purples and varying hues of pink littered the surface of her area from a hot pink stapler to a lavender tape dispenser she'd found on sale at one of the local office-supply stores. Along with the splatters of color on her desk, she'd plastered several inspirational messages and posters on her bulletin board that hung on the wall beside her.

"No, Kim, I'll be sure to add him to the prayer list this Sunday." Nikki pressed the phone receiver to her ear. "I'll make sure he knows." She doodled on a sticky pad. "Sure, no problem. Bye, now." Nikki replaced the receiver as Pastor Connor entered the receptionist area from his office carrying a file. "I spoke with Kim. She wanted you to know that her brother, Tom, is back in the hospital. She's very upset. You might want to visit him next week if you have the time."

"I'll add him to my visitation list." Pastor Connor thumped the file in his hand on the counter before meeting her gaze. It was Friday afternoon, and his usual panic about Sunday's sermon had set in. "Nikki, are you sure you double-checked the references for me? All I need is a repeat performance of that sermon last fall. I received more emails over that mix-up than I did the year Tara Hunley played Mary in the Christmas pageant and sent the three wise men sprawling across the stage when they tried to take baby Jesus from her."

"Tara was always a little high-strung." Nikki took the papers from the pastor's hand and sat at her desk behind the counter. "I'll do another check and have it back to you in thirty minutes."

"Perfect." The older man sighed, running his hands through his thick white hair. "I'll be in my office when you're done." Turning, he strolled down the hallway.

"You humor him too much." Purdy lifted the partition and slid behind the counter where the desks were located. Purdy Thomas had worked for Pastor Connor for over twenty years.

"I know, but it's what we do. He panics about the references on Friday, and I do a cursory check for him.

That way I stay his favorite." Nikki flashed a smile at Purdy.

Purdy wagged her finger at her. "I got your number, young lady. Don't be thinking you'll grab my job one minute before I'm ready to retire."

"Who me?" Nikki widened her eyes, giving Purdy a Tweety-Bird look.

Sarah Thomas, Purdy's fourteen-year-old granddaughter, stepped out of the copier room with the folded bulletins for Sunday, catching the last of the conversation. "I can't imagine you retired, Grams."

"Me neither," Nikki said.

Sarah smiled, glancing at the bulletins in her hands. "Well, that's another hour towards my Silver Medallion community service." Walking to the counter, she laid the bulletins in three neat stacks.

"So, what's the grand prize this semester?" Nikki asked.

"A new computer, a hundred dollars that we're supposed to use toward college—" Sarah made air quotes with her fingers—"And a silver medal."

Nikki teased. "You must really want that silver medal, putting in two afternoons a week here."

"It's the computer she's after." Purdy grabbed the bulletins and placed them in a basket. "Her computer is too slow. Plus, she's helping at a few other places around town, like the Senior Citizen's Center. You know lots of people need help after the hurricane."

"Oh, maybe I need to enter the contest." Nikki's

eyes widened. "I could use a newer computer."

"Nope, it's only open to eighth graders who live in Orange Blossom. So far, there are five of us who are in the lead."

"Don't worry, Sarah. The way you're racking up the hours. I'm sure you'll do fine." Turning toward her screen, Nikki pulled up the needed document. She knew the references were right—she'd checked them twice already, but she'd do it once more to appease Pastor Connor.

As she flipped through the large Bible, the door from the parking lot swung open. Glancing up from the page, she discovered Marilyn Kemp leaning on the counter, out of breath.

Purdy can handle this one. Nikki didn't like Marilyn. She'd read all about loving thy neighbor, but Marilyn made it near impossible.

"Hello, ladies. I hope y'all are doing fine and well."

"We are," Purdy answered short and sweet.

Sarah grabbed the bulletins and moved into the copier room, shutting the door behind her.

Nikki suppressed a giggle.

"What on earth have you done to your hair?" Marilyn asked.

Not wanting to get too deep into her reasoning, Nikki decided to give Marilyn the abbreviated version. "It's something we're doing at the Animal Ark Rescue." Pushing a strand of her hair behind her ear, she added, "It'll wash out in a day or two."

"Oh, well, let's hope so." Marilyn slung her oversized satchel onto the counter in front of her. "So, I thought you'd like to know that a most eligible bachelor has moved into town. He's good-looking and loaded." Marilyn's eyes widened with excitement.

"And why would I want to know that? I'm sliding towards sixty-five faster then I care to mention." Purdy stuck a pen behind her ear, giving her a too-busy-to-be-bothered look. "And I'm most certainly not interested in getting involved with anyone now." Purdy turned and strode to her desk. Sitting, she pulled out the financial books, the big thick heavy ones.

Nikki hoped this would deter Marilyn. It did not.

"He's not your age, but I thought Nikki might be interested. Besides, don't you go on those visits once a week inviting people to church?" Marilyn shot Purdy a look. "I mean, we wouldn't want him to miss out on our upcoming bachelor auction and picnic for the center simply because he's new in town, would we?"

Purdy's lips stretched tight into a frown. "No, I guess *we* wouldn't."

Nikki thought about stepping in to help, but before she could, Purdy pulled open one of her desk drawers and dug out a stack of cards. Nikki recognized the light blue color of the newcomer cards. They blended with all the blue and gray surrounding her. Walking over to Marilyn, Purdy set the pile in front of her on the gray counter. "Here, feel free to fill one out."

"Oh, that's a good idea." Marilyn snatched a card from the stack. Fishing out a pen from her satchel, she filled out the form.

Nikki shook her head in amazement at the glow on Marilyn's face. The woman looked as if she'd won the lottery.

A twinge of pity for the poor guy stirred in her heart. It had to be the man who'd bought the Mitchell mansion a few weeks before the hurricane. That place must've cost a small fortune. Thankfully for him, it withstood the 120 mile-an-hour wind.

"All right," Marilyn held out the blue card and waited for Purdy to come and take it. "Be sure to have Pastor Connor go over and invite him to church."

"Aye-aye, captain." Purdy scowled, scanning the card. "Why is this so important to you? Worried for his soul?"

Marilyn swatted away her words. "Of course not, he's an angel. I just need a way to get to know him better, and church is the perfect place to meet men."

"Well, you could invite him to church yourself. You don't need to have the pastor do it. Plus, that would give you a great excuse to see him," Nikki teased.

"I can't." Marilyn's bottom lip protruded, forming a pout. "We got off on the wrong foot."

"Oh, I see," Nikki pressed her lips together trying hard to keep her thoughts to herself. She could only imagine what Marilyn had done to the poor man.

"Maybe, it'll work out."

Marilyn slid her satchel from the counter and slung the strap across her shoulder. "Keep your fingers crossed," showing them her own crossed fingers.

~

Dan parked as close to the Cowboy Community Church office as possible. But a horse trailer parked lengthwise and a silver SUV that resembled the one his realtor drove took up most of the spaces.

He groaned as he grabbed his cowboy hat from the passenger seat of his truck. Not again. The bad thing about small towns—there was nowhere to hide.

Ambling past the horse trailer, he lingered to admire it, peeking in the windows. It looked new. He kicked the tires, ran his hand over the paint job. Shoot, he even read the license plate, LUV2RIDE. But he could only stall for so long before he'd have to go inside.

He gripped the metal handle and pulled open the door, hoping all the while he was wrong. Stepping over the threshold, he stopped short, avoiding a collision with the blond-haired realtor by inches.

Marilyn glanced at him and beamed. "Well, what do you know? Here is one of our newest members of our community. Get in here and let me introduce you to these wonderful ladies."

Dan steeled himself as she trotted over and grabbed his arm. He removed his hat and tried to straighten his hair, but it was impossible with Marilyn hanging on him.

"Ladies, I'd like to introduce you to Dan Harris Thibodeaux."

"Nice to meet you. I'm Purdy Thomas." A woman with salt-and-pepper hair stood and walked over to the counter with her hand stuck out.

Dan, unsure of what to do, extracted his arm from Marilyn's grasp and took it. "Nice to meet you, too." Giving Purdy's hand a firm shake, he smiled at the spunky woman. A flash of bright red hair behind a computer monitor caught his eye. He leaned on the counter to keep Marilyn from reattaching herself to his limb. "Well, hey there, neighbor."

Nikki glanced from the large book she studied. "Oh, hi. What brings you here?"

"Oh, you two have met?" Marilyn asked, her tone flat.

"Yeah, Nikki brought me dinner and a show last night," Dan teased. A chuckle escaped his lips.

Nikki nodded. "It was entertaining, trying to get Blue off your bed. You should've seen Dan. He was a natural with him."

Purdy's brow knit together, and she looked between Dan and Nikki. "You took him dinner? But you don't cook."

Nikki's face flushed.

Marilyn scowled. "You were in his bedroom?"

"We were getting Blue. When Dan opened his front door, Blue invited himself in."

Dan ignored Marilyn's comment and turned to Purdy. "She's a good cook. I'd say her spaghetti hit the spot." He winked at Nikki.

A grin spread across her bow-shaped lips. "You're not going to let me live that down, are you?"

"It's not every night a fella has a pretty girl hopping around his living room, screaming."

Purdy and Marilyn exchanged baffled looks.

Nikki rolled her eyes. "That dog is going to be the death of me."

"Let's hope you can find that dog a home before he takes over Dan's." Marilyn sidled up next to him touching her shoulder to his.

A twinkle appeared in Nikki's eyes. "You know *you* could take Blue. I'm sure he'd be a great watchdog." Nikki's grin widened. "And he'd make you a loyal companion."

Marilyn shrieked. "I don't need some flea-bitten mutt, digging holes in my professionally landscaped flowerbeds."

Dan smothered a chuckle with a cough. "Don't you want a guard dog?"

"I wouldn't need a guard dog if I had someone looking out for me." Marilyn leaned more heavily against him.

The purr in her voice caused Dan to straighten. His muscles stiffened, and he took a step back.

Marilyn lurched forward, but the counter kept her from losing her balance. She glanced at him. "The three of us were talking about the bachelor auction and picnic the church is having in October. We're raising funds to repair the Senior Citizen's Center. Since you're not married, you ought to volunteer to be auctioned off."

"I don't think so."

"But you have to. It's for a good cause, and we need every available bachelor. There aren't many in Orange Blossom. Besides, I'm in charge of finding the volunteers." Marilyn stuck out her bottom lip in what Dan assumed was a pout. "Pretty please," she added and wrapped her hands around his bicep.

Nikki popped out of her chair and marched to the counter. "For goodness' sake, the man said no," Nikki said. "Leave it alone. If he decides it's a good cause, he'll do it." Turning her attention to him, she asked, "Right, Dan? Surely, you'll sleep on it before deciding."

Great, two against one. What was he supposed to do now?

"Okay, ladies, I'll think about it, but no promises."

Nikki's face filled with delight, leaving Dan a little wobbly in the knees.

"Oh, good. That's all I ask." Marilyn gave Dan's arm a little squeeze before she released him. "I need to go. But it was good to see you. I'm sure I'll bump into you again soon." She nudged him with her shoulder.

Dan nodded.

"And Purdy, don't forget to talk to the pastor about that little matter we were discussing."

"Sure thing," Purdy said still holding the card Marilyn had filled out.

No one spoke until the door swung closed behind her.

"She sure is something, isn't she?" Dan remarked.

"She most certainly is." Purdy laid the newcomer card on the counter in front of Dan. "Now, what can we do for you?"

"My pastor knows yours and recommended I come introduce myself. He thought Pastor Connor might be able to help me with a situation I have." Dan wasn't about to delve into his personal life here in the middle of the church office. "Is he here?"

"Yes, he is here. Let me go check with him and see if you'll need to make an appointment or if he can see you now. Wait here." Purdy lifted the hinged counter and walked down the hall to the pastor's office.

"So, I thought you worked at the Humane Society." Dan glanced down at the card in front of him wondering why Purdy had placed it there. To his surprise, he read his name.

"No, I work at The Animal Ark Rescue, a no-kill rescue shelter. We're working in conjunction with the Humane Society to find homes for the animals left homeless by Hurricane Harvey." Nikki turned and walked back to her seat.

Dan grabbed the card and examined it. "Well, what are you doing here, then?"

Nikki raised her eyebrows as she peeked around

the monitor. "Working."

He wasn't slow, but Nikki jumbled his thinking. "Let me get this straight. You work at the shelter, but you also work here at the church?"

"Yes, I have two part-time jobs. I tried to get a full-time job with the shelter, but they didn't have the funds. So, Pastor Connor needed someone young to help out around here, and he hired me. I work on the website and run the social media accounts. Those sorts of things."

Purdy called down the hall. "Don't be patting yourself on the back for being young." She appeared moments later. "I might think you're calling me old."

Dan chuckled as Purdy pinned Nikki with a glare.

"The pastor can see you now. Go on in."

Dan stuffed the card with his information into the back pocket of his jeans, glad he had come when he did to meet the pastor. He didn't need his family connection getting out, or he'd have no peace while he was in Orange Blossom.

A teenager poked her head out of the copier room and surveyed the receptionist area. "Is she gone?"

Nikki grinned. "Yeah, Sarah, the coast is clear. You can come out."

Dan smiled at the brown-haired teen. How nice it would be if he could hide when he saw Marilyn. Heading down the hallway, he shifted his focus to the matter at hand. This visit wasn't about introductions but rather about saying good-bye. Maybe Pastor Connor could help him move on. He'd waited three years, but after the scare of almost losing the crate in the hurricane, the time had come.

Chapter Four

Dan sat in his truck looking at the information on the card he suspected Marilyn had filled out. If word got out that he was well off and unattached, he'd never have any peace. Ladies turned so unladylike when money was involved. At least that had been his experience.

And admittedly, he had limited experience. From the time he and Lilly were kids, he only had eyes for her. They grew up together and dreamed about their future together. They'd had five years as man and wife. Then, she was gone.

Dan tore the card into pieces and stuffed them into his front pocket.

Pastor Connor had understood. He'd listened to Dan explain what he needed, and why it had to be now. The hurricane had taken so much from him. It had almost stolen Lilly. No more putting it off, no matter how much it hurt. He rubbed his hand over his eyes and drew in a deep breath to clear his mind.

Shaking off his mood, Dan jumped out of the truck and strolled to the mailbox in front of the yellow rental. Twilight painted the evening sky with swirls of grays and pinks as the frogs croaked a familiar song. Pulling the mail from the box, Dan sorted through it as he walked toward the house. Circulars from the local stores, a few addressed to the previous occupant, made up the majority of the post. A notice from the water company updated everyone on its progress of replacing damaged pipes and listed the communities with safe drinking water.

Dan bounded up the steps to the front porch without looking up and lurched forward when his feet hit an immovable object. Catching himself on the post, he groaned when he discovered his feet entangled with the hound from next door.

Blue moaned and rolled over onto his back so Dan could rub his tummy.

"Why you mangy mutt? How'd you get out?" Scowling, he scanned Nikki's yard but didn't see her anywhere around, but her car was in the driveway. Leaning over, he scratched under the dog's chin.

The pup didn't move anything but his tail, which swished back and forth across the white planks of the porch. Dan could've sworn the dog smiled. "Oh, all right, but just for a minute or two." Dan sat down on the top step next to the sprawled-out pup. He ran his hand down the slick fur of the hound dog and rubbed his soft belly.

The dog wiggled like it tickled. Dan rubbed a little harder, and the dog started a low growl. Dan found himself laughing along with the dog. After a few minutes, Dan stood. "We'd better take you back to Nikki's. I'm surprised she hasn't missed you yet."

Jiggling the front door open, he set the mail on the small table right inside the living room. Blue bolted through the crack, but Dan grabbed his collar. "Oh no, you don't. I've got enough flea bites. I don't need anymore." In one move, he pulled Blue out and closed the door.

"Now, let's see if Nikki is home and maybe cooking." The thought of a hot home-cooked meal appealed to him since the one offered him yesterday had ended up on the floor. "Come on, boy." Dan hustled down the steps but stopped short when he spotted the small hedges, or what used to be the hedges, strewn in front of the flowerbeds.

"What have you done?" Dan scolded, holding an uprooted hedge in his hand.

Blue crouched to the ground peering up at Dan with soulful eyes.

"Don't think looking so pitiful is going to get you out of this, you bag of fleas." Sighing, Dan dropped the plant to the ground and strode over to Nikki's front door, making sure the pup followed. Stepping onto her front porch, he pounded on the wooden door.

Pandemonium ensued. Barking, squawking, and a sound he couldn't identify rang out causing Blue to add his own howl to the mix.

Nikki yelled something, but he couldn't make it out.

"What?" He hollered at the door.

The voice got louder. "Go. Around. Back."

Dan looked at Blue. "Come on, boy. Looks like we're back-door guests." He jogged around the side of the house and found the wooden gate shut tight. But he noticed a gaping hole in one of the boards. He eyed the hole then Blue. *Yeah, Blue could fit. Must be how he escaped.*

Dan caught sight of Nikki's flaming red hair through the slats of the gate before she opened it.

"Hey. What brings…" Nikki pushed the gate open. "Blue."

"Yeah, he was waiting for me on my porch when I got home. He took it upon himself to dig up the new hedges."

Nikki used her leg to hold back the large white dog that stood at her side. Her flexed muscles caught his attention. He wished she'd wear jeans instead of shorts.

"Sorry. I'll try to do better keeping everyone in the yard."

Dan stepped inside the fence followed by Blue and shut the gate. He forced himself to keep his eyes on her face. "I think he wiggled through that hole." Pivoting, he walked over to the broken board and swiveled to face her.

"Oh." Nikki followed him, a train of four dogs behind her.

"I can fix it if you want. It won't be my best work, but it'll keep him in." Dan nodded towards Blue. "And out of my hedges."

"That'd be great." Nikki touched his arm. "Thanks."

A tingle surged through him, making him aware of how close she stood.

She dropped her hand.

He squatted to inspect the hole putting him at eye level with those legs. After a quick glance at the hole, he stood. "No problem. I have tools and some scrap wood in the back of my truck."

Nikki stepped closer to him. He caught the smell of her citrusy perfume on the light evening breeze. "I appreciate it. I have a hammer and nails somewhere, but they might be with the stuff at the church. Remember I mentioned we've been helping with a rebuild."

"Yeah, I remember. That sounds like something Pastor Connor would put together."

"It's great. A group from one of the cowboy churches in Louisiana comes over to help. Since Hurricane Katrina, they're kind of the experts." Nikki stopped, tilted her head toward him, and squinted her eyes. She stood waiting for his reaction.

Dan didn't want to disappoint her, but he had so much work to do at his own place. And he hated leaving all the long hours to others. He'd managed to sidestep the invitation once, but he wasn't sure how to explain his situation to her without lying, which he refused to do. Or reveal who he was, which went against his better judgement. Neither prospect sounded good to him, so he opted to ignore the hint. "I'd better go get the tools and wood."

~

Nikki watched as Dan made a hasty retreat. She hadn't meant to touch his arm or stand so close. So, maybe she had picked one of her nicer flowy shirts to wear hoping she might run into her new neighbor. But she wasn't really that attracted to him, not really. Sure, he had rock-solid biceps, but so what? Lots of guys did. And, he was renting, just passing through.

Purdy asked a million and one questions after he had left the office. Where was he from? What did he do? Did you hear him call you pretty?

Yes, she'd heard. It had made her heart skip a beat or two. Dan Thibodeaux thought she was pretty. Now, what was she supposed to do with that? After all, she'd sworn off men. Her fragile heart had been broken like a jackhammer tearing through concrete one too many times. She didn't need to do a foolish thing like flinging her heart out there again.

The love of a dog—now that was true and uncomplicated. The love of a man left you tangled up, disappointed, and confused to the point of not being able to recognize who you were. No thank you.

Dan returned with the needed tools. Placing a scrap of wood over the hole, he took two nails from his pocket and placed them in his mouth. Taking the hammer in one hand, he pressed the wood against the broken plank, and with the other hand, he pulled one of the nails from his lips.

"You know I'm sure Pastor Connor wouldn't mind if you wanted to tag along with us tomorrow."

"Tag along for what?" Dan mumbled around the nail in his mouth.

"You know, our community-rebuilding project. We'll be going over to the Senior Citizen's Center to do some cleanup and tear down part of the building that has water damage."

"I thought you said it was a rebuild project." Dan swung the hammer at the nail he held tight between his thumb and finger.

"One of the buildings near the river received water damage from the surge. We need to tear out the sheetrock before we can rebuild."

"I'm in the same boat." Dan tapped away at the nail. "That's why I'm renting. My place is being rebuilt too."

"Oh, do you have your own home?" Nikki noticed his hesitation. She didn't think it was a difficult question. "I mean, I don't know the setup for a ranch hand. I assumed you lived on the—you know—ranch."

"Well, that should hold." Dan stood and stretched, placing his hand on his lower back. "Do I smell something?"

"Oh, no." Nikki raced across the yard to the house, letting the screen door slam behind her. When she opened the back door that led into the kitchen, a cloud of dark smoke billowed out, and the sizzling sound of scorching food met her ears. She twisted the knob on the stove and grabbed the metal handle of the pan. Screeching, she dropped the pan with a clank onto the stove. Lurching for the sink, she twisted the faucet and stuck her throbbing hand under the cool water.

"Are you all right?" Dan stood in the back door.

"I'm fine. Stupid, but fine." Nikki inspected her hand. Blisters raw and red clustered on her palm at the base of her fingers.

Dan closed the distance between them. "Here, let me look at that." He cupped her hand in his.

She studied him as he examined the burns on her hand. He had a five o'clock shadow that accentuated his firm jaw line, and his brown hair hung in his dark green eyes. Her fingers itched to push it aside.

He shifted his weight and moved her hand closer to the window. His leg pressed against hers, his arm tight against her own.

She tensed.

"I'm sorry. Did I hurt you?" Dan asked unaware of the effect he had on her.

"No." She pulled her hand from his. "It'll be fine."

Dan didn't look convinced. "Do you have an aloe-vera plant? That always helps with burns."

"I'm not much of a gardener." She moved away from him to the stove, needing room. "My plants tend to die of neglect. I'm more of an animal person. They can remind me to feed them."

The pan lay cockeyed against the burner with the oil and food pooling to one side near the edge. She reached for it but stopped to pull a potholder from a nearby hook.

"So, I've noticed." Dan took the potholder out of her hand. "You need to take care of those burns. Do you have any ointment?"

"Yes, it's in the bathroom."

"Sit down, and I'll go get it."

Nikki obediently sat in one of the yellow chairs at her small dinette. The set had been her grandmother's when she lived in the house, yellow and tan Formica with yellow seats.

Dan returned with the ointment and a large Band-Aid. He knelt on one knee in front of her and took her hand, turning it over to where the blisters were visible.

"I see you rifled through my medicine cabinet." Why had she said that? She didn't care.

"You've had a wrestling match on my bed. I think we're even." Dan's smile started at the corners of his mouth and spread all the way to his eyes.

Nikki drew in a sharp breath, startled by the compassion she found in them.

"Sorry." He rubbed the ointment onto her hand.

"No, it's fine." She squirmed.

He held her hand firm as he put the bandage in place.

This wasn't supposed to happen, all the flutters, all the blushing. *He's temporary, for goodness' sake.* She just met him. But her eyes linked with his, and she stilled.

"Better?"

"Uh-huh." She didn't move, not wanting to break the connection.

Dan ran his thumb across the palm of her hand and leaned closer to her.

Goose bumps emerged across her skin. For the briefest of moments, Nikki played with the idea of kissing those inviting lips.

Multiple barks sounded from the yard, breaking the moment.

Like a man waking from a dream, Dan surveyed the kitchen. "I have to go." He shot up and darted for the back door.

The Chihuahua ran in, as he went out.

Nikki jumped up and followed him. By the time she reached the screen door, he stood fighting Snowball at the gate. "What about tomorrow?"

"Tomorrow?" Dan yelled above the barking.

"Do you want to go to the Senior Citizen's Center to help?" Blue jumped on him, pinning him against the fence, licking his face. The dachshund and the collie joined the party. Nikki sprinted to the gate to rescue him from the ensuing pack.

"Down, you mangy mutt," Dan commanded, regaining his footing. "Can you keep this dog off me?"

Nikki grabbed Blue's collar and pushed against Snowball trying to keep her back. She winced when her bandaged right hand hit the collar. "You bet I can."

"Now, what were you asking?" He glowered at her; his hands propped on his hips.

"Nothing, it's not important." The gate slammed, leaving Nikki wishing she'd never bothered with her handsome, irksome neighbor. "Jerk."

Chapter Five

Dan berated himself all the way to his house, through the sandwich he made for dinner, and late into the night.

Jerk. Nikki had nailed it. He needed to get his emotions under control. She made him feel things he hadn't since Lilly. Nikki treated him nice for the sake of being nice. She didn't want anything…well, for the most part. She wanted to be a good neighbor and include him in the community. Like a regular guy, and isn't that what he wanted? To be another ordinary…guy?

Dan dragged himself out of bed. Digging through his dresser, he pulled out an old raggedy tee-shirt. If he was going to be working outside at the Senior Citizen's Center, he'd better dress for the heat of the day. Fall mornings in Texas could be crisp, but the temperature would rise throughout the day hitting somewhere in the eighties.

Dan poured a cup of coffee for himself in a go mug

and a second one for Nikki. The least he could do was deliver his apology with a cup of coffee as a peace offering. No matter how hard he tried, he couldn't erase the look on Nikki's face from the previous night from his mind. The knot in his stomach tightened. He hated guilt. He pounded on the front door, hoping he had caught her before she'd left. He needed to be working on his own land today, but—

The door cracked open. Nikki poked her head out, her hair no longer red. "What do you want?"

He could hear the dogs in the background. "I brought you coffee."

"I don't drink coffee." She stepped back and pushed the door shut.

"Wait. I—" The door stopped. Dan looked down at his boots and shifted his weight. "I need to apologize."

The door opened a little wider. Nikki stood in the doorway dressed in jeans and a Texas A&M tee-shirt that hugged her curves. Cowboy boots adorned her feet. "I'm listening." She crossed her arms.

The Chihuahua appeared beside her.

"I'm sorry for the way I shot out of here last night."

She glared at him, unmoved.

Snowball pushed the door all the way open with her nose. Lying in front of it, she functioned as a doorstop.

"I'm sorry for what I said about Blue. He's a fine dog. I was aggravated, that's all."

"Aggravated about what?" Nikki lifted an eyebrow.

Dan ran his hand across the back of his neck. He'd lain awake all night thinking about that very question. What had set him off-kilter? Now, standing here in the morning light face-to-face with Nikki, he understood what had thrown him. But she didn't need to know how attracted he was to her. Nope. 'Cause this wasn't going anywhere. Neighbors, yes. Possibly friends, but that was it. "Things. But I shouldn't have snapped at you or Blue."

She scowled. "Well, that's not much of an answer or an apology."

"May I come in, please? I thought I might tag along with you this morning to the center." He expected this to please her, maybe melt away her anger.

Instead, she stayed planted in the doorway. "Why?"

Confused, he asked, "Why what? I thought you wanted me to come help."

"Why do you want to come?" She leaned against the doorjamb, crossing her right foot over her left, nailing the point of her boot to the floor.

"Really, the third degree? I haven't even had my coffee yet. And I do drink coffee." He held up the travel mug.

"Fine. Go drink your coffee at your house. But don't come to the workday if you're doing it for me. You're supposed to do it out of Christian charity—love for your neighbor, and that sort of thing. If you're after brownie points with me, or if it's some sort of attempt to make up for your behavior yesterday, don't bother." Nikki straightened and grabbed the door to shut it.

Dan stepped onto the threshold and held his palm against the door. "I'm not doing it for you. Or at least not only for you."

Nikki gripped the door, refusing to meet his gaze.

"It's just that I want to help. I'm displaced too, remember? I know how it feels to see your home in pieces, strewn across acres, even miles."

Nikki glanced at him. Her eyes soft with mercy as she bit her bottom lip. Indecision played on her face. "Okay, you can come. On one condition."

"What's that?" Dan asked.

A smile tugged at the corners of her mouth. That lovely bow-shaped mouth.

"I need to use your truck."

~

Sucker was the first word that popped into his brain.

Dan rested his hand on the steering wheel and glanced at Nikki sitting in the passenger seat of his truck. The Chihuahua squirmed in her lap with his head hanging out the window. The crisp morning air rushed through the cab causing goosebumps. He turned onto Deadwood Drive and headed towards Harry's Hardware store. How had all this happened?

The dog kennels in the bed of the truck shifted

when he rounded the next curve. They had loaded six cats each in their own carrier back there as well as a pack of dogs. He had drawn the line at the two parakeets.

"I sure do appreciate you giving all of us a lift to the Senior Citizen's Center. It's a sure thing I'll be able to place some of the animals with some of the volunteers working today. I placed four of them last weekend when we were working over at Sue Vann's house. Even Sue took a cat."

"Great…that's great." Dan leaned forward and adjusted the heat. At least his feet would be warm.

Maneuvering one last curve, he drove into the parking lot of Harry's Hardware store. Nikki moved the Chihuahua from her lap and cuddled him in her arms. "I'll put him in the back with the others." She pushed open the door as Dan turned off the engine.

Dan had counted seventeen animals in total. The girl wasn't an animal lover; she was an animal hoarder. And where they had all come from, he couldn't fathom. Her house wasn't that big. He'd watched in amazement as she carried one after another out the door. Now, he had an idea of how Noah felt with his boatload of critters.

When he'd asked, she assured him that some of the animals came from other members of the rescue shelter who were fostering. But he wasn't sure he bought that story.

Nikki stood by the truck and propped her elbow on

the driver's side window leaning in a bit. "Aren't you coming in? Didn't you say you needed a pair of work gloves and oil for the chain saw?"

"Yeah, I did say that." But Dan didn't move. He crossed his arms and stared at Nikki. "You know what? I feel like I've been hoodwinked."

Nikki pulled back and stuffed her hands in her jean pockets. "How so?" Her brows furrowed, forming a tight V between her bright blue eyes.

"Don't play innocent with me—you had all this planned. You had to know I'd feel terrible for snapping at you, and you used it to your advantage." Dan wanted to kick himself for falling for her nicey-nicey act. *No one brings their neighbors dinner anymore.*

"You're right. Busted." She placed her forearm across her brow in mock distress. "I planned the whole thing. You getting mad. You storming off. You coming over this morning to apologize. You caught me. I'm an evil genius who can manipulate people's thoughts." Nikki dropped her arm and grinned.

"Okay, so you didn't plan it, but it sure feels like you took advantage of it."

"Maybe a little, but I had decided to ask you to use your truck yesterday. Before you got nasty. I was finishing breakfast before coming over to ask." A slow grin traveled from her lips to her eyes. "I can't help it if you were impatient and beat me to the punch."

Dan leaned his arms on the steering wheel, trying hard to hang onto his momentary ire. If he could be irritated with her, perhaps he'd be able to stop those other twinges that happened whenever she was around.

"My usual ride had to help family this weekend. So…I figured you had this little darlin' sitting in the driveway right next door." Nikki moved closer to the window. "Come on." She nudged his elbow with hers. "You're not really mad over this, are you?"

"No, I just expected to be working my own land today. Not chauffeuring a bunch of flea-ridden animals around." Dan hesitated and hoped Nikki hadn't caught his reference to his *own land*.

"Look, I told you if you came along, to do it for the right reasons. So, don't blame me if you're going to get into trouble with your boss. I didn't know you were supposed to be working today."

The sound of a car engine caught Dan's attention. The vehicle pulled into the parking space behind the truck, so he couldn't see the car without looking into the rearview mirror, but Nikki rolled her eyes and let out a groan. That couldn't be good.

"Hurry, jump out of the truck." She opened the door for him.

Dan grabbed his keys from the ignition and hopped out without question.

As they neared the door, he opened it, letting Nikki enter first. He glanced over his shoulder before going in and spotted a silver SUV. Marilyn.

"Thanks," Dan whispered into Nikki's ear as they stepped across the threshold into the hardware store.

"Now we're even," She whispered over her shoulder. "Another one of my evil plots."

When Dan made eye contact with her, she wiggled her eyebrows at him. The gleam of mischief in her eyes made them sparkle.

His heart crackled with electricity. Man, was he sunk.

Chapter Six

Nikki moved toward aisle five in Harry's Hardware Store where they stocked the nails. Passing aisle three, she spotted Dan inspecting a pair of work gloves. At that moment, Marilyn appeared on the same aisle, feigning surprise at finding him there.

Suppressing a giggle, she hustled to the safety of aisle five before Marilyn dragged her into the conversation. She had to hand it to the woman. When Marilyn was on the hunt, she became unstoppable. Nikki figured her persistence made her a good realtor. But not a great date.

After making the rounds through the back aisles of the hardware store and grabbing the bucket of nails, she headed to the counter and planted herself near the cash register. She pushed the bucket onto the counter and off to the side with her other items, making sure not to use her bandaged hand. The evil thought she'd entertained between aisles five and seven was too rich to ignore. Nikki couldn't help herself. Dan wouldn't appreciate her humor, but the situation was too perfect, and it needed to be done.

She hated to admit it, but she agreed with Marilyn. And with her here, they could mount a two-pronged attack. She'd stayed away from the subject of the bachelor auction yesterday, giving Dan time to warm up to the idea. Her first impression of him was that of a loner, not keen on the spotlight. But they needed Dan in the bachelor's auction. He was too good-looking to sit on the sidelines. At least, she thought so. Besides, all the money went to the Senior Citizen's Center to pay for the rebuild of the interior. Plus, the grandmas would love him. He had that adorable, can't-say-no-to grin.

Marilyn's laugh drifted toward her before she caught sight of the two emerging from the aisle. Now was the perfect moment to broach the topic.

Dan carried a couple of small jugs of chain-saw oil tucked under his arm, and a pair of leather work gloves wrung in his hands. With his jaw clenched, he walked beside Marilyn, his body tense. But to his credit, when she finished talking, he nodded politely and smiled.

Marilyn sighed as they approached the counter.

He's going to hate me. Nikki had no doubt about that fact, but it needed to be done. The seniors needed their walls. "Hey, how are you this morning?" Nikki greeted Marilyn.

"Better than I was." Marilyn beamed at Dan.

Dan stepped between the two women and placed his gloves and the jugs of chain-saw oil on the counter.

He scanned the store looking for Harry, avoiding eye contact with either woman.

Marilyn continued. "I needed a few things before I headed over to the Senior Citizen's Center. Dan tells me y'all are headed in that direction with the animals from the rescue. That'll be a good place to find some more adoptive families."

"That's what I thought too," Nikki said.

Marilyn wrapped her hands around Dan's arm. "You're so sweet to help Nikki like this. I know Michael is tied up with helping his own family in Shreveport this weekend."

Dan's lips flattened. "Michael?" He shot a glance her way.

Nikki started to explain, but Marilyn talked right over her words.

"Yes, Michael and Nikki have known each other forever." Marilyn looked to Nikki for conformation.

She nodded. "Yep, forever."

"You two dated at one point, didn't you?" Marilyn cocked her head to one side and grinned.

Oh, now Nikki understood why Marilyn found the subject of Michael so interesting this morning. "Yes, when we were in high school, but that's ancient history."

Marilyn's smile grew. "And let's not forget Brian who truly is history. Didn't he leave Texas when you two broke up?"

"Yes, he did. Brian left, and Michael and I are just

friends. Speaking of dating—" Nikki highjacked the conversation. "How are you doing with the bachelor auction? Have you added any new victims to your list?"

Dan shifted his weight and leaned against the counter. "I wonder where Harry is?" he mumbled.

Nikki bit back a giggle. He didn't like the hot seat, and his discomfort showed all over his body.

"No, but I was hoping—" Marilyn shot a glance in Dan's direction.

"Have you made a decision yet?" Nikki asked. Both women swiveled to face Dan.

A pang of compassion pulsed through Nikki. She'd laid the trap, and now he had nowhere to run.

The side door opened, and Harry buzzed into the store. "I'm coming. Sorry, I was out back helping with the propane tanks. Never fails. The minute I get swamped out there, someone shows up in here."

"No problem. We just need to make these purchases so we can get back on the road." Dan pushed his items forward on the counter.

"Oh, y'all are heading over to the community rebuild at the center. There ought to be a big turnout today. Weather's pretty, and I know of at least four churches participating. I only hope y'all don't get in each other's way." The older man parked himself behind the cash register and rang up Dan's gloves and jugs of chain-saw oil. "Gonna do some hard labor today, I see." Harry winked at Dan.

Nikki caught the amused look that washed over

Dan's face.

His shoulders relaxed as the focus shifted off him. "Man, I do hard labor every day. Any man worth his salt does. Like the Good Book says, 'If a man won't work, he won't eat.'"

"Does rattling around in an old store count?" Harry's gray bushy eyebrows rose two inches.

Nikki liked Harry. He always played Santa in the town Christmas parade.

"Sure does," Dan said.

Harry grabbed a brown paper bag from under the counter and tucked Dan's merchandise inside it. "Here ya go."

Nikki picked up her bucket of nails and moved it closer to Harry, intending to go next. But she stopped when an idea presented itself. "Marilyn, why don't you go first. You have several things. I don't want to keep you." She had to stall for time. Dan couldn't leave before Marilyn could convince him to agree to the auction. After all, it was for a good cause.

"Well, how sweet." Marilyn walked past Dan to the counter, her back to him.

Nikki toyed with the handle on the bucket of nails. It shifted with each movement, inching closer to the edge. "So, Marilyn, you never did say if you had any new volunteers."

Dan scowled at Nikki.

"Actually, I did have one new volunteer—the gentleman who purchased the Mitchell house on Picket

Lane."

"You mean the mansion? That's great," Nikki said.

Turning to Dan, Marilyn added, "So, how about you? I could use the help." She batted her eyelashes.

Nikki suppressed a grin.

Dan looked between the two women. His brows furrowed. "What would I have to do?"

"All that's required is for you to show up at the center dressed for a picnic. The volunteers and members are bringing the baskets."

"How long will the picnic last?" Dan widened his stance and hugged the brown paper bag to his chest.

Nikki piped up, "About an hour. Once all the bachelors are sold, the eating will begin."

"I don't know if I want to spend an hour with a complete stranger." Dan ran his hand down the back of his neck.

"That's not a problem. I'm going to make sure you'll be eating your lunch with me."

Surprised, Nikki jerked the handle on the bucket, sending it smashing to the floor, The nails spilled out like the tide rolling to the shore. Apparently, Marilyn didn't notice Dan cringe, but Nikki did.

He stammered. "Oh no, no, no, I couldn't ask you to do that. It wouldn't be fair to the other guys if it was rigged. I'll have to take my chances like everyone else. Besides, I'm sure the guys are lining up to have dinner with you."

Marilyn cooed, "It's a friendly competition. I

wouldn't worry about it, since I may have already told a few of the ladies that I wanted you all to myself."

Nikki glanced up from her position on the floor where she'd knelt to pick up the nails and read sheer panic in his eyes. She swept the nails into a small pile with her good hand and held the bucket handle with the bandaged one.

"Will that be all for you?" Harry asked with a hint of amusement ringing in his voice.

Marilyn's attention turned back to the transaction. "Yes, thank you so much." Once Harry had handed Marilyn her bag, she faced Dan with a triumphant smile. "I'll put you down for the auction. And don't worry. You'll have a good time. I'm going to make sure of that." She winked at him before pushing open the door that led to the parking lot.

Dan froze, hugging his bag to his chest, looking as if a horse had kicked him in the gut.

Rising, Nikki cringed. Why couldn't she have left well enough alone? She ought to be ashamed of herself for siccing Marilyn on Dan like that.

Dan hadn't said a word since they'd left the hardware store. Nikki consoled herself with the fact that his participation would raise a lot of money, but that didn't prevent her anxious thoughts. No, she'd pushed him too far. This time she'd stepped over the line. She leaned her elbow on the truck door trying to relax. "If what Harry says is true, there should be a great turnout. Plenty of people to adopt some of my crew."

Dan cut his eyes toward her but didn't comment.

They pulled into the parking lot of the Senior Citizen's facility to find two church vans and a slew of trucks covering the debris-speckled asphalt. Dan maneuvered his truck into a spot near the walking track and jammed the gearshift into park. "How's this?"

"Perfect." Nikki touched the door handle but hesitated. "Would you mind helping me set up the temporary pen?"

"I guess I don't have much of a choice, do I?"

Nikki noted the sharp edge in his voice and couldn't blame him for his sour attitude. She'd brought this on herself.

"Kind of like the decision to participate in the auction." He faced her and draped his arm across the back of the seat. Dan could have touched her if he wanted to. His closeness unnerved her.

"Well, if you don't want to find one of them in your yard every evening, you might want to help me."

"Is that a threat, Miss Davis?" He raised one eyebrow and cocked his head to the side.

"No, of course not." Nikki rolled her eyes. "I'm sorry, okay? Marilyn got carried away. I'm sure she'll move on to the rich fellow who bought the Mitchell property. She's probably already picked out the names of their kids." Nikki clasped her hands in her lap and waited for Dan to react. When he didn't, she tried again. "Besides, the auction is for a great cause." She nodded toward the building at the edge of the parking lot.

"What if she doesn't move on? I've already had a less than favorable experience with her, and I don't want a repeat."

"Oh, I didn't know." Nikki fidgeted in her seat, ashamed of her actions. "Marilyn can be a bit of a bulldog when she sets her sights on something."

"Or someone." Dan frowned. "And I don't like being on the receiving end of her determination."

"But under it all, she's a...good person." A twinge of guilt nagged at her.

"Well, I'm not willing to test that theory. And *you* are going to help me avoid that picnic with her."

Nikki shrugged. "I supposed I don't have much of a choice, do I?"

"Not a one." Dan's green eyes blazed with purpose.

"I didn't think so." Nikki swallowed. "What do I have to do?"

"Nothing illegal." A smile crept across his face. "You simply have to make sure you outbid her when it comes my turn."

"I'm not sure I can do that. As it is, I'm barely making ends meet, plus I have more mouths to feed." She pointed to the back of the truck. "I wasn't planning on bidding."

"You mean you pulled me into this, but you were ... abstaining?"

"Well, yeah." Nikki shrugged, but the set of Dan's

jaw told her he didn't like that answer.

"Not on your life. You're going to outbid that woman because you got me into this mess. And you owe me that much."

"How do you figure?" Nikki crossed her arms, intrigued.

Mimicking a woman's voice, Dan said, "'Oh, Marilyn, have you found any new victims?'" He cocked his eyebrow. "Victim is right."

Nikki didn't appreciate the reprimand but couldn't deny the truth of what he said. She blamed it on her mischievous nature. "And how am I supposed to outbid her? With my good looks?" Heat rose on her neck and warmed her cheeks. Had she just asked Dan about her good looks? Did they even make a shoehorn big enough for her mouth? Nikki glanced at Dan, resisting the urge to crawl under the front seat.

Dan's eyes took on a whole new gleam. "Maybe. But I thought cash might work better."

"I don't have that kind of money. Marilyn won't bid less than a couple of hundred to get what she wants."

"In that case, I'll make sure you have a couple of hundred to spare."

"Where are you going to find that kind of cash? My friend Michael worked one summer as a ranch hand, and he didn't make much." Nikki hoped he wouldn't go into debt to avoid an hour with Marilyn.

Dan dropped his arm from the back of the seat and

took her hand in his.

"Don't worry. I've been at it awhile, so I make a pretty decent salary. Besides, I've always been a saver. You should see my bank account." Dan squeezed her hand.

A surge of awareness flooded her. She had an uncanny urge to lean into him and plant a big sloppy kiss right on those firm lips. But instead, she looked into his bright eyes and let herself warm to the thought of having Dan all to herself the day of the auction. She couldn't leave him in the clutches of Marilyn, could she? It was her civic duty to save him. Besides, what harm could come from one date? "Okay, Rockefeller, I'll do it."

Chapter Seven

Dan carried the pieces of the temporary pen to the open area next to the walking track. Setting them on the ground, he pulled the sections into place and snapped them together with a clip. It took less than five minutes to put the contraption together; the trick would be herding Nikki's band of furry misfits into it.

He glanced over his shoulder and found his outgoing neighbor talking to a group of gray-haired men wearing toolbelts. When she turned and spotted him, she waved, and her sweet lips lifted into a smile. With her hair pulled back into a ponytail, she looked like the all-American girl.

Guilt covered him like a scratchy coat. He'd used her good nature to his advantage. But he was desperate. He couldn't afford to play around with Marilyn, and he couldn't afford to offend her. She held the power to make his life a complete nightmare during his stay in Orange Blossom. Nope. Nikki needed to outbid Marilyn fair and square … sort of, and everyone would be happy. He hoped Nikki wouldn't get too curious and start asking questions.

The sound of the barking dogs pulled his thoughts back to the task at hand.

He headed to the truck and spotted Nikki walking toward him. Before he could reach the vehicle, Blue groaned his displeasure at being locked in a kennel.

Four kennels and six cat carriers sat in the bed of his truck. One kennel held the Chihuahua and the dachshund along with a few other small dogs. Another held Blue and the collie, while Snowball, the large sheepdog, got her own space. There were a few other dogs in the fourth one to bring the grand total to eleven.

Nikki reached the truck before he did but waited until he joined her.

"Could you lift me into the back of the truck? I'm afraid to put pressure on my hand." She wiggled the fingers that peeked above the bulky bandage.

"Sure. No problem." He reached around her and pulled on the latch to release the tailgate.

She moved to the side out of the way, so he could lower it.

Once the tailgate was secure, he patted the metal, and she stepped in front of him, resting her hands on his shoulders. "Okay, up you go." Her waist seemed small under his large hands, and he concentrated on not squeezing her too hard as he lifted her to a seated position on the tailgate, never letting his eyes stray from hers.

Standing there in front of her with her hands on his shoulders, the urge to kiss her swept over him like a magnet drawing him toward her lips.

Nikki let go. "Thank you," she whispered.

A soft pink blush grew on her smooth white cheeks, adding to her All-American mystique.

"Sure. No problem." These few words seemed to be the only ones in his vocabulary today. Aggravated for feeling like a tongue-tied schoolboy, he stepped back and let her swing her legs onto the metal and stand.

As Nikki unlocked the kennels, she attached a leash to each dog and handed the leash to him. He lowered the animal down to the ground and escorted him to the temporary pens. One by one, Dan took the canines to their new location.

Several people stopped to talk to the dogs and pet them while he made his trips back and forth to the truck.

Maybe Nikki was right. Perhaps tonight they'd go home with fewer animals or maybe even none. Dan smiled. *Wouldn't that be nice.* He settled the cat carriers on some nearby picnic tables with their carrier doors facing out, so everyone passing could see them. On his last trip to the pen, Dan spotted a young man wearing a vintage Mickey Mouse tee-shirt standing at the pen, talking to Blue. He leaned in, over the metal barrier, and scratched Blue on the head between his ears.

Blue closed his eyes as the young man spoke soft

words to him.

Dan thought about cautioning the young man not to bump the barrier, but Blue with his tongue lolled to the side was enjoying the attention, and he didn't want to interrupt. The scene brought a smile to his lips. A little piece of him would be sorry to see the lug go. He hated to admit it, but the crazy dog had grown on him—kind of like Blue's foster mom.

"Hey, a little help," Nikki called from the back of the truck.

Dan turned to find her standing with her hands on her hips, staring in his direction. He took off in a jog. Too late. Within seconds, four other men answered Nikki's request for help. His jaw tightened, and he slowed his steps. No need to hurry. She had all the help she could want. Shoving his hands in his pockets, he waited for the tall, lean gentleman with a mustache to set Nikki's feet on the ground. The man took his sweet time letting go of her.

Dan didn't like it. Not one bit.

"Thanks, Carl," Nikki said.

"My pleasure." Carl smiled as he sauntered off toward the debris-covered tennis courts.

"It looks like we might get lucky today and re-home a few of the dogs." She nodded in the direction of the pen.

Dan glanced that way and discovered a group of teens who had surrounded the pen full of dogs. "Yeah, looks like it."

Nikki's gaze fell to the ground, and she kicked at a piece of tin lying at her feet. "Look, Dan. I want to thank you for all your help. After everything you've done for me— fixing the fence, bringing Blue back when he escaped, bandaging my hand." She looked up and met his gaze.

Those beautiful blue eyes that looked like fields of cornflowers held him mesmerized.

"I'm ashamed of myself for getting you involved in the auction and Marilyn. I thought it was for a good cause, and it might give you a chance to meet some of the townspeople. I mean while you're here, you might as well make yourself at home, right?" Nikki shrugged. "Anyway, I'm sorry. I'll try to butt out of your business and not be the typical nosy neighbor."

Dan groaned. "You're not a nosy neighbor, and you don't need to apologize. I'll be happy to do the auction. Sorry I overreacted." He shrugged. "I'm a very private person, and large functions make me nervous." At least the last part was true. He was a private person, and large functions of any kind did make him antsy. Give him a hundred acres and a horse, and he thrived, but put him in with thirty people at a party, and a turtle had nothing on him for retreating into his shell.

"So, we're good?" Nikki asked.

"Yeah, we're good," Dan said. "But I still need you to outbid Marilyn. I don't want to hurt her feelings, but it's better for everyone if I skip being too social with her."

Nikki nodded her agreement. "I'll be glad to help."

~

After lunch, the day sped by as the workers cleared the larger pieces of debris from the area. Many items had to be hauled away because they couldn't be left on the side of the road for the dump trucks and crane that made weekly rounds since the Hurricane.

It took eight guys to move a damaged horse trailer that the high winds had dumped on the property. Eight guys, some straps, and a tow truck. Most of the volunteers were bagging the smaller pieces of debris and prepping limbs for disposal. Dan's chainsaw had come in handy.

Nikki leaned over for the umpteenth time of the day and scooped into her mud-covered gloves a knot of plastic necklaces, remnants of some little girl's treasures. She sighed and tossed them into the black trash bag, wondering where that little girl might be right now.

On August 25th, life had changed for everyone in her community. She counted herself blessed. She still had her home and belongings, but many did not. Orange Blossom would never be the same, but her town would survive this crisis. Her community had a strength, drawn from its faith and deep roots. God had his hand on this small town, and he'd never let go.

Nikki stood, dropping the bag and placed her hands in the small of her back. She scanned the area for Dan, wondering how things were going with the other men. Nikki had wanted to help him feel connected; that's why she'd invited him to come today, but she feared she'd pushed him too hard. It didn't escape her attention that over the two weeks he'd lived next door, he'd had zero visitors. Not a one.

Perhaps, it was none of her business, but she couldn't bear to think of him all on his own. She had her mother and older brother, but so far, he hadn't mentioned anyone. He'd spoken of being displaced because of the hurricane, but there was a huge difference between being displaced and being alone.

The late September sun hung low on the horizon, setting shadows on the ground under the trees. Her thoughts ran to the dogs and to Dan helping her into the back of the truck. How different it had been having Dan lift her onto the tailgate—his hands wrapped around her waist and his muscles tensing under her touch—than when Carl had lowered her down.

She shook her head to dispel the thought. After all, before long he'd be gone. But for some reason being around Dan made her aware of his every movement like the radar in bats. And that radar told her he'd have kissed her if she hadn't pulled away. Why had she pulled away?

She leaned over and grabbed the trash bag, wanting to kick herself. Hadn't she thought about kissing her handsome neighbor more than a few times? Perhaps the memory of their first meeting held her back. She had caught him digging through a box filled with pictures of a young, beautiful woman. Someone, she was sure, who had been important to him. Maybe the woman in the pictures was still important to him. But if that were the case, where was she?

Dan strolled around the corner of the building carrying his chainsaw, wearing a pair of clear protective glasses.

She giggled. Even covered in wood chips and sweat, the man looked good.

Waving, he veered toward his truck.

She let her gaze follow him. A small section of the metal dog pen hung open. She did a quick head count as she trotted toward the furry band. Only ten dogs were sitting in the pen.

Blue was missing.

"Dan," she called, panic in her voice. She pointed to the other dogs.

He scowled and shot around the truck to the pen.

"It's Blue. He's missing," Nikki said.

Dan shoved the open section back into place and snapped the metal band around it to keep it secure. "How did it get open?" His voice rang with irritation.

"Don't know. I was over there, picking up trash. You know as much as I do," Nikki answered not hiding her own frustration. "Anyone could've come along and opened it, or Blue could've figured it out himself."

"I thought you were working over here so you could keep an eye on them," Dan said.

"Look, it doesn't matter how he escaped. We need

to find him. He's my responsibility until I locate him a new home, and I don't want to have to report to the rescue that I lost one of these guys on my watch. Or worse, that he's hurt. He could be standing in the middle of the road as we speak." A fresh wave of worry gripped her. She turned toward him fighting back tears.

"It's going to be all right." He rubbed her shoulder. "You're right. We need to find him."

The even tone of Dan's voice worked to calm her. Taking two deep breaths, she forced herself to focus on the problem and not on what might have happened.

"You go look in the parking lot. If he's not there, go see if he's hanging around the snack table or over where the ladies served lunch."

"That's a good idea. He a bottomless pit." Nikki bit her bottom lip trying to keep her anxiety in check.

"I'll go search the side of the road. But I'm sure he's fine." He dropped his hand from her shoulder.

Another anxious thought emerged, Nikki's eyes grew large, and she gasped. "There's a pond on the neighboring farmland at the back beyond the trees." She pointed toward the woods.

"Would he go there?" Dan asked.

"Yes, he loves water."

"Okay, I'll go check the street then the pond. If we don't find him in those spots, we'll ask some of the others to help us look."

Nikki touched his forearm as he turned to go. "Thanks, Dan. I appreciate this."

"It'll be all right. We'll find him." His face softened, and he covered her hand with his.

She smiled at him and found comfort in the warmth in his gaze. Her bat radar buzzed and beeped, warning her that the tingling sensation in her stomach had returned. Nikki pushed aside the sensations and forced her mind back to the job at hand—finding Blue in one piece.

Chapter Eight

Dan jogged to the end of the long, concrete drive. The Senior Citizen's Center sign on the right and the hedges on both sides of the entrance blocked his view. Moving around them, he inspected the area closest to him. No sign of Blue behind the sign or under the hedges. No evidence of digging either.

To the left, the road ran straight as far as he could see before it dipped down and curved out of view. Scanning the grassy areas that hugged the black asphalt, Dan jogged a little further down the side of the road to see beyond the curve. No Blue.

Sprinting to the other side of the entrance, he repeated the exercise cupping his hands around his eyes to block out the setting sun. He whistled and called the dog's name, but no response. Since there were no cars in sight, he moved to the middle of the road on the yellow line, so he could see both sides of the road. Nothing but the two piles of debris waiting to be picked up.

Before he could move off the pavement, a red Jeep rounded the curve to the left. The driver slowed when he spotted Dan standing in the middle of the road.

"What's going on?" the young guy asked. The license plate on the front of his vehicle announced that the young man went to Texas A&M.

"I've lost a hound dog, dark, floppy ears. Goes by the name of Blue. Have you seen any dogs fitting that description?" Dan approached the driver's side of the Jeep.

"No, I'm coming from Vinton, north of here, and I didn't see any dogs along the road. Are you sure he came this way?" he asked.

Dan shook his head. "Not sure where he ran off to, but I thought I'd better start here. Just in case. I'd hate for anything to happen to him."

"Makes sense. I'll keep a lookout for him."

"Great. Thanks. Oh, wait." Dan dug his wallet from his back pocket and pulled an old business card from the fold. "Here, you can reach me at this number. If you see him, call. He couldn't have gone far. And I'll meet you."

"Sure." The young man scanned the card in his hand. "Mr. Thibodeaux." He glanced up. "You're not Dan Harris Thibodeaux, Edward Harris's grandson, are you?"

Dan hesitated. He didn't like the look in the guy's eyes. "Why do you want to know?"

"I'm on the magazine staff at Texas A&M. As an

old agricultural school, it would be great if I could score an interview with one of the wealthiest and most successful ranchers in the state. You and your grandfather are legends in the industry."

"Sorry. I can't help you." Dan walked away from the vehicle, but the kid followed him inching the jeep along beside him.

"Look, I won't take much of your time, and it'd help me out of a tough jam with my editor."

"I can't—" Dan muttered. He hated to be in the spotlight of any kind.

"We can meet whenever its convenient for you." The young man pulled into the driveway of the Senior Citizen's Center. "Mr. Thibodeaux, sir, I really need this. Please."

Dan stopped and studied the young man. He sighed, regret already filling him. "Fine. Call me next week, and we'll set up a time for the interview. Thirty minutes, no more."

"Great." The guy's face glowed with excitement. "And if I spot the dog, I'll let you know."

"Sounds good." Dan nodded.

The guy backed up, waved, and drove off.

Dan gave both sides of the road one last glance and jogged back down the driveway to the center. Perhaps Nikki had found the scoundrel by now. He spotted her in the yard by his truck wearing a worried expression. It told him all he needed to know.

Catching Nikki's gaze, he nodded toward the stand

of trees at the back of the property that led to the neighbor's pond.

She nodded her understanding and headed in that direction.

If the mutt wasn't at the pond, Dan didn't know where else to look.

Nikki ran ahead of him as they neared the fence line.

He lengthened his stride to catch up with her, but before he reached her, Blue flew out from beneath the underbrush near the fence that separated the two properties, wet and covered in mud.

Nikki ran toward the dog, but Dan, reading the situation, slowed.

Realizing her mistake, Nikki clambered to retrace her steps, twisting to move out of the dog's path.

But Blue, covered in stinky pond scum, galloped toward her, tail wagging, tongue lolling and launched himself at her. With one motion, Blue had Nikki pinned to the ground.

"Get off me, Blue. Bad dog. Bad dog," Nikki sputtered under the loving licks of the filthy hound.

Dan pressed his lips together to stop the laughter, but he couldn't hold it back. The sight was too grand. His chest shook as he doubled over, holding his sides with his hands, struggling to catch his breath.

Nikki lay trapped under the dripping hound, wrestling to regain control.

Blue's tail swooshed back and forth a mile a

minute. Apparently, he'd enjoyed his little outing to the pond and wanted to show his gratitude to Nikki for letting him have his fun. Dan wasn't about to get in the way.

"Don't just stand there, hee-hawing like a donkey. He stinks. Come get him."

"Oh, I don't know. He seems so happy. I hate to be a party pooper."

Nikki grabbed Blue's collar which was covered in slime. "Gross." She wiped her hand on the ground beside her. "Blue, off." She made her voice deeper than normal and tried again. "Blue off."

"Is that supposed to be an imitation of me?" Dan asked.

"No." She pushed at the eighty-pound dog sitting on her abdomen.

"Come, Blue." Dan leaned over and patted his thighs.

Blue gave Nikki one last lick on the cheek before trotting over to Dan.

"Sit, boy." Dan smiled when the crazy mutt sat.

Nikki pushed up onto her elbows. "Thanks. So. Much." She huffed and rolled to a sitting position.

Dan knelt beside the dog and scratched the one spot on his head not covered in mud. "Aw, you can't be mad. He was giving you a little appreciation. Weren't you, boy?" Looking toward her, Dan pointed to Nikki's shirt. "You're glowing." The black and green stains shimmered in the sunlight.

Pulling the cotton cloth away from her skin, she stood and inspected it. She shrugged unfazed by the smeared mud and algae. "I supposed that's the price of the love of a good dog. What can you do?" She smiled holding the hem of her shirt to her nose. "Ew, I don't think this can be saved."

The muddy shirt wasn't the only casualty in the dog's play. Small droplets of mud had found their way onto Nikki's face. The smudge on the tip of her nose had Dan's hand itching to wipe it away. But instead, he pointed. "You have a little schmutz…"

She reached and wiped one side.

"No, it's …" He gestured toward her nose.

"Just get it."

Dan rose and moved closer to her.

She stuck her face out toward him and closed her eyes.

Fifteen thoughts raced through his mind, and none of them involved removing the smudge. He swallowed and leaned in.

"Well?" she asked. "Did you get it?"

"Not yet." His voice was rough even to his own ears. As he leaned down, his lips a whisper from hers, Blue stuck his head between them, smearing a streak of pond scum down both of their pants. A whiff of the putrid smell from the dog wafted upward.

Opening her eyes, Nikki pushed the dog back with her leg. "Oh, Blue, haven't you caused enough trouble?"

Dan moved the dog out of the way. "Here, let me get that smudge." Catching her by her shoulders, he turned her toward him.

She stilled and met his gaze, her blue eyes full of warmth.

For a split second, he thought about picking up where Blue had interrupted, but the moment was gone. Instead, he gently wiped away the spot of dirt. "There, that's better." Smiling, he released her.

A glimmer of disappointment shone in Nikki's eyes.

"Well, we'd better go back." She tsked at Blue as she studied him. "Look at you. How will I ever find you a home if you keep getting into mischief?" Nikki gave Dan an appraising look but didn't offer any comment about his appearance. Returning her gaze to Blue, she patted her thigh. "Come on, boy. Let's pack up."

Dan followed behind her with Blue at his side. Leaning over, he scratched the top of his head and whispered, "thanks. I owe you one." No matter how much Dan wanted to kiss Nikki, it wouldn't be fair to her. A part of his heart would always belong to Lilly.

~

Everything stunk to high heaven. Nikki leaned close to the open truck window trying to catch a breath of fresh air as they made their way down the two-lane road.

Back at the Senior Citizen's Center, she'd dumped a couple of bottles of water over Blue trying to wash away the mud and lessen the stench, but there hadn't been much she could do about her clothes or the huge streak across Dan's jeans. The fumes permeated every nook and cranny of the space, making her eyes water.

A low hum floated to her side of the truck drawing her attention. Dan turned toward her and flashed a smile before focusing back on the road.

She couldn't help studying him. Funny, he seemed so relaxed, not concerned about their present situation at all. She'd half expected him to complain about the smell even though she could do nothing about it. Or tease her about what had happened near the pond when she was running toward the mud-covered pooch. Or fuss about the fact that she hadn't placed any of the animals today, making the effort of toting them to the center a big fat flop.

Instead, he sat with his arm perched on the open window, and his eyes focused on the road, humming a tune she didn't recognize. The breeze circulating in the truck sent the ends of his hair curling around the edges of his baseball cap.

He must've sensed her staring. A smile pulled the corners of his lips upward, and he shot her a sideways glance. "What? Do I have a spot on my nose?" He chuckled.

After loading the dirty dog into the bed of the truck, they were both wearing splotches of pond scum in a variety of locations.

Nikki grinned, encouraged by his attempt at

humor. "Well, probably, but that wasn't what I was thinking about."

"Oh, what were you thinking?" He pushed his baseball cap back a little further on his head and glanced her way without taking his eyes off the road for too long.

"I was wondering if you were going to church tomorrow, and if so, I was going to offer you a ride." She studied him as he cocked his head to one side.

He rubbed his hand across his chin. "That's very sweet of you, but I can't. I need to work."

"I shouldn't have asked you to use your truck. You came to apologize, and I took advantage of you. Now, you'll have to air everything out before you can carry anyone else in it."

She groaned and turned her face toward the window. The trees passed by like galloping horses as the truck ate up the miles to her house.

"Nikki, if I hadn't wanted to go today, I wouldn't have. Besides, as you've reminded me several times, you did warn me about helping at the Senior Citizen's Center for the right reasons. Not as a gesture to you."

Nikki shrugged. "Well, yes, I did say not to go for me as part of your apology, but to go because you wanted to help."

"Right. So, you don't need to feel guilty about it. Besides, don't people get special credit with God for helping their neighbors?" Dan took the steering wheel with his left hand; his elbow propped in the open window and ran his right arm across the back of the seat.

"I don't think it works like that." Nikki giggled. "But we are called to do good. And—" she turned her shoulders toward him, leaning her body against the seat. "You did great today. Several of the men mentioned how handy you were with that chain saw. Having the back area cleared of the fallen trees is impressive."

Dan squeezed her shoulder with his hand. "I appreciate that. I enjoyed being in the company of other like-minded men."

Nikki's heart raced. Not simply because of his touch but because his words lead her to think he was a believer. "So, normally on Sundays, you do go to church?"

"Most Sundays. There are those few exceptions. You know, when something like a gang of unruly animals and a kindhearted, pretty woman sidetrack me."

"Hey." She swatted at him but didn't hit him. "You said no guilt."

He laughed causing crinkles around his eyes to appear. "You're right. It's been a good day."

So that's what she read on his face—contentment.

"I agree. Even with having to chase Blue, it's been a good day." She took a drink from a water bottle she'd pulled from the cooler at her feet. "You want one?"

"Yes, please."

Nikki pulled a second one from the red and white

cooler and opened it for him before placing it in the cupholder closest to him.

After a second long drink, she peered at his profile. "I've been kind of curious. How do you know Pastor Connor?"

"I don't really. My preacher at the Cowboy Church of Sine River has mentioned him once or twice. When he found out I'd be in Orange Blossom, he told me to look him up."

"Oh, it seemed that you were in his office for a long time the other day. I figured you two were old friends. And when Pastor Connor asked me to block out the second Saturday of November for him, since the first weekend of that month is the annual potluck, I thought you two might have made plans to go horseback riding or hunting or something."

Dan straightened and placed both hands back on the wheel. "No, nothing like that. I had some personal business I needed to see him about."

"Oh, sorry. I shouldn't have asked." Nikki held up her hand to stop him from saying any more.

Dan sighed. "I have someone's ashes, and I'd like to put them to rest. He agreed to help. After the hurricane, I thought I'd lost the urn, but I recovered it from the damage. It made me realize that I needed to take care of this before I missed the opportunity. They left instructions in their will, and I want to honor them."

She squirmed in her seat and placed her water bottle in the cupholder in front of her. "I'm sorry. I know better than to ask. Discretion is part of my job description. Pastor Connor insists that what goes on in the church office is private, and we need to keep it to ourselves. I shouldn't have asked." She glanced his way. Her hands clutched together in her lap, praying he'd hear her heart.

He sat rigid, eyes on the road. "It's all right. But please don't mention this to anyone else. I don't want to have to explain myself to the people of Orange Blossom, and if word gets out, others will want to know all the details." He rolled his shoulder and settled further into the driver's seat. "And frankly, it's none of their business."

Chapter Nine

Two weeks passed without Dan seeing Nikki or any of her furry companions. He'd spotted her once or twice going from her car to the house or caught the sounds of her in the backyard with the hounds. But the few times he thought about going over to check on her, he'd talk himself out of it. Leaving things as they were, friendly but distant, seemed easier on his heart.

The atmosphere on the truck ride home had been strained after he'd mentioned the ashes. He'd wanted to confide in her about Lilly, but he feared that would only lead to more questions. So, he'd kept his mouth shut. Which in retrospect had been the wrong thing to do. She must think she did something wrong or that he was moody. Either way, he'd been rude once more.

He'd arranged to meet his ranch foreman, Rod Carson, at the Silver Spur that Saturday to finalize the plans for the rebuilding of his family's home. He'd deal with that first before dealing with his neighbor.

Dan Thibodeaux threaded his way to the spot

where the ranch house had once stood. It had been home to four generations of the Harris family.

The ground sank under the weight of his steps. Broken boards, snapped limbs, and pieces of twisted metal sat piled in heaps near the long, gravel driveway, waiting for disposal. Trees stood splintered and torn, victims of the howling winds of the hurricane. Soon, they'd be cut into pieces to make way for what would come next.

A work crew had been at it the entire month of September, and now they had cleared enough of the area to start work on the structures. A new barn. A new house.

He shook his head. Every time he came here, his heart plummeted another couple of feet.

So many of his memories from his life with Pops and Nana and Lilly connected him to this place. He squatted and picked up a handful of dirt, breathing in the fall scents of the land he loved, letting the dirt spill out through his fingers.

He couldn't count the number of times as a boy he and his mom had come to visit his granddad, Pops Harris. And when he'd moved here to learn the family business of ranching, this stretch of land had become home.

He could still hear Pops' voice when he shut his eyes and concentrated. Dan could hear him teaching him how to knot a rope, so the cows couldn't pull lose. He could hear the joy in his voice when Dan had told him about his engagement to Lilly. And he remembered the glow on the old man's face as he watched them exchange their vows in the gazebo by the river that threaded through the landscape.

Now, the gazebo sat splintered—another piece of home wiped away by Hurricane Harvey.

He closed his eyes trying to hear his grandfather's voice. But instead of Pop's voice from the past, he heard the rumbling of a truck engine and the crunch of the gravel under the tires as a vehicle approached.

He stood and turned to see an old black Ford pickup. Rod parked beside Dan's truck. Dan had known Rod for as long as he could remember. He'd been the one to teach him to ride, and he'd even shown him how to talk to horses—Dan chuckled. And how to talk to women.

Rod waved and trotted out to where Dan stood by the area the cleanup crew had cleared. "It's looking good, huh?" Rod stopped next to Dan and thumped him on the back as a friendly hello.

"Yeah, it's hard to believe they've done as much as they have. I mean, it took me and Marge a week to dig out the things I wanted to keep. Well, rather the items that hadn't been carried off to another county."

"I know. So many people have lost so much. Pictures, collectibles—shoot, even animals scattered from here to yonder." Rod looked down at his worn brown boots and shook his head. "I'm pleased as punch that we were able to locate that crate. Don't know what we'd have done if it had been slung to the ends of the earth."

"Yeah." This time Dan thumped Rod's back.

"Speaking of critters."

Dan smiled. He had an idea where this conversation was headed.

"Have you seen that pretty animal-loving neighbor of yours recently? Has she got any of them placed yet?" Rod's eyes lit up with mischief.

"Now, don't go trying to make more out of this than there is. You know my heart will always belong to Lilly."

He slid his hands into the pockets of his faded jeans. "I know, but, son, you need to start thinking of what's to come. Lilly wouldn't want you to mourn her for the rest of your life. She'd want you to be happy."

"I know." Dan swallowed the lump that formed in his throat whenever he thought of his late wife.

"Besides, it's been three years since she passed. You've grieved as you should have, but it's time to let that dream go and find a new one." Rod squeezed his shoulder. With a lighter tone to his voice, he added, "Shoot, I'm not talking about getting hitched. But maybe a date or two wouldn't hurt." He lifted his shoulders. "Would it be so bad to take a pretty woman out to dinner? Who knows, it could be fun."

Dan chuckled. He couldn't help himself. The plaid-wearing, jean-clad man who had taught him the most about ranching and women had only loved one woman his whole life, Dolly Lynn Carson. "What do *you* know about dating? It's not exactly like you've had a lot of experience." Dan poked Rod's arm with his elbow.

"Now, don't go thinking I don't know nothing about dating and romance. Shoot, I've been married for over forty years. It's because I've been married so long, I can tell you that it's time."

Dan shook his head and ambled over to the spot where the foundation would be poured the following week. Rod trailed after him. "You know God's Word says it's not good for man to be alone. You might want to take that into consideration next time you see your neighbor."

Dan shot Rod a sideways glance without commenting. He didn't like how his heart drummed louder each time Rod mentioned Nikki. It made him feel disloyal to Lilly, the woman who had loved him for himself and for no other reason. He changed the focus of the conversation. "It looks like they got the dimensions right."

"Yep, and the additional space to the main living area as well as the mud room next to the laundry was a great idea," Rod said. "Did you want to head over to the lower pastures and finish that leg of fencing?"

"Good idea. I want to have the last herd shipped back from Burchum's place before November. Once the temperature drops up north, the herd will need hay, and I don't want to put Burchum out. He's already done so much."

As Dan and Rod moved back toward the driveway to the trucks, Dan asked, "So, would a bachelor auction count as a date?" Dan kept his eyes glued to the ground in front of him, knowing he'd piqued his friend's curiosity.

Rod stopped a few feet from his truck. "Are you pulling my leg? I can't imagine you doing anything like that, ever."

"Well, it's for a good cause."

"Uh-huh." Rod studied him for a moment. "I see." Nodding, he ambled to his truck.

"As it happens, Nikki and another woman cornered me at the hardware store a few weeks back. So, I didn't have much of a choice." Dan opened his truck door, pulled out a pair of leather gloves, and stuffed them into his back pocket. He didn't know why he felt compelled to share this news with Rod. It only gave him more ammunition to poke fun at his expense.

"I see." Rod repeated. He stood with his hand on the truck handle and gave Dan his full attention.

Dan closed his door and leaned against the truck meeting Rod's gaze. "What?"

"There is no way you would ever stand up in front of a crowd of strangers and let someone auction you off. No matter how much pressure they put on you. That Nikki must be some kind of woman." Rod opened the door and retrieved his own set of gloves along with a baseball cap. Plopping the hat on his head, he pulled the brim down, anchoring it in place.

The heat rose on the back of Dan's neck causing him to look away. Ignoring Rod's comment, he continued, "But I do have a small problem."

"What's that? You're afraid she can't afford you?" Rod chuckled, poking one glove into each of his back pockets.

"No, I sort of left out a few details about myself when I met her."

Rod cocked an eyebrow. "What did you leave out?"

Dan shrugged. "Quite a lot, unfortunately."

Slamming the door, Rod walked to the back of the truck. Reaching over the tailgate, he grabbed a leather tool belt and slung it over his shoulder. Leaning his forearms on the metal, he nailed Dan with a glare that caused him to pull his own cap down on his forehead.

"Does she know about Lilly?"

"No." Dan pressed his lips together and shifted his weight. "I haven't told her about Lilly."

"Well, she knows who you are though, right? I mean you've told her about your family and the business."

Embarrassed by his lack of honesty, Dan kicked a piece of gravel and let his gaze rest on a stand of trees on the other side of the drive. "That's the subject I avoided the most. I didn't want her or anyone else for that matter to treat me any different because of the money."

"Okay," Rod said. "I can understand that. Your Pops complained about that same problem. One minute the other men treated him like another good-ole-cowboy, but once they got wind of the money and the business, he became Mr. Harris. He always wondered if they were being nice because they liked him or his money." A look of compassion swept across Rod's face.

"Exactly." Dan met his gaze. "I wanted to be plain ole Dan. Not Mr. Daniel Harris Thibodeaux."

"I get it. So, who does your pretty neighbor think you are?" Rod stood straight, a playful glimmer dancing in his eyes. "Some ranch hand with no prospects?"

"Not quite," Dan chuckled. "She basically thinks I'm you."

Chapter Ten

"Ghosted," pronounced Purdy's granddaughter as she threw her backpack onto the church counter and leaned her elbows on its surface.

Confused, Nikki blinked at the teenager standing in front of her. "Ghosted? What does that even mean?" Sarah had entered the conversation halfway through and didn't bother to wait for Nikki to finish telling Purdy what had happened over the last two weeks with Dan. Which for the most part was nothing.

The fourteen-year-old girl rolled her eyes and tsked. "It's when someone ignores you. Like you've ceased to exist." She huffed when Nikki frowned. "You know, like you've died and become a ghost."

"Oh." Nikki frowned as Sarah's observation sank in. "So, you think Dan is ghosting me?"

"From what you said, yeah. And it's working too." She grinned. "He's got you salty."

"Salty? I'm lost." Frustrated, Nikki turned toward Purdy who sat smirking on one of the stools behind the counter. "Can you tell me what she's talking about?" Nikki didn't consider herself old or out of touch, but Sarah's presence in the church office on Wednesdays had proven her wrong on both accounts. She wrestled to keep her patience with the teen in check.

"What she means is that you're upset. He's got you upset over the fact that he's been—" Purdy glanced at her granddaughter. "Ghosting you."

Sarah nodded, and a satisfied grin settled on her lips. "Good job, Grams."

Nikki leaned her hip against the counter and crossed her arms. "I'm not salty; I'm curious is all. We're next-door neighbors for goodness' sake. How could he go almost two weeks without seeing me, once?"

"I don't know. You do seem a bit out of sorts, but I can't blame you. That guy would be hard to put out of one's mind. He's got that air about him, a real man's man." A gleam of mischief twinkled in Purdy's eyes.

Nikki scowled. "Don't be ridiculous. That's not why I'm worried. I mean, we ran into each other almost every day the first few weeks without even trying. Between Blue escaping and his helping with the senior's center."

Sarah opened the small front pocket on her backpack and pulled out a tub of lip balm.

Purdy watched as she applied it. "When did you start wearing makeup?"

"Grams." Sarah smacked her newly colored lips

together. "It's not makeup. Mom said I could use it to keep my lips from drying out. Fall weather and everything."

"Fine," answered Purdy, "but put it away and move your backpack over to my desk. The Sunday bulletin is ready for you to copy and staple together in the copier room."

Looking past her grandmother toward Nikki, Sarah said, "If I were you, I'd go see him. Make him explain why he's ignoring you. That's what I told Izzy to do when Mitch ghosted her."

Nikki leaned closer to Sarah. "How did it work out for Izzy?"

Sarah tilted her head. "Let's just say they have a date for homecoming next month."

Purdy looked from Sarah to Nikki and back. "You'd better get to work, or Pastor Connor will have no reason to add today to your service hours for the Silver Medallion Competition."

The teen came in most Wednesdays and Thursdays after school to help around the church office to earn service hours toward the competition held for the eighth graders throughout the county. Over the past three years that Nikki had worked for the Cowboy Community Church, they had sponsored several students in the competition. However, none had kept her and Purdy on their toes like Sarah.

The teen grabbed her backpack and moved it to the floor next to her grandmother's desk. As she passed

Nikki, she stopped. "If you like this guy, and it's plain you are low-key obsessed, I'd have a face-to-face with him."

Nikki met Purdy's gaze as Sarah disappeared into the copier room. "You, Purdy Thomas, are a saint of a grandmother. Half the time I have no idea what she's talking about. How do you do it?"

She shrugged. "I don't know what half the words she says mean either. Thank goodness for Google. That crazy app has kept me sane. The first time she told me I was a girlboss, I didn't know whether to be insulted or pleased." Purdy giggled. "But now, I've learned some of the slang her group uses, and I feel more comfortable entering into the conversation with them."

"It's like a whole different language." Nikki walked to her desk and gathered the sermon notes she'd been typing for Pastor Connor. "I think I'll get a head start on the ritual this week and give him the typed notes early."

Purdy shook her head. "Brave girl. It'll only give him an extra day to fret over them."

Nikki swept past her and lifted the divider, passing through to the other side of the counter. "I'll only be a second unless he's done with the notes from this month's business meeting."

"Oh, I already have those on my desk, but he might want you to go through the mailing list. He's thinking it's time to put together a new church pictorial directory. The last one is five years old. Some of the kids pictured have grown taller than him." Purdy laughed.

Nikki walked down the hall to the pastor's office. Purdy's voice floated to her as she greeted someone at the front counter. Funny, Nikki hadn't heard the front door open.

"Well, long time no see, stranger." From Purdy's words and upbeat tone, Nikki figured it must be one of her friends. Several ladies in the church stopped by from time to time for a chat.

Nikki knocked on the wooden door and waited for a response. Upon hearing "Come in," she stepped across the threshold. But before closing the door, the sound of laughter floated down the hallway. One of the voices held a husky timbre to it. A few minutes later, Nikki headed back to her desk carrying six ancient pictorial directories and two files with information on the current church families. She studied one of the lists as she went.

"Look who's here," Purdy called out before Nikki had emerged from the hallway.

Glancing up from the contents in her hand, she stopped. Lifting her chin, she sashayed by the man holding his cowboy hat in his hands.

"How are you, Nikki?" Dan asked. Not waiting for a response, he continued, "I was telling Purdy how busy I've been with all the house renovations and fence work we've had to do on the Silver Spur."

She glanced his way as she plopped the items in

her hands onto her desk with a thud. "Well, don't let us keep you." She sat in her chair with her back flagpole stiff and refused to look his way. "What nerve," she muttered.

"I'm sorry, dear. What did you say?" When she looked up, Purdy nailed her with a withering glare before turning her attention back to Dan. "You're not going to believe this, but we were just talking about you."

Wide-eyed, Nikki jumped up and rushed to the counter to keep Purdy from saying anything more about their previous discussion.

"I hope it was good," Dan said.

"Oh, yes, it was about how—"

"So, you've been working at the Silver Spur? That's the first time you've mentioned where you work." Nikki cringed when she realized she'd steamrolled her way into the conversation. The heat of embarrassment splotched her cheeks.

Dan's head tilted her way. "You're right. But I supposed there are a lot of things about me you don't know." A lopsided grin pulled a corner of his mouth upward. "But I'd like a chance to remedy that. That's why I stopped by. I wanted to check on our arrangement for the bachelor's auction this Saturday. We do still have an agreement, don't we?" His green eyes sparkled.

Nikki stepped back from the counter and crossed her arms. "I don't know." She glanced at Purdy, not wanting to give away their plan. After all, Purdy might think it was cheating to arrange who was going to win the auction ahead of time. "I mean, we've barely seen each other in two weeks, and …" she faltered.

"I know. And I want to apologize for not being around much." Dan glanced over at Purdy who rose from the stool and walked to her desk, busying herself on the computer. "Can we step outside and talk?"

Nikki scowled. "There's nothing to talk about. I offended you, and you proceeded to ghost me. You didn't even give me a chance to make things right."

His brow furrowed. "I'm not sure what *ghosted* means, but you're right. I owe you an apology and an explanation."

The door to the copier room swung open, and Sarah stuck her head around the door. "Grams, the paper's jammed again," she yelled. Catching sight of Dan, she stepped out of the room and leaned her back against the wall next to the open door studying him. "Is this the ghoster?" She grinned, her braces sparkling in the light.

In a flash, Purdy dashed from her desk to where her granddaughter stood, gaping at Dan. "Yes," she whispered. "That's Dan. Now, don't be rude." Grabbing the teen's arm, she hustled her back into the copier room and closed the door.

Dan pointed to where Sarah had stood. "Who was that? And what's a ghoster?"

"Don't pay her any attention. That's Purdy's

granddaughter. She works here a few afternoons a week to earn service hours toward the Silver Medallion competition. It's this thing the eighth graders do. Anyway, she speaks her own language." Nikki waved her hand in the direction of the closed door. "Forget about them. What were you saying?"

A grin lifted Dan's lips. "That I wanted to apologize for avoiding you." He looked down at the hat in his hand. "If you want to know the truth, it took every ounce of will power for me to stay away."

"I find that hard to believe," she said, but her heart skipped a beat anyways.

"Plus, I haven't been completely honest with you and would like the chance to set the record straight. I thought Saturday during our lunch date would be a good time." He placed his hat on the counter and leaned in, motioning for her to come closer.

The fact that he'd referred to Saturday's lunch as a date did not escape her notice. *A date.* A date with Dan. She tilted her head letting the thought playout in her mind. Meeting his gaze, she smiled. "We have a deal." Leaning closer and lowering her voice, she said, "I'll be sure to outbid Marilyn and anybody else who might place a bid."

Reaching over, he took her hand in his and intertwined their fingers. The warmth of his hand in hers sent a sweet, tingling sensation skittering through her.

"I don't think you have to worry about too many

women bidding on me." His gaze met hers. "After all, I'm a ghoster." He grinned.

She soaked in the feel of his hand in hers and the warmth she found in his smile, not wanting the moment to end, but she needed to know if this was a sincere attempt to repair their broken friendship or if he simply wanted her to save him from Marilyn. "So, how do you want to handle Saturday?"

"I'm not sure." He rubbed the back of her hand with his thumb. "How does a bachelor auction work?"

"Well, they set the lunch baskets out with assigned numbers. Then they assign a number to each bachelor. As the bachelors come on stage, they hand him the corresponding basket and the women bid on the man and the basket together."

"Oh, so a woman could be bidding on the basket she likes best, and the man is extra, like dessert?"

Nikki laughed. "Usually, it's the man the woman is bidding on, not the basket. But I suppose it could be the other way around."

"So, when do they collect the money from the winners?" Dan asked.

"After the auction. I'll need the cash or check to pay—"

"You're definitely extra." Sarah stood behind Nikki. "Way extra for the Senior Citizen's Center bachelor auction."

Pulling her hand from his, Nikki stepped back to face Sarah who had appeared from out of nowhere. "I didn't hear you come out of the copier room."

Sarah gave a knowing grin. "That's obvious."

"Where is your grandmother?" Crossing her arms, Nikki pushed down the irritation that threatened to rise at the young girl's sass. Yes, she was embarrassed about being caught in an awkward situation at her place of work by a teen who thought she had all the answers. But more than that, she hated the doubt that ran through her mind about Dan's intentions.

"She's finishing the last few bulletins before I run them over to the sanctuary for Sunday's service."

"Here they are." Purdy emerged from the copier room with a pile of bulletins. Handing them off to Sarah, she asked, "Is everything all right?"

Nikki nodded. "Everything's fine. Dan just wanted information about the auction Saturday."

Grabbing his hat, he said, "Well, I'd better be going. I'll make sure to take care of everything after the auction Saturday. Remember, don't be shy. I've got it covered." Dan placed his hat on his head and walked to the door. Turning, he added, "And thanks for hearing me out. I'll be looking forward to Saturday."

When Dan left, Purdy couldn't contain her curiosity. "So, did he apologize?"

"Yes," Nikki answered. "But he's right. I don't know that much about him."

"It sounds like you'll find out more on Saturday," Purdy conjectured, settling on one of the stools. "I'm sure it's nothing too earth-shattering."

Nikki glanced toward the front entrance. She hoped Purdy was right. Maybe he'd mention a couple of old girlfriends or perhaps a few innocent adventures that went wrong. But somehow Nikki doubted it would be that simple. Because no matter how hard Dan Thibodeaux tried to pass himself off as another good ole cowboy, Nikki had the distinct impression he was anything but simple.

Chapter Eleven

Dan stepped onto the lowest stair of the gazebo at the Senior Citizen's Center so he could see above the heads of the other bachelors. He hadn't found Nikki before they called the men together to give them some last-minute instructions. To be honest, the mere thought of stepping out into the center of the gazebo holding a frilly backet to be auctioned off like a nine-hundred-pound steer had his stomach in an uproar. Now, as he scanned the crowd, he still couldn't find Nikki.

This was not the day for her to be late. What if Marilyn didn't have to outbid her because Nikki wasn't here? A stream of doubts flooded through his brain as he continued to watch the crowd milling about on the south side of the gazebo.

Lord, please let Nikki show. I know I've treated her poorly, and I've let you down, but if you could see your way clear. Just as he thought about making a promise he shouldn't make, he spotted Nikki jogging across the parking lot with Blue in tow.

As she darted around the groups huddled together, the hound dog sideswiped two gray-haired ladies, causing them to lurch forward and almost fall.

Dan grimaced hoping the ladies were all right.

One of the women followed Nikki and the dog, frowning as she watched her pull Blue along behind her.

Nikki found a spot in the third row of the crowd to the right of the gazebo. She said something to Blue who sat facing her with his head tilted staring intently into her face.

Relief swept through him. What would he have done if she hadn't made it? He stepped from his perch and took his place in line with the other bachelors. The center's director, a Mrs. Peterson, worked her way down the line of eligible men with Purdy's granddaughter, Sarah, trailing behind her. He'd met Mrs. Peterson when he'd accompanied Nikki to the workday.

When they reached him, Dan flashed the teen a smile.

"Oh, hi," Sarah said. "You're Dan, right? Nikki's friend, the ghoster."

"That's right." He stood still while Mrs. Peterson pinned a badge to his red-checkered shirt. Glancing down, he discovered a large number five on the tag.

"Oh, that's good." Sarah pointed to the number. "That basket is a big one."

The bachelor standing next to him chuckled, and

Dan grinned. "Really? 'Cause I'm hungry." Patting his tummy, he wiggled his eyebrows.

Giggling, Sarah held her arms wide. "Yes, it's huge." She gestured. "Plus, you already know who you'll be having lunch with, so you know you'll have fun *and* a good meal."

Dan stood straight and glanced at Mrs. Peterson who was pinning a badge on the man next to him. She scowled, meeting his gaze.

"So, you know who's going to bid on you, do you?" The fifty-something woman tightened her grip on the wicker basket containing the numbered badges.

"I do have an idea of who will be bidding on me." Dan looked down the line of the twenty bachelors. "But I'm sure some of the other men also have sweethearts or friends who have mentioned they'd be bidding today, right?"

No one made direct eye contact with him or Mrs. Peterson, but a few of the men shifted their weight and shrugged while one or two mumbled an answer.

Mrs. Peterson huffed. "I suppose that's only natural." But before she could say anything else, Marilyn appeared with a group of ladies surrounding her. "Marilyn, you know you're not supposed to be back here." The woman frowned.

"I know." Marilyn waved off the rigid woman's reproof. "But I wanted to let Mr. Thibodeaux know I was here, and that I hadn't forgotten my promise."

Mrs. Peterson sighed. "I see. Well, there's not

much I can do about people making arrangements about the bidding, and I suppose since it all goes to a good cause there's no point in making a fuss about it, either." She sniffed and lifted her chin. "But don't linger, Marilyn." Moving to the next man in line, she repeated the process.

Sarah's face clouded in confusion. "But I thought …" She eyed Dan and pointed toward Marilyn who busily chatted with the other women. "You had plans—"

"To eat every bite in that basket. You are one hundred percent correct." He tilted his head. "You'd better catch up to Mrs. Peterson; she may need you."

"Oh, I'd better. She won't give me all my service hours if I'm not with her every second." She hurried off.

As Dan turned his attention back to the group of women, Marilyn wrapped her hand around his bicep and cooed, "Isn't he divine, ladies?"

A steer at auction had nothing on him. No wonder they snorted and stomped the ground.

Her three cohorts giggled like a bunch of schoolgirls. All of them had to be near forty or past. Purdy's granddaughter acted more mature than this herd of females.

Dan caught the curious stares of the other bachelors out of the corner of his eye. "Look, Marilyn, I need to get ready, so if you don't mind—" Lifting her hand, he pulled his arm away.

An older man wearing a cowboy hat, leather vest, and a rope tie with a silver clasp stood on the top step. "All right, gentlemen, I'm Bill Temple, and I'll be your auctioneer this afternoon. The mayor has instructed me to thank every one of you for participating in today's auction. I know many of you, especially you, Sam—" the auctioneer pointed to a stout, older man at the head of the line. "don't particularly love to be the center of attention, so the committee of the Senior Citizen's Center and the mayor himself would like to extend their hearty thanks." The gray-haired emcee with the smooth baritone voice tucked a clipboard under his arm and clapped for the bachelors.

Mrs. Peterson, Sarah, and Marilyn's group joined him. Marilyn wiggled her fingers in Dan's direction then headed back toward the crowd followed by Sarah who had finished helping hand out the badges.

Exhaling, Dan relaxed and turned his focus onto the next part of this nightmarish event, the actual auction.

~

Nikki weaved her way to the front of the crowd closer to the gazebo, pulling Blue behind her. The dog stopped every few feet, waiting for the next person to pet him. She yanked on the leash. "Come on, Blue. We're late as it is."

The hound wagged his tail. She could've sworn he smiled at her. "Don't try to get on my good side now." She found an open spot big enough for her and Blue without crowding anyone else. Blowing out a breath, she relaxed her grip on the leash and scanned the scattered groupings of people.

Marilyn and her friends rounded the west side of the gazebo and sauntered over to four empty lawn chairs nestled in the front row.

She frowned. Why hadn't she thought to bring a lawn chair? Groaning, she shifted her weight, her wedge-heel sandals pinching her feet. She'd been torn about what to wear. After all, it wasn't a date, but still, she wanted to look nice. She'd settled on a pair of slim fit jeans with a purple peasants blouse and her new sandals.

She glanced down at Blue who rested in the grass with his head on his front paws. He had one ear turned toward her and the other one directed toward the couple sitting beside them.

Irritation stirred in her. She'd almost been late because of Blue's shenanigans. "Why couldn't you've been this easy when I tried to get you into the car?" Reaching down, she stroked the dogs' droopy ears.

He yawned closing his eyes.

Straightening, she searched the crowd to see if she recognized anyone. Pastor Connor and Purdy had both told her they were coming. Even Tabitha, her boss at the rescue, had planned to be here.

Turning around, she rose onto her tiptoes to see past the guy standing behind her. Nikki spotted Pastor Connor sitting with his wife and two grown daughters closer to the back of the crowd. She motioned with her arms, making her purse flap against her hip, but he didn't look her way. Nikki continued scanning the faces of the crowd and spotted Purdy and Sarah standing a few feet behind the pastor, with hands above their heads signaling in her direction. She smiled and waved, happy to see them.

Both gestured for her to join them.

Shaking her head, she pointed toward Blue. *No sense in disturbing His Majesty while he was calm.* Besides, she wanted to be close, so she wouldn't miss anything.

The auctioneer bounded onto the stage carrying a clipboard. He walked to the podium and grabbed the mic. Moving to the center of the structure, he planted himself where everyone could see him.

Ralph, one of the bachelors, led the men onto the stage. The line of men formed a semi-circle along the railing of the gazebo behind the auctioneer, giving everyone a clear view of all the eligible guys.

Nikki's gaze flowed over the line of men until she found Dan wearing a crisp, red-checkered shirt and a tan cowboy hat pushed back on his head. A large number five hung over his chest.

He turned and looked straight at her.

She nodded to acknowledge that she'd seen him.

A slow smile spread across his lips, and he dipped his chin.

The auctioneer lifted his hands above his head and

waved his arms to grab the crowd's attention. Speaking into the mic, he said, "Gooood afternoon, ladies and the few gents who weren't forced—I mean, eligible—to be on the stage."

The crowd chuckled.

"I'm your auctioneer this afternoon, Bill Temple." He grinned, revealing a gap between his front teeth. "My, my, what a fine group of lovely women we have here today and so civic minded."

Another low rumble of laughter skittered through the crowd.

"I know these gents will be proud to share one of these delicious baskets with you on this bea-u-ti-ful October day." He swept his arm in the direction of the table sitting to his right.

The table showcased over twenty baskets of various shapes and sizes. The senior citizens who used the center and several of the volunteers had prepared the meals and decorated them.

"I'd also like to say a big thank you to all the bachelors, the ladies who prepared the baskets, and to all of you for coming out to support our local Senior Citizen's Center. Let's give everyone a big hand." He paused until the applause died down. "I know all of you broke your piggy banks and brought an extra checkbook, so you could help with the refurbishing of the center. So, I won't keep you waiting any longer. If my lovely assistant, Miss Sarah Thomas, would come up, she'll be passing out the baskets to the bachelors.

We'll get started."

Sarah hurried up the five steps and took her place beside the table where the baskets were displayed.

The auctioneer walked to the podium sitting to his left and deposited his clipboard on it. Attaching the mic to the stand, he motioned for the first gentleman to come forward.

Ralph White, who was known for his antics, moved to the center of the gazebo, and curtsied as pretty as you please to the audience while batting his eyelashes. Placing his hands on his hips, he sashayed forward like a New York model, turned, and strutted back to the center.

Everyone laughed, and a couple of the ladies whistled.

Nikki lifted her hand to her mouth to smother a giggle. Leave it to Ralph to set the tone for the whole day.

Sarah scurried over and handed Ralph a basket decorated with yellow lace and sunflowers. He took it. Holding it by the handle, he let it dangle daintily from his fingertips.

Shaking his head, the auctioneer pulled a three-by-five card from his pocket. "Ralph is a local carpenter. And he promises one odd job in addition to a fun-filled lunch." Looking up, he smiled. "Let's open the bidding at fifty dollars."

After a few minutes of bidding, Ralph sold for a solid two hundred bucks.

Nikki's heart faltered. If Ralph, the town clown, brought in two hundred, how much would Dan go for? After all, he did have those biceps going for him. She pulled at the collar of her favorite purple blouse, hoping Dan could cover the amount.

She glanced toward Marilyn who sat relaxed in her green aluminum-frame chair.

Digging into her purse, Nikki produced her wallet. She dumped the contents into her hand and counted. It didn't take long. Two fives, four ones, and a dollar's worth of change was all she had. Nothing like the cash floating around here. She snapped the wallet closed and forced it back into her purse. Crossing her arms, she struggled to push down her panic.

Blue sat up, tilting his head.

"I know, boy. I shouldn't worry. Dan said he'd cover it, but I wish I'd asked him how high to go. I mean I'd feel awful if I bid his entire paycheck."

Blue stretched and moved behind her before easing back down onto the ground. His leash pulled against her knees.

The next two guys each brought in seventy-five dollars and the fourth man, who was a local firefighter, went for three hundred.

The firefighter did have a certain appeal, and he'd worn his uniform, which made him look handsome in that hero sort of way. But even with that, he still didn't hold a candle to Dan, at least not in her opinion.

"All right, folks, here is a new member of our little

community. Dan Harris Thibodeaux."

Dan walked to the center of the gazebo and shot a glance in her direction.

The auctioneer continued, "Dan loves to work outdoors. And he is rumored to be quite handy with a chain saw."

Her palms damp with sweat, and she licked her dry lips. She'd never bid on anything before, and she didn't want to disappoint Dan. He'd never forgive her if he had to spend the afternoon with the notorious Marilyn. Especially since Nikki had been the one to coerce him into this mess.

Marilyn and her crew let out a few squeals of excitement, and before the auctioneer even asked for a starting bid, she raised her hand. "One hundred dollars."

"Well, look at that. I have one hundred." The auctioneer pointed his gavel at Marilyn. "Do I hear one twenty-five?"

Nikki swallowed. "One twenty-five." She raised her hand.

The auctioneer nodded toward her.

Marilyn turned in her chair and glared her direction. "One fifty."

"One sixty." Someone called from behind Nikki.

Turning, Nikki recognized the tall brunette as the lady who owned the coffee shop Dan frequented.

Nikki shot Dan a worried look. He slipped his hand near his badge, giving her a thumbs- up on the sly.

Encouraged, she said, "One seventy-five."

Marilyn scowled. "Two hundred."

"Two twenty-five." The coffee-shop owner called, nodding to the auctioneer.

"Two fifty." Nikki met Marilyn's gaze.

Blue rose and leaned against Nikki's leg.

Marilyn jumped up from her seat. "Two seventy-five."

"Too rich for my blood." The coffee-shop owner held her hands in surrender and took her seat.

"Three hundred." Nikki stood straight and crossed her arms.

Blue pulled on his leash.

"Three hundred and fifty." Marilyn called crisp and clear with a slight lift of her chin.

Forgetting she was bidding with someone else's money, Nikki propped her hands on her hips set on winning. "Four hundred."

"Four fifty," Marilyn called out before she leaned over and whispered to her friends. The women grabbed their purses and rummaged through them, pulling out wallets and billfolds.

She had them. "Five hundred."

Marilyn did a quick count of the cash she'd been handed. "Five forty and thirty-seven cents."

Nikki's eyes widened.

"I have a bid of five hundred forty dollars and thirty-seven cents. Do I hear five fifty?"

She hesitated, not sure if she should go that high.

What had she done? How had the amount grown so rapidly? She turned toward Dan who stood gawking at her, holding a white wicker basket clutched to his chest.

"Going once."

Dan lurched forward. His mouth gaped open. His eyes glued to her.

"Going twice."

"Six hundred." Nikki's voice cracked as the words burst past her lips.

Dan's body deflated.

The auctioneer's gavel banged on the wooden podium. "Sold for six hundred dollars to the woman with the dog wrapped around her knees."

Chapter Twelve

Dan leaned back on his elbows with his legs stretched out in front of him. The day had proved to be as beautiful as the auctioneer had predicted. Nikki sat next to him on the cloth tarp, watching Blue sniff around the base of a large oak tree.

He'd grabbed the tarp from his truck after the auction ended, when he realized Nikki had come a bit unprepared. But she'd made up for it by choosing the perfect spot toward the back of the Senior Citizen's Center's property for their picnic. It was far enough away from the gazebo and the other groups and couples lunching together for them to talk privately. He couldn't have chosen a better place for the conversation if he'd tried.

"Blue," Nikki called to the dog. "Come drink some water. Come, boy."

Blue trotted over, dragging his orange leash behind him. Nikki held out an empty plastic bowl that moments earlier had contained chicken salad with pecans and grapes. Reaching for her bottle of water, she shook the dribble that remain at the bottom and poured it into the bowl.

Dan shifted onto his side, propping on one elbow and poured the remainder of the water from his bottle into the plastic bowl as well.

"Thanks." Nikki set the bowl on the edge of the tarp while Blue lapped up the liquid as if he'd been playing in a desert.

The meal had been superb including the two slices of pumpkin pie—one for each of them.

"So, you wanted to talk?" She ran her hand down Blue's back while the dog pushed the plastic bowl around with his nose, looking for more water.

"Sorry, buddy," Dan said. "That's the last of it." As if he understood what Dan had said, Blue lowered himself to the ground beside Nikki, placing his head on her leg. "You spoil that dog," Dan observed. "He knows you'll pet him until your hand falls off, and he's not ashamed to let you."

Nikki grinned and looked down at Blue with an unmistakable warmth in her eyes. "I've grown very fond of him. He's a bit of a troublemaker, but he brings a lot of joy too."

"Like tying you up with his leash during the auction? Or almost making you late for the whole thing? Or wallowing around on a complete stranger's bed?" Dan shot Blue a knowing look. "He's a real joy giver, that one."

Laughing, Nikki scratched behind the dog's ears.

Dan loved the sound of her laughter. It had a light jingle to it, making it almost musical. He missed it those weeks he'd kept to himself, trying to figure out what it was about this woman that had him so tangled up inside. Indeed, he'd missed a lot of things about Nikki and her furry crew. Like how she had a knack of painting each situation with the bright color of hope. He couldn't remember a single time when she'd complained. Not about the animals in her care, not about having to work two jobs, and not about him. Her can-do spirit drew him like a thirsty hound to a bowl of water.

If he let himself, he could—

The touch of Nikki's hand on his arm brought him back to the moment. "From the look on your face, those must be some heavy thoughts. Anything you want to share?"

He cleared his throat and sat up, resting his arm across the top of his knee, searching for the best way to start this conversation. *How should I tell this beautiful woman who makes my heart race that I'm not who she thinks I am?* "Here goes." Dan took a deep breath. "I need to clear up what you think you know about me."

"To be honest, I don't know much about you at all." Nikki grabbed the plastic bowl and placed it into the white wicker basket without disturbing Blue. "You're hard to get to know. I mean, apart from you working on a ranch and rebuilding your house, I don't know much about your life, now or before we met."

"Well, that's what I want to clarify. It's time I set a few things straight."

"Okay, let's start with an easy question, then. Do you have any siblings?" Nikki asked.

"Siblings?" Dan frowned. Apparently, Nikki had the wrong idea about what he meant.

"Yeah, you know, brothers or sisters?" Nikki cocked her head to one side, giving him a quizzical look as she tucked a strand of honey-blond hair behind her ear. "I have a brother. He's married and lives out of state." She waited.

"I have two younger brothers, Wade and Brent. One is in the military and the other runs a security service."

"So, you're the eldest son. Well, that explains a lot." She moved, jostling the dog who rolled over onto his side and let out a deep sigh.

Dan smiled. "You stopped petting him."

"My hand is about to fall off," she said.

They both laughed.

Dan's cheeks ached when they caught their breath. He couldn't remember the last time since Lilly he'd been this comfortable around a woman. Lilly had been his best friend. They'd known each other since childhood. They'd grown up together and shared every aspect of their lives, even their first kiss. He never expected to find anything close to what they had. But now with Nikki, he could see the possibilities.

"Okay, here's another one. Do you like what you do?" Nikki asked.

Dan nodded. "Yeah, I do. I love working outdoors with the animals, both horses and cattle. And I like the people who work for me." He waited to see if she caught what he'd said.

"What about your boss?" Nikki's eyes sparkled. "'Cause, you know, I *have* to like my boss. He's a pastor." She giggled.

"Yeah, it is sort of a requirement, isn't it?" He grinned and shifted positions, not sure how to turn the conversation back in the direction he needed it to go. "I do like my boss, but that's what I need to straighten out. You know how I said I worked at the Silver Spur?"

"Oh, I meant to tell you I know where that's located. I did a search for it on a map app. It's not too far from Zion Hill about forty miles north of here. I can see why you picked Orange Blossom, though. It's close to the ranch, and it's convenient for buying the materials needed for rebuilding."

"Yeah, Zion Hill is a small community. Smaller than Orange Blossom." Dan nodded. "But they are rebuilding as best as they can." He took her hand in his. "Look, Nikki, there's something I need to explain, and I'd better do it now before I lose my nerve."

She squeezed his hands. "I'm listening."

"It's about where I work. You see, I don't just work at the Silver Spur." He gazed into her cornflower-blue eyes, willing his heart to quit racing. He licked his dry lips and squeezed her hand that lay in his. "I kind of …"

A horrific yelp cut through his words.

Glancing over to where Blue had been lying, Nikki jumped to her feet. "Where's Blue?"

"Darn that dog," Dan muttered. Rolling to his knees, he hoisted himself to a standing position. But before moving, he listened.

"Blue," Nikki called. "Blue."

Another yelp. Dan held up his hand to silence her. Tilting his head, he tried to figure out from which direction the sound came.

After a moment, sharp, panicked barks broke the silence.

"The lake." Nikki tore out across the field toward the fence that separated the two pieces of land without so much as a backward glance.

"Wait, Nikki." Dan jogged behind her but couldn't keep up. He didn't like the thought of Blue and Nikki at the lake. It stirred up too many bad memories.

As she reached the fence, she vaulted over the top rung and disappeared into the brush on the other side.

Too bulky to fling himself over the fence like Nikki, he stepped on the bottom rung and swung his legs over the top. Twisting, he jumped to the ground. Not sure which way to go, he called, "Nikki, Blue."

No answer.

Spotting a narrow trail to the right, he inspected the path for any signs of the dog or Nikki. A closer look showed paw prints headed away from the fence. A little further down the dirt path, he discovered heel marks that could come from a pair of wedge sandals.

Beating back tree limbs and thorny vines, he kept his eyes glued to the path. The further he went, the more worried he became. What trouble was Blue into now?

A series of yelps rang through the woods and grew louder with every step he took. "Nikki, Blue!" He yelled. "Nikki, Blue."

Barks replaced the yelps. Firm, hard barks, one right after another. Something was wrong.

Dan picked up speed, his cowboy boots kicking up dust as he shot down the narrow trail, emerging from the woods a few feet from the shoreline of the lake.

Blue stood on the edge, barking wildly at the water.

There near the center struggled Nikki, her hands beating the surface, trying to keep her head above the water line before she disappeared beneath the cold reflection of the trees.

Every nightmare he'd ever had about Lilly's accident rushed into his mind. Without taking off his boots, he plunged into the cold water, swimming with all his might. Pushing the water with his cupped hands, he propelled himself toward the spot where she'd been.

Nikki emerged a few feet from him, grabbing at the air as she went under a second time.

Not again, dear Lord, please.

Diving into the murky water, he saw flailing legs. He grabbed them, pushing Nikki heavenward until her head broke the surface. Drawing in a breath, he caught her by the shoulders and rolled her limp body onto her back, placing her head against his shoulder. "I've got you, Nikki. Don't go. Please, don't go."

Choking in air, her limp body stirred to life, and she fought against him, struggling to free herself from what held her in the water. The fear on her pallid face tore at his heart. Lilly had worn that same expression, but he'd been too late.

He held tight. "It's me, Dan," he whispered in her ear. "I've got you. You're safe."

Her body sagged. "Is Blue…okay?"

"For now," Dan said.

The barking stopped the moment Dan entered the water. But now the dog paced along the edge. He'd look toward them, dipped his paw into the water, then backed away and resumed his pacing.

With his free arm, he swam toward the shore. When his feet touched bottom, he stood in his waterlogged boots and lifted Nikki into his arms. Sloshing out of the lake, he placed her on the hard ground.

She rolled over and kissed the dirt beneath her before flopping out her arms and taking in a few deep breaths.

Dan crumpled to the ground beside her listening to her inhale and exhale—the best sounds he'd ever heard.

Nikki eased up on her elbow to face him. "Thank you. I don't know what I would've done if you hadn't followed us."

"What happened?" Dan asked.

"I don't know. Blue was tangled in something when I found him in the lake. I got him loose. One minute I was pushing Blue toward the shore and the next minute, I lost my footing. When I tried to stand, it was too deep." She gazed down at the grass. "I'm not a very strong swimmer."

Pressing his lips together, Dan fought to compose himself. "Well, first thing Monday, you're taking that stupid dog back to the rescue and leaving him there." He pushed against the ground, sitting upright. Anger filled him. He'd been scared out of his mind when he found her going under. "He's nothing but trouble. You nearly died saving that dumb mutt."

Nikki shot up. "I simply lost my footing. That's not Blue's fault."

Blue wandered over to them when he heard his name.

"Yes, it is. He's the whole reason you're here. If he hadn't run off in the first place, we wouldn't be sitting here drenched, again. He's a nuisance. You need to get rid of him."

Nikki placed her arm around Blue's neck. "I admit he's a bit high maintenance, but that's no reason to abandon him." Nikki chanced a glance at Dan.

"Besides, he's the one who sounded the alarm when I got into trouble. He's a hero."

"A hero? Are you kidding me? You need to get rid of him." Dan's jaw tightened.

"Yes, a hero. What is wrong with you? Why are you so angry?" Nikki released Blue and stood.

Dan rose to face her. "What about you? What if I hadn't followed you? Or known what to do?" He grabbed her shoulders and pulled her toward him. "You were sinking, Nikki. I didn't know if I could reach you in time, and it scared me." He met her gaze. The compassion in her eyes buckled his knees.

"What's this really about?" She rested the palm of her hand on his cheek.

He loosened his grip on her shoulders as he fought to keep his voice steady. "Lilly." He swallowed the lump in his throat. "It's how she died. She drowned in a boating accident."

"Lilly?" Flickers of confusion played on her face. "Who's Lilly?"

"My wife. *Was* my wife. She died three years ago. Drowned. I couldn't save her." His lips quivered.

Nikki leaned into him and wrapped her arms around his middle. "I'm so sorry, Dan." She ran her hand along his back and rested her head against his chest.

Without hesitation, he slid his arms around her shoulders and pulled her closer, the anger seeping out of him. He closed his eyes and let the feel of her comfort his soul.

The hound walked around them before settling next to Dan with his paw on his foot.

He leaned over and scratched the dog behind the ears. Glancing up, he said, "I'd better drive you back to town and have someone take a look at you."

"That might be a good idea." Nikki gave him a weak smile. "I'm feeling a little light-headed."

In one swift motion, Dan scooped her off her feet into his arms.

"Oh, I don't think this is necessary."

"Nikki, you almost died today. You don't get to argue."

"Point taken." She slid her arms around his neck and leaned her head against his shoulder.

Dan looked back. "Come on, you hero. Time to go."

Chapter Thirteen

When the truck pulled to a stop in Dan's driveway around eight o'clock that evening, Nikki pushed the passenger side door open and stepped out on wobbly legs. Grabbing her purse and the white wicker basket, she shut the truck door with her hip.

Dan climbed out, dragging the cloth tarp from their picnic with him.

Purdy had given Blue a lift back to the bungalow and promised to feed the animals when Dan had insisted Nikki go to the emergency room. She didn't mention Tinkerbelle to Purdy, knowing the alligator only needed to eat once a week, and she had until tomorrow to feed her.

The trip had been overkill, but Dan wouldn't take no for an answer. Once there, he proceeded to fuss over her like a mother hen. He questioned every move the nurses made. *What are you doing? What is that? When will the doctor be here?*

She walked toward the porch of her house, ready to

plop onto her couch and forget all about the last few hours. "Thanks for looking after me," she called over her shoulder. "I'll see you tomorrow."

"Where do you think you're going?"

She stopped and turned toward him, hugging the wicker basket to her. "Home."

Dan stood in front of the truck folding the tarp. She could barely make out the scowl etched on his face in the glow of the porch light. "No, you're not. You're staying at my place tonight, so I can keep an eye on you."

"That's not necessary. I'm fine. Even the doctor said everything checked out." Nikki waved off the suggestion, hoping he'd be satisfied with her answer and pivoted to leave.

He shook his head. "Nope. I'm afraid not. The doctor also said to keep you under surveillance for twenty-four hours and to make sure you get plenty of rest." Dan finished folding the tarp and laid it on the hood of his truck.

Nikki moved toward him determined to sleep in her own bed. "Well, don't you think I can accomplish that better at home? Not to be rude, but I don't think I'd sleep as well on your couch."

"You won't be on my couch." Dan cocked his right eyebrow.

For a moment, her heart stuttered. Surely, he wasn't suggesting anything untoward.

"You'll be in the guest bedroom. There's a nice

homemade quilt on the bed and several down pillows. I'm sure one of them will be to your liking."

"I'm telling you it's not necessary." She tightened her arms across her chest.

Dan spread his feet wide and crossed his arms in like manner, determination written all over his face.

It was clear she'd lost, but she gave it one last-ditch effort anyway. "What about the animals? Who's going to take care of them if I'm over here?"

He didn't hesitate. "Me. Since Purdy already fed them, I'll go over and take them out one last time before bedding them down for the night. And in the morning, I'll go over and feed and water them." He tilted his head and met her gaze. "Will that work?"

"Yeah," she said. "But I'll need a few personal items like some clean clothes." She looked down at the stiff jeans she'd been wearing since her swim in the lake. "And some pajamas and a toothbrush."

"I'll get them," he offered.

"Nooo, I don't think so." She shook her head as the heat of a blush rose to her cheeks. Hopefully, he couldn't see it in the dim porch light. There was no way she was going to let this man, her next-door neighbor, go through her unmentionables or tote around her toothbrush.

"And before you say it, I'll get dinner, too." Dan stepped toward her, stopping within reach. "I could really use some dinner."

"Oh, me too." The mention of food made her

stomach grumble.

"Okay." Dan touched her shoulder which made a tingling sensation zing through her. "Why don't we go over to your house first? I'll take care of the animals while you grab the things you need for the night. Then we'll go over to my house, and you can clean up while I order two large pizzas."

Now, how was she supposed to argue with that? The mere act of standing here in the driveway discussing it had drained her. A wave of exhaustion poured over her. As if he sensed it, he took the basket and her purse from her.

"Which pocket are your keys in?"

"The front one."

He dug in the front pocket of her purse and pulled out her keys. Picking up the tarp from the hood of the truck, he jogged to his porch and deposited all three items on the top step. Returning, he took her by the hand and led her to her house.

~

The pizza arrived while Dan was in the shower. She'd forgotten that he'd been wearing damp clothes all day too. Well, that accounted for his grumpy attitude toward the nurses.

After her shower, she'd put on a pair of sweatpants and an old ratty Texas A&M tee-shirt she'd bought as a freshman several years ago when she thought she wanted to be a teacher. She loved the old shirt. Now, comfy and clean, she pulled two sodas out of the refrigerator, placed them on the counter, and grabbed a couple of napkins from the pile of restaurant napkins that sat stacked near the toaster.

The smell of the pizza permeated the tiny kitchen.

She flipped open the lid on the top box and leaned over it to inhale the aroma. Her tummy rumbled, pushing her to find the plates. Humming, she opened the cabinet to the left of the sink, thinking it was the most likely place for them to be, but instead, she found a couple of stainless-steel pots with lids. She continued her search, opening and closing the cabinet doors—first the top, then the bottom ones.

"Hey, whatcha looking for?"

Nikki jumped, whipping around to face him. "Oh, my word. Are you trying to scare me to death?"

Dan stood in the doorway wearing a gray tee-shirt that hugged those biceps she admired so much, and a dark blue pair of gym shorts that stopped at his thighs. Barefooted, he had a towel draped around his neck. When she met his gaze, a smile appeared on his firm lips that ran all the way up to his dark green eyes, igniting them with a spark.

Feeling a little wobbly again, she leaned against the counter hoping that the thundering in her chest couldn't be heard.

"Boy, that sure does smell good." He sauntered over to where she stood and reached above her head, standing mere inches away. "Were you looking for these?"

She lifted her chin. "Yes, the plates." He handed one to her and kept one, never moving his eyes from hers. "I thought I'd looked there." She tried to take a step back to put some distance between them, but her feet seemed glued to the spot.

What if he kissed me? Both terrified and exhilarated by the thought, she straightened.

"Maybe you just missed them." A sparkle twinkled in his eyes. She could tell he wanted to say something, even do something, but he didn't. Stepping back, he broke the connection and moved to the other end of the counter where the pizza boxes sat. Pulling out a couple of slices from the top one, he placed them on his plate. "Do you want to eat in here or in the living room? We could see what's on TV."

She shrugged, trying to calm the drumming in her chest and grabbed a few slices for herself. "I'm not much of a TV watcher. How about we sit in the living room and talk. You did say you wanted to tell me a little bit about yourself."

"That's true." Taking one of the drinks from the counter, he led the way to the sofa. She followed him, hoping he'd be open to the topic she had in mind.

Placing his plate in the one clear spot, he gathered the piles of mail and circulars that littered the coffee table and moved them to the smaller table by the door to make room for her plate.

"Thank you," she said.

He plopped down on the cushion beside her,

pulling the towel from around his neck and throwing it onto the armchair that sat angled to the couch. "You're very welcome." Lifting her hand into his, he prayed. "Lord, I don't know how to thank you for what you did for Nikki and me today. Life is so precious, and you reminded me of that again. Please bless her and bless this food. In Jesus' name, amen."

Nikki pressed her lips together and blinked back the tears that threatened to come. The sincerity in his voice touched her. "In case I didn't say thank you, let me say it now. Dan, I'll never be able to repay you."

He looked down at her hand still in his. "You don't have to repay me. I'm glad you're safe." Releasing it, he took a drink of his soda.

She couldn't imagine the pain that had run through him finding her struggling like that—not with his past. Not with what he'd told her. She lifted a piece of pizza to her lips and took a bite. The tangy sauce danced across her taste buds. She loved this kind, not sweet but spicy. Wiping her mouth with a napkin, she decided to broach the topic that had been burning in her mind since he'd rescued her. "So, tell me about Lilly."

Dan cut her a sideways glance and finished chewing before answering. "I figured that's what you wanted to talk about." He laid the half-eaten piece of pizza on the plate on the table and leaned back. "Let's see. The short version is that Lilly was my best friend. She understood me better than anyone else." Dan folded his hands in his lap as the sadness slipped into his eyes.

"So, how long were you married?" Nikki leaned back against the cushion and slid her feet under her, holding her plate in her lap. She thought this might take a while, and she didn't want to rush him. If she wanted to know about Dan, she had to know about Lilly.

"We were married for five years. But we'd grown up together. I'd known Lilly since we were six years old." He shook his head, a soft smile spreading across his lips that hinted at heartache and lost chances.

"Oh, that is a long time." Nikki played with her napkin searching for what to say next. "Did you two go to the same schools? Is that how you met?"

"At first, yes. We met in Mrs. Stillman's first grade class. She stood up for me when another boy had accused me of stealing his candy bar from his lunch box." He chuckled. "She'd been a terror. But, of course through the years, we were assigned to different teachers, and when we hit middle school, she went to public school, and my dad moved me to a prep school. He wanted to make sure I received the best education …" Dan paused.

"I understand. Parents always have high hopes for their kids. They want them to do better than they did. Have more than they do." Nikki thought about her own mother who worked as a high school English teacher, and how disappointed she'd been when Nikki decided against teaching as a career. "Following in their footsteps but on a little higher ground. That's what they expect or hope for."

He ran his arm along the back of the couch, leaning closer. Meeting her gaze, he said, "Wise beyond your years."

She blushed. "So, tell me more about your Lilly."

"By the time we'd started high school, I knew she was the girl I'd marry."

"And she felt the same way?"

"Yeah, to my amazement. I couldn't get over the fact that a creature so beautiful and so smart would give someone like me the time of day. But she did. When we finished college, I proposed, and she said yes. One of the happiest days of my life." His gaze left hers and drifted to somewhere beyond the walls of the house.

Nikki listened, picturing the woman from the photos in her mind. He was right. She was beautiful. "You told me she died three years ago. Are those the ashes you need to scatter?"

Dan squirmed and leaned forward, placing his forearms on his knees, not looking at her. "Yeah. Until recently, I couldn't. But after the hurricane, I thought I'd lost the opportunity. She requested in her will if anything ever happened to her, that I'd scatter her ashes by the river that runs through Silver Spur Ranch." He ran his hand down the back of his neck. "I can't tell you how relieved I was when I found the wooden crate with her urn."

Nikki wanted to reach out and comfort him, to soothe the hurt that hung on him. Instead, she put her plate on the coffee table and snatched one of the throw pillows, hugging it to her chest.

"She said, that way we'd always be together if her ashes were spread on Silver Spur."

Confused, she asked, "Why would she want you to spread her ashes where you work? What if you quit or something?"

Dan looked up startled. Leaning closer, he took one of her hands from the pillow. "There's something I've been trying to tell you."

"Okay, I'm listening." Nikki leaned forward a bit, giving him her full attention.

Dan rubbed the back of her hand with his thumb. Clearing his throat, he tried forming the words. But nothing came out.

"It's okay, Dan. If you're not ready to share more about your life with Lilly, I understand. The fact that you've shared this much means a lot." She placed her other hand over his and squeezed, trying to reassure him. "We can talk about something else."

"It's not about Lilly," Dan said. "It's about me. There's something I need you to know about me, about who I am."

"Okay." The way he acted she wasn't sure what to expect.

But before she had time to let her mind run wild, he said, "It'd be easier if I showed you. Are you doing anything Saturday afternoon?"

"No." She smiled, not sure where all this would

lead. "I think my calendar is clear. Why? Where are you taking me?"

"Home." He grinned. Standing, he clutched his plate of cold pizza. "I'm going to heat this up. Would you like me to zap yours?" Dan disappeared into the kitchen with both plates.

Alone with her thoughts, Nikki wondered what Dan's life must be like on a ranch. She imagined him on horseback herding cows. A smile lifted her lips. But something nagged at her. Why would Lilly want her ashes spread at Silver Spur Ranch, and what had he meant about taking her home?

"Here you go." Dan handed her the warm plate.

"Smells good, thanks."

After polishing off both pizzas, Nikki and Dan settled in to catch the local nightly news. She fought for as long as she could to keep her eyes open, but the voice of the newscaster droned on and on.

Dan shook her shoulder. "Hey, you fell asleep on the couch. Let's get you to bed."

Nikki groaned and turned her back to him. "I'm fine here." The patter of his bare feet retreating on the wooden floor echoed around her.

The next thing she remembered, he lifted her head and placed a soft pillow beneath it. "Um, thanks," she whispered.

The weight of a blanket draped over her, and firm hands tucked it in around her.

"Sweet dreams, Nikki." Dan mumbled.

His breath tickled her ear. She dragged her eyelids open and smiled into his face mere inches from her own. "Thank you for everything. Especially for saving me." She lifted her hand to his cheek, the stubble of his five o'clock shadow rough to her touch. "You're a hero like Blue."

Dan chuckled. Placing his hand over hers, he lifted it, kissing her palm before tucking it under the blanket. "Not quite like Blue. I can't yelp and have you come running."

Closing her eyes, she sighed. "But I think you can."

Chapter Fourteen

Cracking open her eyes, Nikki surveyed her surroundings—a TV, two armchairs, a coffee table. Right, she was at Dan's. She rolled over and checked the clock near the TV. Nine-thirty?

She huffed laying her head back against the pillow. All she wanted was more sleep. The late morning sun streamed into the living room despite the closed wooden blinds on the windows. She placed her arm across her eyes. Her muscles ached when she moved. The doctor at the emergency room had recommended a day or two of rest. And from the way her body felt, she agreed. But before she could get comfortable, her eyes popped open. *Oh, no. The animals.* By now, they'd all be starving including Tinkerbell who hadn't eaten this week. A groan welled inside her as she threw her sore legs over the side of the couch. The smell of food cooking drifted into the room from the kitchen. She inhaled. Coffee.

She darted to the hall bathroom where she had left

her duffel bag. There she washed her face, brushed her teeth, and changed into a pair of jeans and a long-sleeved tee-shirt with a picture of a pooch with oversized eyes on it. Checking her reflection in the mirror, she dug a brush from her toiletry bag and tried to tame her locks. After a few futile attempts, she pulled them back into a ponytail before following her nose to the kitchen.

"Hey there, bright eyes." Dan grinned. "I like your tee-shirt."

"Thanks. Sorry for oversleeping. I can't tell you the last time I slept this late on a Sunday."

"I know what you mean. I'm surprised you did, sleeping on that lumpy couch." Dan walked over and handed her a cup of coffee. "I added sugar and creamer. Hope that's okay."

She held the mug between her hands and let the steam rise to her nose. "It's perfect." Sipping the hot liquid, she eased toward the table, pulling out a chair. "I hate to be a spoilsport, but I'd better head over to my house."

"Oh, why?" Dan scrambled the eggs in the skillet.

"The animals."

"Oh, right," Dan said.

"The dogs need some outside time, and I'm sure all of them are starving." The image of Tinkerbell formed in her mind. Even though she was a baby, she didn't need to get too hungry and go looking for something to eat on her own. Alligators could be testy if they weren't fed at least once a week. And if Tinkerbelle got out to forage for food, Nikki did not relish telling the neighbors she was hunting for a lost, hungry alligator—no matter what size she might be.

One neighbor in particular. Her gaze drifted toward Dan who dropped two pieces of bread into the toaster.

"You don't think they could wait another half hour?" He glanced at her over his shoulder.

"No." The word came out sharper than she'd intended. Standing, she headed to the living room to slip on her shoes.

The noise of a skillet clanking on the stove top rang out, right before Dan called from the kitchen, "Wait, and I'll come with you."

"Oh, that's not necessary." She leaned over to tie one shoe then switched feet. "Why don't you stay and finish cooking. That way when I'm done, everything will be ready for us to eat." She stood and grabbed her duffel bag, hoping that he'd see the logic in her plan.

Dan came from the kitchen into the living room. "Don't be silly. By the time you're done, the eggs will be cold anyway. So, why don't I come help, and that way you can finish twice as fast. And get back to resting. It hasn't been twenty-four hours yet." Not waiting for an answer, Dan dashed into his room. When he emerged, he wore a pair of blue jeans in place of his shorts, and he wore a pair of black boots she'd never seen on him.

Of course, he couldn't wear his usual brown boots.

They were drying from their swimming adventure yesterday. Her lips tugged into a smile at the thought of her hero-turned-nursemaid.

"Ready?" Her hand rested on the doorknob.

"Yeah, and when we're done, we'll come back and eat. Deal?"

Nikki nodded and stepped onto the porch with Dan behind her. As they walked to the driveway, a car slowed down and honked. Turning, Nikki spotted Dawn, one of Marilyn's gal pals, cruising past with her window rolled down.

Dawn slowed to a crawl, pulled her sunglasses down an inch or two on her nose, and lifted her eyebrows. A devious grin crept across her lips right before she floored it and disappeared around the corner.

"Who was that?" Dan asked. "A friend of yours?"

"Not exactly. She's Dawn Miller, one of Marilyn's friends. I'm surprised you didn't recognize her. She was part of your fan club with Marilyn yesterday. She whistled at you."

He chuckled. "Let's say my mind was occupied with other things, like not making a complete idiot out of myself on stage."

Nikki frowned. She didn't like the fact that Dawn had seen them leaving Dan's house. What if she misinterpreted things? And from that smile on her face, Nikki could only imagine what was going on in the woman's mind. A wave of worry swept over her. "You don't think she got the wrong idea, do you?" Nikki glanced over her shoulder at Dan.

"Nah, we're neighbors. There's nothing strange about you being at my house at ten in the morning. It's not like you were sneaking out the window in the middle of the night. Besides, we know that nothing happened. It was a medical emergency." Dan fell in step with her.

Nikki squeezed the duffel bag under her arm. *Neighbors don't visit with luggage.*

As if reading her mind, Dan nudged her elbow. "Don't worry. There's no way she knows that you slept on my couch last night. It'll be our secret."

Dan followed Nikki across the two yards to her back-porch door that led into the kitchen. When she opened the door, Snowball, Blue, and the Chihuahua ran out, knocking her off balance. She teetered, but Dan caught her by the shoulders from behind.

When she entered, Nikki scanned the kitchen floor for any loose reptiles that might be lying around hissing or stray body parts from some unfortunate animal who had become dinner.

Not seeing any, Nikki did a quick head count. Three dogs outside. Looking up, she spotted one of the two tabbies sitting on the top of the refrigerator. The minute she opened the cabinet that contained the canned cat food, the other cat appeared on the floor, rubbing against her legs as she dumped the food into the two bowls. The one on the refrigerator jumped to the counter and joined his friend on the tile. Good, both cats were accounted for.

Dan reached for the water bowl and started filling it.

Nikki moved to the living room and whistled for the other dogs. She wanted to go check the laundry room where Tinkerbelle lived, but she didn't want to alarm Dan. He'd never understand about Tinkerbelle. In fact, he'd probably lecture her on the dangers of hosting such an animal in her home.

The scurrying of paws on the hardwood floors in the bedroom echoed down the hall. Relief flooded her as she knelt to greet the collie and the dachshund. *Okay, so everyone survived. Now, to figure out how to check on Tinkerbelle without Dan noticing.*

When she entered the kitchen with the two dogs following her, she found Dan placing the water bowl next to the cats who were now focused on their food dishes. Seeing him gave her a bright idea. "I think I've changed my mind. Could you take care of the water bowls on the back porch for me?"

"Sure, no problem." He stood.

"And could you take these two with you and fill the food bowls out there as well?" She added, hoping Darling, the collie, would put up her usual fuss about going out into the yard. If she did, it should keep him busy while she checked on Tinkerbelle. "It'll be easier to fill them if you can get all the dogs out into the yard."

"I think I can handle that."

"Oh, that'd be great." She smiled. It should buy her enough time to feed the reptile, and Dan would never need to know.

Dan patted his thigh with his hand. "Come on, guys." He opened the back door to the porch.

Darling stopped in the doorway to sniff his pants leg but followed the other pup out onto the porch.

Once the animals and human were out of the house, Nikki darted to the laundry room and inched open the door, little by little in case Tinkerbelle had escaped the aquarium and was lying in wait.

"Tinkerbelle." She sing-songed. She checked the aquarium from the door, but there was no sign of the baby alligator who measured close to two feet. The lid that had been secure yesterday lay dumped to the side on the white folding table that acted as Tinkerbelle's stand.

Oh, no. Stepping further into the room and shutting the door behind her, she moved the laundry hamper that sat next to her washer. No green log with eyes.

"Where are you?" She called.

Moving slowly, she rose onto her tiptoes and peered behind both the washer and the dryer. Nope, nothing. "Tinkerbelle?"

A hiss emitted from a nearby pile of darks. She crept in that direction not wanting to startle her. The little booger could move with lightning speed.

As she caught sight of Tinkerbelle's tail, the back door slammed. Nikki froze. The green reptile scurried behind the dryer. She couldn't let Dan find out about Tinkerbelle. He'd flip.

"Hey Nikki, do you have any more dog food? The bag in the bin outside is only half full, and these critters are hungry."

She dashed to the door and opened it enough to stick her face out. "I think there might be some in the bottom of the bathroom linen closet." Something moved across her left foot. Resisting the urge to scream, she pressed her lips together and rocked her weight from one foot to the other.

"The linen closet? I would've never looked there." He chuckled and turned toward the hall. Stopping, he pivoted and moved back toward her. Leaning his hip against the kitchen counter, he crossed his arms. "What are you doing?"

Nikki straightened and opened the door another inch or two. "Nothing, just ..." She looked around for inspiration. "Checking my laundry."

"Um, is that all?" One of the tabby cats rubbed against Dan's leg, and he nudged it away with his foot.

A cough-like noise came from behind her, followed by a deep bellow.

Dan straightened. "Nikki, stand very still." He inched toward her. "Now, don't be scared, but there's an alligator right behind you."

"Oh, do you see her?"

Dan stopped. "You know there's an alligator in there with you?" His eyebrows winged upward. "Do not tell me this is one of your rescues."

"Okay, I won't. I'll just keep that information to myself." Nikki twisted at the waist and looked over her shoulder trying to locate Tinkerbelle. "Do you think you can get a pillowcase out of the linen closet? A big one. And a scoop of dog food. She tends to like the beef flavored."

~

Dan muttered under his breath with each step. "What is she thinking?" He shook his head. "She's not thinking. Keeping an animal like that in her laundry room." He flexed his hand trying to remain calm. "I'm surprised she doesn't have a rattlesnake tucked away somewhere in her bedroom." He pulled open the white slatted door to the linen closet and grabbed the first pillowcase he found. "Totally irresponsible." Snatching the fifty-pound bag of dog food from the closet, he flung it over his shoulder, slammed the door, and lugged the bag to the kitchen.

Placing the pillowcase on the counter, he tore the top of the bag open and used his hands to scoop the dried kibble into the pillowcase. Finishing, he glanced toward the laundry room door to find it shut. "Great. That's just dandy. Locked herself in with a killer." Tapping on the door so he wouldn't startle the beast, he whispered, "It's ready."

"Okay, good." Her voice, soft and low, floated back to him. The nearness of the sound told him she hadn't moved far.

"I'm going to count to three. When I open the door, hand it to me," Nikki whispered.

"Okay."

"One, two—"

A scream filled the air. A scuffle erupted followed by a bang, then a crash.

Dan dropped the pillowcase. Turning the knob, he pushed on the door. It wouldn't budge. "Nikki, are you all right?" He jiggled the knob again.

Lowering his shoulder, he lunged forward with his full weight. The door swung open, and he stumbled through, landing face-first on a pile of jeans beside a laundry hamper. Groaning, he rolled over to a sitting position, his irritation growing.

Nikki stood over him with both hands clamped over her mouth, eyes wide, choking on her giggles.

"This is not funny." Glancing around, he spotted the alligator in the aquarium. He pointed to the beast. "And what in heaven's name are you doing with an alligator?"

"That's Tinkerbelle." She leaned over and offered him her hand.

He ignored the offer and pushed to a standing position while the fire in his belly worked its way to his mouth. "That is not a Tinkerbelle. A Tinkerbelle is a fuzzy rabbit or a cuddly kitten or even possibly an it's-so-ugly-it's-cute potbellied pig. But an alligator is not a Tinkerbelle. It's a predator who can jump, climb, and—this is the important part—bite."

"You're right. Especially about the climbing." Nikki scowled at the beast who closed both eyes, unconcerned. Turning her attention toward Dan, she asked, "Are you all right?"

"Yeah, my pride's bruised a little, but I'll be fine. I'm amazed you took in an alligator." If he could, he'd get rid of the thing, right now before it did any harm. "What were you thinking?" He shook his head in dismay.

"Well, Tinkerbelle is a baby, not more than a year-old, and she was injured." Nikki shrugged. "She was separated from her mother during the hurricane, and one of the preserves is working on the paperwork to take her in. I'm expecting a call any day."

Dan studied Nikki. The woman loved all God's creatures, even those who didn't love her back. Or in this case, those who would gladly eat her for dinner. He chuckled. "You, Nikki Davis, are quite the animal lover." He nodded toward the aquarium. "How did you get that toothy critter back into its glass cage?"

A smile tugged at her bow-shaped lips. "Well, when I screamed, I scared Tinkerbelle so bad that she scrambled to her safe place."

"The aquarium?"

"Yep. Once she was in, I grabbed the lid and secured it with the clamps."

"So, why'd you scream?" Dan asked.

A yellow tabby emerged from behind the dryer and darted from the room.

Nikki grinned. "Let's just say, an alligator can jump close to five feet in the air. But so can a terrified cat."

155

Chapter Fifteen

Dan drove the post hole digger into the ground. Most of the digging they did by machine, an auger attached to a tractor, but sometimes he or Rod would need to clear the wayward clumps that the machine left behind.

The cooler October morning had warmed to eighty degrees by midday as it often did in southern Texas. Dan worked the tool, pushing the wooden handles together and lifting the clods of the dark earth to the side of the hole. He preferred to do this type of work in the fall when the days were like this one with blue skies as far as he could see.

He had to admit the weather wasn't the only reason for his good mood. His Sunday afternoon with Nikki had led to more than he'd anticipated. She'd surprised him with her candor. A smile tugged at his lips as the image of Nikki holding the wriggling Chihuahua in her lap on the way to the Senior Citizen's Center popped into his mind. The woman had a heart the size of the state he loved. Enough room to care even for an alligator. A chuckled rocked his chest.

"What's so funny?" Rod called from the seat of the tractor.

"Nothing."

Rod climbed down from the machine with a thermos of coffee in his hand. "Would that be the same nothing that had you grinning from ear to ear when we were setting the fence posts on the east side of the pasture? Or is it the same nothing that had you humming when we were unrolling the wire?"

Dan leaned his chin on top of his hand holding the post-hole digger. "It is the same nothing."

"I thought it might be." Rod nodded. He twisted off the lid of the thermos and turned it upside down to use as a second cup. Setting his own coffee mug and the lid on the metal of the tractor, he poured them each some of the steaming-hot liquid.

Dan took his black. Picking up the stainless-steel cup, he blew on it before taking a sip.

"Good, huh?" Rod took his own sip.

"Yeah, Dolly makes a mean cup of joe." Dan shifted his weight, contemplating how to broach the subject that had been picking at his brain for the last two days.

"So, what's got you in such a terrific mood?" Rod asked, drawing the last word out. He leaned his back against the tractor and braced himself in place with his legs.

Dan walked over and sat next to him, leaning the tool against the tractor. "I spent some time over the weekend with Nikki."

"Ah, that explains a lot." Rod chuckled. "I'd say from all the symptoms you're displaying you're smitten with her."

"Yeah, I am." He turned to face his friend. "Nikki's so different. She makes me laugh, but she also makes me think."

"That sounds like a good combination." Rod took another sip eyeing Dan over the rim of his mug. "Why does it feel like there is a but hidden in there somewhere?"

"Because there is." Dan frowned. "You know how I felt about Lilly. *Feel* about her. Is wanting more with Nikki being disloyal to what Lilly and I had? It feels like it is, and I don't want to be disloyal to Lilly."

"No, of course you don't." Rod stroked his chin with his free hand.

Dan waited, the embarrassment of the situation building in him. How could he have fallen for the girl next door? Could it be more cliché? Wasn't that what teenage boys do? Thirty was too old for a crush.

"What do you think Lilly would say?"

"I'm not sure," Dan stammered, surprised by the question. "I hadn't thought about it."

Rod turned his shoulders so he could face him. "Think of it this way—what would you want Lilly to do if she had lived and you had been the one to die? Would you want her to put the rest of her life on hold out of some misguided sense of loyalty?"

Sighing, Dan shook his head. "I wouldn't want her to put anything on hold for me."

"No, you wouldn't. And I'd venture to say you'd even want her to be happy. Find someone to walk through this life with her, to love her the way you would've." Rod turned back and surveyed the open pasture beyond the newly-set fence posts. "This life is a hard rodeo. Lilly wouldn't want you to go through it without someone cheering in your corner."

"You're right, I know. But I can't help feeling that pursuing a relationship with Nikki would somehow lessen what Lilly meant to me. She anchored me and made me a better version of myself. I can't ignore that."

"You don't need to, Dan. No matter who is in your life, Lilly will always be a part of you. Like Carol is for me."

"Carol?" Dan scowled. "I don't remember you ever mentioning a Carol."

Rod grinned. "No, but she's with me every day." He patted the left side of his chest above his work-shirt pocket. "Right here. I loved her with my whole heart, but it wasn't meant to be." He shrugged. "So, I grieved, and I moved on and I tried to stay open to what the Lord had for me."

"And you found Dolly." Dan crossed his arms staring down at his boots. Could he move on? His heart had been shattered into pieces. Even now after three years, he couldn't say it was whole again.

"I did. Not right away. And not without a lot of prayer and mending. But yes, I found Dolly. Or she found me. Now, I can't imagine what my life would've been like without her. Carol was my first love, but Dolly's the one who makes me love life."

The image of Nikki at his door that first night rushed into his mind. He wasn't sure how it had happened or when, but the free-spirited, God-loving, animal-hording woman who drove him mad had won a place in his battered heart.

Rod stood and drained the last of the coffee in his mug. "So, have you told her who you are yet? Or does she still think you're me?"

Running his hand down the back of his neck, Dan groaned. "Well, I tried to come clean over the weekend, but it never seemed like the right time."

Scowling, Rod took the stainless-steel cup out of Dan's hand and flung what was left in the bottom onto the ground. "That's not good. You're not being fair to Nikki." A grin lifted the corners of his mouth. "You do know I could have you prosecuted for identity theft." Twisting the lid on the thermos, Rod tucked it back into the box attached to the tractor. "You need to get this worked out."

Dan pushed off the metal side of the machine and stood. "I know. But I have a plan. I'm going to show her instead of tell her."

"And how do you propose to do that?"

"I invited her out to Silver Spurs this Saturday. With any luck, I'll have it all straightened out before you can file the paperwork on the identity theft."

Rod laughed and slapped Dan on the back before climbing into the seat of the tractor.

Dan grabbed the post-hole digger from where it leaned and strode to the next spot marked with orange spray paint.

The engine of the machine started, and the green tractor rumbled over the ground toward him. The work of repairing the ranch had been long and hard. But between him and Rod and the construction crew working on the ranch house, the progress had been steady. It resembled the work the Lord had done on him over the past three years—long, hard, and steady.

Rod's words swirled in his mind as the roar of the tractor rang in his ears. Yes, Lilly would want him to have a life, to have someone to love. But was he ready? And better yet, was Nikki?

~

His boots slapped against the tile floor as he headed toward the wooden counter that divided the front room of the Animal Ark Rescue from the back. Dan spotted Nikki at a desk situated against the right side of the room behind the counter. She sat facing a computer, brows furrowed, studying the screen.

An older woman dressed in a tee-shirt with the shelter logo on it rose as he approached. Smiling, a cascade of wrinkles formed around her eyes. "Hi. What brings you to the Animal Ark?" She leaned her elbows on the counter and clasped her hands together.

Dan removed his cowboy hat and leaned one arm on the counter. "I've come to see a lady about a dog." He nodded in Nikki's direction.

The woman, Tabitha, according to her name tag, followed his gaze. "Oh, I see." Leaning closer, she lowered her voice. "You must be Dan. I've heard a lot about you."

Keeping his own voice low, he asked, "Was any of it good?"

Tabitha swatted the air and chortled. "All of it." She glanced over at Nikki who had yet to look away from the computer screen. "You've been the hot topic. Seems you're a hero. And a great neighbor. Taking care of her all weekend and everything." Tabitha's eyebrows winged up. "Now, I see what all the fuss was about."

The heat of embarrassment rose on his cheeks.

She winked. Standing straight, she called out Nikki's name, crisp and clear.

Glancing up, Nikki made eye contact with Tabitha.

"Would you mind taking care of this gentleman?" She glanced toward Dan. "He seems to want to talk to you about a dog."

A glow radiated from Nikki's face when her gaze landed on him.

His pulse raced. He'd thought of little else since his conversation with Rod. That's why he needed to see her, be near her.

"I'll be in the back checking on Chester. He's been pulling at those bandages again." Tabitha's eyes darted between them. Turning, she strolled to a door and disappeared into the back among a chorus of barks and mews.

Nikki rose from the chair. "Well, hello. Checking up on your patient?"

Grinning, he reached for his cowboy hat from the counter and rolled it in his hands. "Maybe." He leaned his leg against the counter as she settled across from him. "I was wondering what you were doing for dinner tonight."

"Well, if I go with what's in my refrigerator, I'll be enjoying a lemon slice and some baking soda." She placed her chin on her balled fist and gave him a half smile. "Why? What did you have in mind? Not a picnic, I hope."

"No. I've had my fill of picnics. I thought we could try some of the local cuisine. I hear The Flying Pig Barbeque is top-notch. A friend of mine, Rod, lives close to Orange Blossom and introduced me to their pulled pork. Besides, how can you go wrong with a place who's famous for their flying pigs?"

"True. Once you've hit flying-pigs status, you've reached the pinnacle of the barbeque culinary world." Warmth invaded her eyes, and a teasing smile spread across her bow-shaped lips.

Dan's fingers itched to trace the line of that smile. Instead, he rolled his cowboy hat in his hands and shifted his weight. "So, it's a date then?"

Nikki sobered. "A date? Are you sure?" She met his gaze. "After everything you've told me about Lilly, I'm a little surprised that you'd call it a date. I'm sure you didn't mean a date, date," she stammered. "It doesn't matter. I know what you meant."

"No, I am asking you out." He placed his hat on the counter and took both of her hands in his. "Nikki, would you do me the great honor of going out with me to see pigs fly this evening?" He grinned, breaking the tension.

Squeezing his hands, she beamed. "I'd love nothing better."

Chapter Sixteen

The red-checkered tablecloths at The Flying Pig were covered in clear plastic to protect them from the barbeque sauce. It could leave a wicked grease spot.

As they walked past several tables all outfitted with napkin dispensers, Dan pointed to the large painting that spanned the entire back wall. There in full color were five pink pigs with wings, flying and doing somersaults against a background of blue sky and white clouds. "Now, I've seen everything," Dan said.

Grinning, Nikki nodded. "I know. This place is as famous for the pigs as it is for the barbeque. You wouldn't believe the number of tourists who come through here to see that mural."

Scanning the room for an empty table, Dan spotted Pastor Connor and his wife. He waved. "Do you want to go over and say hi?"

"No, they look like they're deep in conversation. Besides, he can grill me tomorrow at work," she said.

Dan chose a table for two near the back corner, so they could have some privacy. He pulled out Nikki's chair and waited until she was settled before taking the seat across from her.

The waitress hustled to the table. "Hello, folks. What can I bring you to drink?" Her salt-and-pepper hair was pulled back in a loose bun.

"I'll take a tea, Frieda," Nikki said.

The waitress turned her attention to Dan. "And you?"

"I'll have the same."

Once Frieda moved on to the next table, Dan leaned back in his chair trying to relax, but couldn't keep his right foot from jiggling. He shifted in his chair and willed himself to keep both feet flat on the floor. "So, how were things at the Animal Ark today?"

Nikki unrolled her silverware and placed the paper napkin on the table. "Fine, I suppose. Chester—he's a Great Dane—keeps pulling at the bandages on his front paw. It's always hard when we get one that's injured. Even with a cone around his neck, he can still reach it."

"I imagine working with animals can be challenging for many reasons."

Nikki nodded. "The days are never dull."

The image of the green alligator housed in her laundry room popped into his mind. "So, have you heard anything about Tinkerbelle's adoption by the preserve?" A grin pulled at his lips.

"As a matter of fact, I received a call today. They

said I could bring her over this weekend. One of the rangers is supposed to call me with the details. He'll help me with her release." Nikki pursed her lips. "Hey, I have an idea. How would you like to go with me?"

"I don't know. I'd probably be in the way."

"Come on. It'll be fun. Besides, how often do you have the chance to release an alligator back into the wild? What—once a year?" She smiled, a twinkle dancing in her bright blue eyes.

"Okay, you're right. Besides, it sounds interesting. Much more exciting than wrangling cows."

Leaning her chin on her hand, she met his gaze. "What about you? How was your day?"

"Pretty productive. Rod and I worked the fence line trying to replace posts and repairing the damage from the hurricane. I'm shocked at the number of missing posts. It's like starting over."

"Oh, it sounds like a lot of hard work. I'm surprised you're not worn out."

"Normally, after a day like today, I'd be sleeping in front of my favorite show with my feet propped up." He chuckled.

"Oh, I see." She leaned toward him.

"But tonight, I had better plans." Dan took her hand that rested on the table and intertwined his fingers with hers.

A blush painted her cheeks as she glanced downward, breaking their connection. The pale pink on her fair complexion added to her beauty. And knowing that he was responsible for placing it there made it even more appealing.

Nikki pulled her hand from his and grabbed the menu.

He hadn't meant to embarrass her, but he had. It'd been so long since he'd dated, it didn't surprise him that things weren't going well.

"We'd better decide what we want. If Frieda passes by our table and we haven't decided, we'll be lucky to get anything before closing."

Once he made his choice, he slid his menu to the edge of the table. Leaning forward on his elbows, he studied Nikki as she ran her finger down the list of meat selections and sides.

Rod's words rang in his heart. Lily would want him to be happy again, if only he could let go. She had been his past, but Nikki could be his future. Dan needed to find out. He had to let go.

After finishing their meal, Dan suggested dessert, not wanting the evening to end too soon. Everything sounded delicious. Apple pie, red velvet cake, fudge, and something that had caramel drizzled over ice cream on top of a warm, chocolate brownie.

Looking over her menu, Nikki smacked her lips. "I know what I'm having."

"Me too." Dan grinned. "And I bet I can guess which one you picked."

"Of course, you can. There's only one right choice when you're dining at The Flying Pig, and that's the brownie caramel melt delight." She shrugged. Laying her menu aside, Nikki glanced toward the front. "I wonder where Frieda went?"

"I don't know." Dan twisted in his seat. As he scanned the room, the glass door pushed open, and a tall, dark-haired man about his age entered the restaurant.

"Oh, there's Michael. How nice." Nikki sprang to her feet and waved.

"Michael?" Dan scowled.

"Yeah, you remember my friend that Marilyn mentioned. Michael Guillory."

It can't be. Dan recognized the last name the minute it left Nikki's lips. His Pops had done business with Matthew Guillory for years before his passing.

A smile spread across Michael's face when he spotted Nikki. He nodded and threaded his way through the tables filled with people to reach her.

Nikki's eyes sparkled as he neared.

Dan didn't like the way she looked at him; nor did he like the way the guy looked at Nikki. He sat back in his chair with his arms crossed.

"Nikki, you're a sight for sore eyes." Reaching out, he took her in his arms and pulled her into a bear hug.

Dan's shoulders stiffened.

She slid her arms around his waist and gave him a squeeze. "I sure missed you."

Michael snorted. "More like you missed my truck."

"Maybe," she teased before releasing him.

"So, what are you doing at The Flying Pig?" Michael glanced toward Dan.

"Oh, my goodness. How rude of me. Michael, this is Dan. Dan, Michael."

Dan stood and shook hands with him.

Neither man spoke.

"I see you made it back in one piece. How is your family?" Nikki sat and motioned toward an empty seat at the next table. "Grab a chair and join us."

Michael turned and addressed the couple seated at the table. "Do you mind?" He gestured to the metal-framed, padded chair.

"No, help yourself."

Michael swung the chair around so that the back of the chair faced the table. Throwing one leg across the seat, he lowered himself down like he was mounting a horse.

"Have you eaten?" Nikki asked. "We were about to order dessert. Would you like to join us?" Nikki turned to Dan. "You don't mind, do you? It's just that I haven't seen Michael in weeks. He's been in Shreveport helping his parents with their property. Hey, you two have that in common. You both know all about ranching."

Dan mumbled his consent but kept a sharp eye on him. Didn't the guy realize they were on a date? Of course, it didn't seem to bother Nikki at all. In fact, her mood had improved since Michael had made his appearance.

Had he misread her signals? She'd been so pleased when he'd asked her out. But now, since Mr. Bear Hug had shown up, she beamed and glowed and radiated, like a darn mason jar full of lightening bugs.

Frieda approached the table. "Hey there, good-looking. When did you roll back into town?"

"Earlier today." Michael smiled. "And how is my favorite waitress?"

"Doing great. We had that bachelor auction, and I won Ralph White's odd job. Got him in the kitchen unclogging a sink." Frieda cackled. "I love it when a plan comes together."

"Me, too." Michael stole a glance at Nikki.

Dan had the feeling Michael had some plans of his own, and he'd bet his last dollar Nikki stood at the center of those plans.

"So, what can I bring you three?" Frieda asked.

Shaking her head, Nikki tsked. "It's like you don't even know me, Frieda. I'm hurt." Nikki placed her right hand over her heart.

"The usual, it is. One brownie caramel melt delight." Frieda glanced from her pad. "And you two? The same, I suppose?"

Both men nodded.

Dan leaned forward in his chair, placing his forearms on the table. "Michael, where in Shreveport do your parents live? I've had some business dealings in that area and know a few of the ranchers."

"The Guillory Ranch is southwest of Shreveport. Out by the Borden Dairy. My folks own about 500 acres of the best grazing land in Louisiana, if I do say so myself." Michael smiled and tossed a wink in Nikki's direction.

Dan swallowed hard. It was the same family. Shoot, he'd probably even met Michael when they were boys. This wasn't good.

"You know," Michael furrowed his brow, studying Dan. "You do look familiar. Have we met before?"

Dan panicked. He didn't want to lie, but he hadn't told Nikki about owning the ranch, and this wasn't how he wanted her to find out.

Before he could answer, Nikki piped in. "Well, Dan works on the Silver Spur ranch near Zion Hill."

"You don't say." Michael's eyes stayed glued to Dan. "My dad used to do business with the owner of Silver Spur. He was an older man. I think he's passed."

Dan opened his mouth to tell him that his grandfather had indeed been gone for years, but Frieda appeared carrying three dessert plates on her left arm before he had the chance.

"Here you go." Frieda stopped next to their table. She pulled the plate from the top first and slid it in front of Nikki before she set the other two in front of the men.

"This looks divine." Nikki poked her finger into the whipped cream and took a taste. "Heavenly."

Michael chuckled. "You never could wait."

"Why should I?" Nikki picked up her fork and cut into the brownie. The caramel dripped into the middle. She closed her eyes as the first bite melted on her tongue, and she let out a satisfied sigh. "Oh man is this good." She grinned at Dan who had taken his own first bite.

Dan had eaten some fantastic desserts over the years with Marge as his cook, but this gave his tongue a chocolate sensation he'd never experienced.

"Man, oh man." Michael licked his lips, trying to remove the caramel from the corners of his mouth. "There is nothing like having dessert before dinner."

Giggling, Nikki poked his elbow with hers. "That's terrible. You've ruined your dinner because nothing will compare after eating this."

"Who cares." Michael sighed. Leaning back, he patted his stomach. "It was so worth it."

When they'd eaten the last bite, Michael took Nikki's hands into his. "I'd better go, but I'm glad I got to see you." He gave her hands a squeeze before he released them. He nodded toward Dan. "Nice to meet you." Standing, he placed the chair back at the table behind them and turned to face Nikki. "Remember, I'm only a phone call away. So, if you or those critters of yours need a ride, give me a ring."

Dan couldn't take it any longer. He didn't like the way Michael so freely touched Nikki. A hug here, a hand squeeze there, the guy was out of line. It didn't seem to bother him that t he'd interrupted a date. Dan decided to set the record straight.

"If Nikki needs a ride, I'll be glad to give her one. I'm right next door. So, there's no need to put you to the extra trouble with me so close." Dan stood and shot out his hand for Michael to shake. "But it was very nice to meet you."

Michael reached across the table and grabbed it. Dan held firm, giving Michael's hand a firm squeeze.

He could feel his eyes narrow as he maintained a grip on his hand. "I'll be sure to take care of Nikki. You have nothing to worry about."

Michael pressed harder on Dan's hand. "Well, Nikki and I have been friends for years. So, it's kind of my job to keep an eye on her. Besides, you won't be her neighbor for long, right? Then what?"

"Oh, don't worry. I'll still be around. So, she won't be needing your truck anymore." Dan released Michael's hand. Dropping his hand to his side, he flexed it to get the feeling back.

Michael cocked an eyebrow. "I see. But don't you think it should be up to Nikki who helps her? Whether it's me or you?" Michael's eyes narrowed. "Or are you afraid of a little competition?"

"Stop this right now." Nikki grabbed Dan's forearm. "I can't believe the two of you." Heat rose on her cheeks and tinted the tips of her ears pink.

Dan wanted to stop and take a seat. After all, violence never solved anything.

But Michael took a step toward him. Poking Dan

in the chest, he smirked, "Or don't you think Nikki's worth fighting for?"

Chapter Seventeen

Nikki hadn't been so embarrassed in her entire twenty-eight years of living. What had Dan been thinking? And Michael, he didn't act any better. If she could've climbed under the table, she would've. Two grown men, behaving like schoolboys on the playground fighting over a football. "I'm so ..." She sputtered, disbelief swirling in her. "I can't believe ..." She clinched her teeth together and let out a low growl of anger. "Have you lost ..." Unable to form a complete thought, Nikki plopped back against the seat. Crossing her arms, she stared out the passenger-side window of Dan's truck.

Every time she thought about what had happened, the anger blazed in her. She couldn't even look at him. It was bad enough that they'd faced off in the middle of one of her favorite restaurants, but to have the whole spectacle played out in front of Pastor Connor and his wife had added fuel to her humiliation.

"Look, I know he's a friend of yours, but that guy

has it bad for you." Dan tightened his grip on the steering wheel. "You must've known. He flirted with you the whole time."

"For your information, that's how Michael acts. He's super friendly with everyone. Didn't you hear how he talked to Frieda?"

"Yeah, I heard." Dan scowled, keeping his eyes on the road.

"Do you think he wants to date her?" Nikki snapped. "I've known Michael my whole life. And when his parents moved to Shreveport after his senior year to take over the ranch from his grandfather, it was one of the saddest days of my life."

"Was his grandfather's name Matthew, by any chance?"

"I think so. Why?" She huffed.

"I think my grandfather did business with his." Dan let out a deep sigh. "Okay, I get that he's outgoing. But the way he looks at you is not how a guy looks at a friend."

Nikki tucked her chin and glared at Dan's profile in the dim streetlights that streaked the truck cab as they rolled passed. "That's not the point. I don't care if he looks at me upside down wearing sunglasses. I get to choose my friends, and no one—including you or Michael—can tell me who to hang out with. And if you think you can, you're both nuts."

Dan cut his eyes toward her. "May I remind you that this was supposed to be a date, our first date? Did you expect me to sit there and let some other guy flirt with you? A guy, whom I might point out, invited himself to join us."

"He did not." Nikki huffed, straightening in her seat. "I invited him. But had I known how you'd act, I wouldn't have bothered." She sat for a moment before continuing. "Look, Michael and I did date. But it didn't work out for us. Because he was so friendly, all the girls thought—like you—that he was flirting."

"So, his *friendliness* has been a problem for you too?" His eyebrow's winged up.

"That and the fact he has itchy feet. Since his parents moved to Shreveport, he hasn't settled down anywhere." Nikki shrugged. "He's been across Texas and the southern states with work, but every now and again, he comes back to Orange Blossom."

"So, he comes back for you." Dan's jaw tightened.

"No," Nikki said. "He comes back to the area to see his parents. It's not that far to Shreveport, and he wants to reconnect with his brother who lives here."

"Okay, if that's what you think."

"Look, I know enough not to take him too seriously. Michael likes to make people feel good about themselves. It's a gift, and he didn't mean to put me through all that drama the year we dated in high school."

Dan's head jerked her direction, causing him to veer off the road. "You dated back in high school?" He pulled the tires back onto the pavement. "That's like ten years ago or something, right?"

"Yeah, that sounds about right." Nikki shifted in her seat, hoping Dan would keep his eyes on the road.

"So, let me get this straight. He keeps coming back to Orange Blossom. And when you whistle, he still comes running after all this time?" Dan chuckled.

"Hey, he's not a dog."

"No, it's worse. He's a man who has a bad case of infatuation-itis. A real bad case."

"Don't be silly. I've already told you he doesn't think of me that way. I'm more like a sister."

"Nikki, a man doesn't make himself available at a woman's whim if he's not interested in her. Trust me, he doesn't see you as a sister," Dan said.

Nikki cocked her head to one side and studied Dan in the beam of the oncoming headlights. "Well, you've rearranged your day at my whim. What does that say about you?"

~

Dan almost swallowed his tongue. How had the tables turned on him so quickly? She had a habit of doing that to him. He stole a glance in Nikki's direction.

She sat there, waiting.

He wanted to tell her how he felt, but even he wasn't clear about the emotions he carried for her. And of course, there was Lilly and the ceremony. It all muddled together. Dan didn't understand how, but Nikki had a knack of putting him in the hot seat. It must be her gift, like Michael's friendliness. "Look, this isn't about me," he sputtered trying to dodge the question.

"Well, it is now." Nikki fiddled with her black purse that sat on the console between them. "And how is this not about you? After the way you acted." She shook her head, her tone calmer, more even.

Dan slowed and pulled into her driveway. It would've made more sense to park in his own driveway, a mere few feet away, but he wanted to give her the full first-date experience. Good food, good company, and he'd hoped a goodnight kiss. But after what had happened with Michael, he'd gave up that idea. Throwing the gear shift into park, he turned off the ignition. "We were talking about Michael."

The front porch light glowed yellow, bathing the driveway and the cab of the truck in a delicate shimmer.

"Yes, and you made some excellent points. I can see why you and others might think that Michael gives me special treatment." A mischievous grin inched across her lips as she ran her fingers down the strap of her purse.

Dan followed the movement of her hand.

"But that doesn't explain why *you* give me special treatment." She glanced toward him, a gleam shining in her eyes.

"That's easy." He reached for her hand, forcing her to release the strap. "I give you special treatment because you're my neighbor. And neighbors should be treated with the utmost courtesy and respect. Let me show you." Opening his door, he jumped out and jogged around the truck to her door. Pulling the latch, he swung it open and bowed like a Victorian footman as he extended his hand to her. "My lady."

Nikki giggled and took his hand. "Thank you, kind gentleman." Stepping from the truck, she dragged her purse behind her as her feet touched the concrete drive. She released his hand and lifted her purse onto her shoulder.

Dan closed the door and stuffed his keys into his front pocket. "Let me walk you to your door."

She shrugged. "No need. I know the way. Besides, the squeak of the screen door opening is going to set off the dogs." She smiled. "And maybe a cat or two."

"It's okay. They don't scare me." Dan lifted his chin. Besides, he wanted to have the chance to apologize now that Nikki had cooled down.

The glow of the porch light washed over her.

"What about Tinkerbelle?" Her smile created crinkles around her eyes.

"Okay, I'll admit it. She scares me." Dan grinned. "Come on." He placed his hand on the small of her back and guided her toward the steps.

Her teasing had encouraged him. Perhaps he hadn't ruined everything with his jealousy. He stopped before they reached the porch. *Yes, he was jealous.*

"What is it?" Nikki glanced at him.

Taking her by her shoulders, he said, "Nikki, I'm sorry for how I acted tonight. And I'd like to answer your question. The reason I treat you special is the same reason Michael treats you special—it's because you deserve it. And because I enjoy spending time with you." Dan swallowed hard. "I've come to count you as a friend, and if I'm honest, a little bit more."

Nikki smiled at him, placing the palm of her hand on his cheek. "I know."

"You know?" Dan couldn't hide his confusion. "How could you?"

"That day at the Senior Citizen's Center, you were going to kiss me, weren't you?"

The porch light washed her in a yellow hue, giving her an angelic glow. Dan placed his hand over hers on his cheek. "Yes, I was."

"But Blue pushed between us, and you didn't. Is it because of Lilly?" Her eyes searched his.

Dan took a step back and pulled her hand from his cheek. Holding it in his, he intertwined their fingers. "Nikki, I want to be honest with you. I loved Lilly with all my heart for as long as I can remember. And now, I've had all these thoughts and feelings about you that I never expected to have again." He looked down at their hands. "I don't know what to do with them. But I do know that I will always love Lilly."

"I see." Nikki let go of his hand and reached down, pulling her purse back onto her shoulder. Stepping toward him, she took him by his shoulders. Tiptoeing, she brushed her lips against his, a mere whisper of a kiss.

Dan pulled back, surprised. Then in an instant, he ran his arms around her and pulled her to him. Brushing his lips over hers, he deepened the kiss. Her lips tasted sweeter than The Flying Pigs brownie caramel melt delight. And no amount of whipped cream or cherries could make this moment any richer.

Nikki broke the kiss and laid her head on his shoulder. "I shouldn't have done that. I know you loved Lilly. Still do."

"No, don't apologize." He grinned down at her, his heart racing. "That was worth the wait. Now, I'm kind of glad Blue interrupted. The wait made it that much better."

"Um, I agree." Nikki sighed. "But what about Lilly? I know you will always love her."

"Yes, but someone recently reminded me that Lilly would've wanted me to be happy. She wouldn't have wanted me to squander the chance to be with someone else."

Nikki lifted her head from his shoulder and took both of his hands. "Then you need to decide if there is room enough in your heart for someone else."

His mind whirled. This beautiful, caring woman who stood in front of him wanted to be a part of his life. "Nikki, there is so much I want to tell you, to share with you." He lifted her hands and placed a kiss on the back of each one.

"There's plenty of time." Nikki looked down at the concrete drive. "But you need to know I won't play second fiddle. Not to a memory. I've been the second choice before, and I won't do it again. It never works out."

"Was that Brian? The guy Marilyn mentioned?"

"Yes."

"I can't imagine you ever being someone's second choice." He drank in her honey blond hair and the glow of her complexion in the dim yellow light from the porch. Dan couldn't imagine a person putting her in second place.

"It was after college." Nikki released one of his hands and, while holding the other, she moved toward the porch steps pulling him with her.

He followed, waiting for her to continue.

"I'd met Brian during my sophomore year. He was handsome, ambitious, full of vision. We met while working on several projects to save endangered species like the Nubian giraffes, the North Atlantic right whales, and the green turtles." Nikki sat on the top step, her purse falling beside her.

"Seems you liked reptiles even then." Dan grinned and took a seat beside her.

A chorus of yelps commenced when the step creaked under his weight.

She smiled. "Yeah, I do have a soft spot for animals of all types."

The temperature had dropped a few degrees, and the eighty-degree day had turned into a fifty-degree night. Dan scooted closer to Nikki and wrapped his arm around her.

She leaned into him. "After college, my mom and I both thought Brian would ask me to marry him. In hindsight, it was a stupid assumption. Brian had never given me any indication that he had thoughts of marriage. Instead, he asked me to wait."

"To wait?" Dan scowled. "For what?"

"For him to make his mark. He wanted to go explore the world and see all those animals we had worked so hard to protect. So, he accepted a job as a research assistant with Grace for Animals." She snickered. "It sounds silly now, but that's what he asked me to do. And I did for about two years."

"Seriously, you waited for that guy for two years?" Dan shook his head and pulled her closer to him. "He was an idiot."

"Yes, he was." She leaned her head on his shoulder and snuggled into his side. "At first, I thought he needed time to miss me. That he'd come around once he'd had his adventure and seen some of the places on his list. You know, come home and settle down."

"But he didn't." Dan ran his hand down her arm to console her.

"No. And the longer I waited, the more foolish I felt. Until one day, I gave him an ultimatum. Me or the job." She sighed. "So, you can see why I won't wait around playing second fiddle. I've already done that, and it hurts too much when hope dies."

"Why didn't he ever ask you to join him?" Dan

asked.

"He did close to the end. But by that time, I had a life here. Orange Blossom is my home. It's where the people I love live. I was born and raised here, and I didn't want to give that up. Not for a maybe." She lifted her head and shifted to face him.

The cool air rushed in where her warm body had been, sending goose bumps down his arms.

"So, cowboy, you need to decide before we go any further—is this a maybe, or is this a yes?"

Dan tried to swallow the lump in his throat but couldn't. His mouth was too dry. "Surely, you're not asking me for a guarantee. We've only known each other six weeks."

Nikki crossed her arms, rubbing them with her hands. The sound of barking grew more persistent behind the front door. She shook her head. "Not a guarantee but a promise. If it isn't working out, you won't string me along. You'll be honest—" She hesitated. "About everything."

Guilt washed over him. *Honest.* She wanted honesty about his feelings, and he hadn't even been honest about his identity or what he did. How could he make her a promise based on lies? He met her gaze.

"I'll take your silence as my answer." Nikki rose from the step pulling her purse onto her shoulder.

He jumped to his feet. "No, wait."

She shook her head. "I already told you. I don't wait. Not anymore." She reached for the handle on the screen door.

Dan placed his hand on the wooden frame, holding the door closed. "Nikki, I like you, more than I know how to say. But I can't make that promise— not yet. I need you to trust me and come with me to Silver Spur ranch Saturday, as we planned."

"But I'm supposed to meet with the park ranger this weekend for Tinkerbelle's release. He said he'd call with a day and time. I'm not sure I can keep our date."

"I need you to come, Nikki. It's important. There's something I need to show you. It's the best way I can explain everything."

Frowning, she shifted her weight and hung her head. "I don't know."

He lifted her chin to meet his gaze, her sky-blue eyes full of doubt.

"I'm not asking you to wait years; just wait until this weekend."

"Why can't you explain here and now?" Nikki asked.

"It'll be easier to show you." He caressed her cheek with his thumb. "How about Friday? Can you come?"

She laid her hand on his. "Yes, I'll meet you at Silver Spur on Friday."

"Good." Dan's shoulders relaxed, and he drew her closer. Leaning down, he touched her lips with his. "You need to know. I'd never ask you to wait …"

She pulled back giving him a sad smile. "But you are." Letting go of his shoulders, she grabbed the door handle.

"Because there's a good reason," he finished as she swung the screen open, forcing him to move down the steps even though he didn't like how the evening was ending.

The screech from the hinges sent the yelping dogs into a new frenzy.

"Nikki, wait," Dan called.

Nikki hesitated in the doorway. With her back to him, she said, "If it's that important to you, I can give you until Friday."

Chapter Eighteen

Pastor Connor leaned against the counter in the reception area of The Cowboy Community Church grinning from ear to ear. "So, how was your dinner last night?" He lifted his eyebrows as a gleam of mischief shone in his eyes.

Nikki didn't want to talk about it, but she didn't want to be rude either. "Interesting." She rose from her desk, holding a stack of papers that needed to be filed and moved toward the steel gray cabinets. She'd hoped she could forget about what had happened at The Flying Pig.

"Interesting?" Purdy straightened on the stool behind the counter and twisted to face Nikki. "What dinner, and what happened to make it so interesting?"

Nikki scoffed. "Men. That's what happened to make it so interesting, and how they can often behave like children." She scowled, irritated all over again about Michael and Dan's actions. They'd nearly come to blows before Frieda showed up with Michael's to-go order.

Laying the papers on top of the cabinet, she yanked open the second drawer. "No offense, Pastor."

Chuckling, he said, "None taken."

"Men?" Purdy asked. "How many are we talking about, and who?"

Exasperated, Nikki glanced from her work of poking the pieces of paper into the right files. "Two men. Michael and Dan."

Turning, Purdy shot Pastor Connor a questioning look. "And how do you know about her dinner?"

Nikki let out a long sigh. It was torture knowing that the man who was not only her boss but also her pastor had witnessed the whole ordeal.

"Maura and I were there. I've been promising her a night out for weeks." He smothered a laugh. "But I had no idea there'd be a show, too."

Nikki pushed down the frustration that threatened to rise, not for her boss but the situation. Finishing the task, she slammed the drawer a little harder than she intended. "Me, either. I'm sorry you had to see such a display of male rivalry."

"Okay, that's it. You're both going to have to spill the beans. What exactly happened?" Purdy asked.

Standing with her back against the filing cabinet, Nikki huffed, "Dan asked me out."

"Oh, well, that's great." Purdy looked from Nikki to Pastor Connor. "Right?"

"Yeah, I think so." Pastor Connor shrugged.

"So, we decided to go to The Flying Pig."

"Good choice," Purdy said.

Nikki pushed off the filing cabinet and walked to the counter stopping close to where Purdy sat. "Yes, and we were having a wonderful time. Great food, good conversation. I'd rank it as one of the best dates I've had in a long time."

"Since Brian?" Purdy asked.

"Yeah, if I'm honest."

"I can tell. You're practically beaming." Purdy patted Nikki's hand that rested on the counter. "So, what happened."

Pastor Connor shook his head and studied the counter in front of him. The corners of his mouth twitched as he struggled to suppress a smile.

"Well, Michael showed up as we were ordering dessert. And since I hadn't seen him in a few weeks, I invited him to join us."

"Oh, that's where you went wrong." Purdy nodded slowly.

"I went wrong?" Nikki snapped. "How did I go wrong?"

"You never invite someone else to join you while you're on a date. Especially another man. Talk about getting territorial." Purdy grinned. "Besides, you have no idea how much courage it takes for a man to ask a woman out."

Nikki bit her bottom lip. She hadn't considered how hard it must've been for Dan to even ask her out, much less the struggle he went through trying to figure out his loyalties. Nikki didn't have any misgivings about his feelings for Lilly. She'd been his lifelong love, but they hadn't been given a lifetime together. "I see your point. Maybe some of what happened was my fault." Nikki groaned, glancing at Pastor Connor. "What do you think?"

He held up his hands. "As the Bible says, one of the mysteries of life is the way of a man with a maiden. I'm as clueless as the next guy."

"Come on, you must have an opinion. You were there."

"Okay, here it is. Dan went out on a limb to ask you out. He's been dealing with the loss of his wife and now since the hurricane, his home. He's been displaced for the last few years." Pastor Connor rubbed his chin. "If I were you, I'd cut him some slack."

"Great. Now, I have guilt." Nikki rested her chin on her fist as she leaned against the counter. "What should I do?"

"Oh no, this is as far as I'm willing to go." Pastor Connor tapped his hands on the counter. "Though I would suggest praying about it." Turning, he sped down the hall to his office, never looking back.

Purdy laughed. "He got out while the getting was good."

"Maybe that's what I need to do." Nikki sighed.

"Is that what you want to do?" Purdy twisted on her stool to face her. "I mean, deep down?"

"No, but I'm afraid of getting hurt."

"Like with Brian?"

"Exactly like with Brian. And Michael. Neither one of them wanted to settle down. I like Dan. He's smart, charming, and has a great sense of humor."

Purdy grinned. "Plus, he can tolerate your animals and your cooking. That's pretty impressive."

"Ha-ha. Funny." Nikki straightened. "And the best part is he loves God. How can there be any question in my mind about dating him?"

"But I take it there is."

"Yeah, we've known each other for a little over six weeks, and I don't know much more about him now than I did the day I met him," Nikki said. "He's so private, hard to get to know."

"Well, Pastor Connor did say he was still grieving. Dan needs time."

"But what if it ends up like my relationship with Brian, and I've waited for nothing? Or like Michael, and he has itchy feet? He is a ranch hand after all."

The front door to the office pushed open, and Marilyn Kemp walked in.

Nikki pressed her lips together fighting the groan rising inside her. The last person she wanted to see today was Marilyn. Turning, she headed to her desk to find something to do. Maybe if she looked busy, Marilyn would ignore her.

Purdy hopped off the stool. "How can I help you today, Marilyn?"

"I was on my way to show a property out on Clear

View Drive and had some time to kill. So, I wanted to confirm a little rumor I heard about Nikki."

Nikki froze as a wave of dread washed over her. *How could she possibly know about last night? It hasn't even been twenty-four hours.* She turned to face the bleach-blond realtor.

"Well, you know we don't like to encourage people to spread rumors." Purdy crossed her arms. "That's how misunderstandings start." She frowned.

"Oh, I wholeheartedly agree. That's why I'm here to get the information from the source. I'm the last person who would want to tell tales. But I figured this one must be true since it came from Michael." Marilyn tossed her satchel onto the counter making herself at home.

Nikki marched back to the counter. "What did Michael tell you?"

"Only that you had a date last night with none other than Dan Thibodeaux." Marilyn gave her a half smile and cocked one eyebrow.

"Yeah, Dan asked me out since we're friends and neighbors. He's simply being nice."

"Oh really? Just friends?" Marilyn shook her head. "I'm not buying it, and neither is anyone else in town."

"What are you talking about?" Nikki's heart plummeted to her stomach. "Who else is talking about me and Dan?"

"Oh honey, everyone." Marilyn smiled, swatting away her words.

Surprised, Nikki leaned her arms on the counter. "What's there to talk about? Nothing's happening."

"Well, let's see. First, you two took a little swim together the day of the bachelor picnic. We all watched you traipse through the parking lot soaking wet."

"A swim? Are you kidding me?" Nikki's voice rose. "I rescued Blue. The pup almost drowned. And I'm ashamed to say it, but Dan had to rescue me."

"Oh, so that's why you two weren't in church Sunday morning. Although, someone did mention seeing you and Dan leaving his house together, carrying a duffel bag." Marilyn tilted her head to one side. "But I suppose he was helping you with the animals or something? Being a good neighbor?"

"That's exactly what he was doing." Nikki furrowed her brows, and her tone grew icy. "Since I'd almost drowned, the doctor at the emergency room told Dan I needed supervision and rest for twenty-four hours. Dan was kind enough to look after me." Nikki wanted to grab those words back the minute they left her mouth.

Marilyn's eyebrows arched. "Hmm, I believe you. I really do. But you must know how it looks. And for Michael to tell me that you two were out on a date in the middle of the week—it struck me as odd. Like there's more going on between the two of you than you're letting on."

"Well, if there is, it'd be none of your or anyone else's business," Nikki shrieked and slapped her hand on the counter in front of Marilyn.

The realtor flinched. "No need to get so upset. I'm simply letting you know what's being said."

Purdy planted her hands on her hips. "Yes, and we know who's saying it."

Lifting her chin, she snatched her satchel off the counter. "Fine. I came as a friend, but if you don't want my help, I'll leave. Just remember when everyone starts saying that you're a little gold digger, don't come crying to me because I tried to warn you." Marilyn shrugged and moved toward the door.

"Wait," Nikki called. "What do you mean a gold digger? I don't understand. Dan's a ranch hand."

"Is that what he told you?" Marilyn smirked over her shoulder. "Far be it from me to spread rumors." Sashaying to the glass door, she stopped before stepping outside. "But if I were you, I'd ask Dan what it is he does for a living."

Chapter Nineteen

Dan stretched, reaching his arms toward the sky. The fencing was nearly done, and the construction crew had made headway on the framing of the house. It'd be several months before he could move in, but seeing the progress gave him hope. He missed being home, even if he'd be on his own.

The feeling of living in two worlds didn't suit him. He'd always been more comfortable as a ranch hand than a billionaire, but he couldn't help wondering what Nikki would think about that part of his life. She came off as bold, but underneath she carried a lot of hurt and disappointment. How would she react when he told her about his family and the money?

"We've finished the last row of fencing on the north side, and Caleb and his crew finished the eastern half." Rod removed his baseball cap and ran his fingers through his hair. "I told everyone to go ahead and knock off for the day. If I never see another post-hole digger, it'll be too soon for me." He shook his head and replaced his cap.

"Yeah, two months' worth of fencing and cleanup, I'm with you." Dan gathered the tools and wire cutters and placed them in the box on the back of the tractor.

Rod sauntered over to help him. "If I didn't know any better, I'd say something was eating at you. What's going on?"

"It's Nikki. We went out on a date the other night and well, it didn't go as planned."

"From what you've told me about her, most things don't go as planned when she's involved." Rod chuckled.

"Well, this time I was the problem."

"Oh, not the dogs or that hound Blue?"

"No, we were at The Flying Pig when a friend of hers showed up." Dan's jaw tightened. "A guy named Michael. Seems they've been friends since high school and at one time even dated."

"Oh." Rod nodded. "So, what happened?"

"I don't know." Dan threw up his hands. "One minute we were having a great meal and talking, and then this guy shows up. The next thing I know, we're ordering dessert for three." Dan kicked the ground with his boot, irritation taking hold of him.

"Yeah, most men don't like sharing their dates with other men." Rod grinned. "I can see why you might have had a thing or two to say about it."

"At least you understand. I couldn't seem to explain it to Nikki who was not only mad but embarrassed as well."

"Women do not like public scenes," Rod said. "Unless they're the ones making them."

Dan's lips lifted in a half smile. "Well, her boss was there, and of course, she knows practically everyone in town." Hanging his head, he studied his boots. "She wanted me to be honest with her. To promise if things weren't going anywhere, I'd tell her. She's had a bad experience in the past."

"Ah, is that a problem?"

Looking up, he met Rod's gaze. "I haven't told her who I am."

Rod's thick eyebrows pulled tight beneath the brim of his cap. "Oh, I thought you'd already taken care of that little hiccup."

"No. Not yet." He breathed out a long sigh. "I invited her here tomorrow, right after that interview for the A&M Agricultural magazine. I did tell her about that." Dan's lips lifted into a half smile.

"I'm surprised she didn't ask more about the interview."

"Me, too. But she acted as if it were a part of a ranch managers job. When she arrives, I plan to show her around and explain why I haven't been totally honest with her."

"Do you think she'll understand why you needed to protect your identity?" Rod stepped onto the tractor and sat in the torn seat. "I'm sure if you tell her about some of the incidents that have happened over the years, she'll understand your need to be incognito."

Dan put the last tool into the box and shut the lid. He looked up at Rod. "I don't know. But I've gotten used to having her around."

"I can see that." Rod straightened in the seat. "So, you'd better make sure that she's gotten used to having you around. It works better if both parties are in love at the same time." Chuckling, Rod turned the key, and the engine sparked to life.

"In love?" Dan shouted over the noise of the tractor engine. "What do you mean?"

Rod waved and pointed the tractor in the direction of the path that led to the former equipment shed.

"I'm not in love," Dan growled and kicked the dirt again with the toe of his boot. But as he watched the wheels of the machine crush the ground beneath them, he wrestled with the truth of his friend's words. Inhaling, Dan released the air in his lungs and let his thought take form on his breath. *In love.*

~

The phones rang nonstop for the next few hours in the church office, and Marilyn's dramatic exit had put Nikki in a sour mood. She'd been short with a few of the congregants who had called with questions about the potluck and barked at the delivery man who carried in their paper supplies. At least Marilyn had made an exit, Nikki thought, glad to have seen her leave. She chided herself for her bad attitude. The woman burrowed deep under her skin. And that remark about her being a gold digger acted like a rash, making her brain itch. Nikki had been turning it over in her mind for the last two hours as she fielded the incoming calls.

"Yes, Mrs. Thatcher, I'll add your name to the list for the potluck. A sweet potato casserole. Got it." Pulling up the list on her computer, Nikki typed in the woman's name under the column for side dishes. "No, it's no problem." Nikki pressed the receiver to her ear. "Oh, I'm all right. Why?"

Purdy swiveled in her desk chair to face Nikki and gave her a quizzical look.

"I'm just a little tired, Mrs. Thatcher. But thanks for asking." Another pause on Nikki's end before she added, "I'll see you Sunday." Hanging up, she leaned back against her chair. "I can't believe how many calls we've had."

"Me either. And thanks to your expert communication skills, I already have the deposits from Sunday's tithe ready for the bank."

"Yay, me and my great skills," she said with a hint of snark. Seeing that Purdy had finished, Nikki decided to broach the subject of Marilyn's comment. "Can I ask you something?"

"Sure, but it has to be quick. I want to run by the bank before I go pick up Sarah from school."

"Wow, it's that time already?" Nikki leaned forward and checked her cell phone for the time. Where had the afternoon gone? As she placed her cell phone back on the desk, she asked, "What do you think

Marilyn meant by that comment about me being a gold digger? I've been racking my brain to come up with a reason she'd say something like that to me."

"Is that what's bothering you?"

"Pretty much. Of course, those accusations that Dan and I had acted inappropriately didn't sit too well with me either." Nikki rolled her eyes. "Who would think something like that?"

"Consider the source." Purdy tsked. "The only ones wagging their tongues are Marilyn and her girlfriends."

Nikki shrugged. "Probably, but the bit about being a gold digger has me stumped. I can't fathom why she'd say something like that."

Purdy shifted in her chair and inspected the condition of her nails. "I might have an idea, but it's not my information to share."

"Why? Is it some kind of secret?" Nikki couldn't imagine what it could be.

"No, not exactly. And it's not that I've been told anything. I made some assumptions based on Dan's behavior."

Now, Nikki's curiosity jumped into overdrive. "What are you talking about?"

"Remember the day Marilyn came in here to tell us about the new, rich guy who had moved into town?"

"Yeah, I remember she was so excited I thought she was going to drool on the carpet." Nikki furrowed her brows and pinned Purdy with a stare. "But what does that have to do with me being a gold digger?"

"Well, when she handed me the visitor's card, I glanced at the name on it." Purdy shifted in her chair.

Nikki waited.

"It was Dan's name and address." Purdy tilted her head. "So, when he came in behind her, I put the card on the counter in front of him. I intended to tell him about it, so he'd expect a visit. But when I went to point it out to him, the card was gone."

"So, what does that have to do with the gold-digger comment?"

Purdy frowned. "Don't you understand? The billionaire Marilyn referred to that day wasn't the guy in the Mitchell house, but Dan."

"No, you're totally wrong. Dan's not a billionaire. He's barely a hundredaire. He's a ranch hand who works for the owners of Silver Spur."

"Are you sure?" Purdy stood and gathered the deposit bags and slips from her desk. "'Cause after he took the card, I looked him up online. And, sweetie, the man's the grandson of Edward Harris."

"The Texas cattle baron?" Nikki's mouth gaped open. Purdy had to be wrong. "The Edward Harris who made billions raising cattle and exporting beef?"

Purdy nodded. "The very one. I'm kind of surprised you didn't do a search on him yourself or check him out on social media at the very least."

"He didn't strike me as the sort of man who'd be on social media. Besides, I didn't expect him to be related to the guy who has a plaque in city hall and his name over a wing at the county hospital." Nikki's eyes grew round.

"And his grandfather's name is on the agricultural building at Texas A&M." Purdy sighed.

"That's why he's doing an interview for their agricultural magazine. I'm stunned. Dan— the guy who fixed my fence, the one I conned into using his truck, and who hauled all those animals to the Senior Citizen's Center for me, is Edward Harris's grandson?" Nikki groaned and hid her face in her hands. "He must think I'm a naïve twit the way I've treated him."

Purdy walked over to Nikki and patted her shoulder with one hand while she hugged the bank bags and slips of papers in the other. "You didn't know. And besides, I think that's the point. He wants to keep his identity to himself."

Nikki's head popped up. "Why didn't he tell me? I would've kept it to myself. Didn't he trust me?"

Shrugging, Purdy dropped her hand. "Can you blame him? After the way Marilyn acted."

Pushing her chair back, Nikki stood. "I can only imagine what people must think." She moved forward five steps, pivoted, and headed back toward Purdy. "I mean, after the way I bid on him at the auction and that whole escapade with Blue in the lake." Nikki stilled. "Marilyn's right. Dawn saw me leaving his house that Sunday morning." She threw back her head and groaned, balling her hands into fists. "I'm so stupid.

How naïve can I be? I'm such a fool, and worse, I've wrecked my good name."

"Look, stay calm. It's going to be all right."

"No wonder Marilyn said what she did about me being a gold digger. The whole town probably thinks the same thing." Closing her eyes, Nikki let the reality of Dan's identity sink in.

She cringed at the horror of how it had all played out. Her attempts at befriending him, making him feel welcome in their community. Her asking for his help multiple times. Their date at The Flying Pig. She bit her lip to keep it from quivering. "What should I do?" Nikki glanced over at Purdy fighting back the tears. "I'm supposed to meet him tomorrow out at the Silver Spur ranch. I even took the day off from the rescue. Do you think I should go?"

Purdy rushed to Nikki. Placing her arm around her, she gave her a side hug. "Yes, you most certainly should go. Give him a chance to explain."

"But he lied to me, Purdy. And he made me look like such a fool. What if he's been stringing me along this whole time?" Nikki whispered, "like Brian."

Giving her a firm squeeze, Purdy sighed. "I think deep down the man you've come to know and care about—Dan the ranch hand—is no different from Dan Harris Thibodeaux, the billionaire."

Nikki scoffed. "I'm not so sure about that, but I guess I'll have to wait and see what tomorrow brings."

"Good girl." Purdy released her and scurried over

to her desk. "I'm sure things will look better tomorrow." Opening the bottom drawer, she pulled out her purse and slung the strap over her shoulder. "I'd better go, or I'll be late getting Sarah. And you know how she feels about that." Lifting the partition, she stepped through to the opposite side. "Are you going to be all right?"

"Yes, I'm sure I'll be fine one way or another." Nikki gave her a half smile and watched her hustle out the door. Swiveling her chair toward the computer, she muttered, "whether I go tomorrow or not."

Chapter Twenty

Nikki debated all morning if she should meet Dan at his ranch. Her embarrassment over the accusations that Marilyn had tossed in her face made her want to crawl under her blanket and hide from the world. Or at least from the people who inhabited her small corner of it.

But Purdy had a point. She needed to give Dan the opportunity to explain, no matter how foolish she felt for being so trusting. After all, he had saved her life. And Blue's. Unlike Purdy, though, she would've never dreamed of looking him up online. To her, what you see is what you get. Well, she'd learned her lesson. First Brian and now Dan. She was tired of behaving like a fool when it came to men.

From now on, everyone went through at least a cursory online search. And as for waiting, she'd set the pace from now on for any relationship.

Snowball hopped onto the couch and nuzzled close to her, pulling Nikki from her thoughts. The large dog made herself comfortable and rested her head in Nikki's lap. Nikki took a sip of her coffee, enjoying the relaxing morning in her pajamas.

"How are you, girl?" She ran her hand down the dog's full white coat. The Maremma sheepdog had such a sweet face. Nikki could always tell what Snowball was thinking from her expressions. Today though, Snowball had been acting strange. She'd refused to eat when Nikki offered her breakfast, and she'd spent the morning lounging in the hallway.

Checking the display on her phone, she sighed. "It's almost time for me to leave, Snowball. I'm supposed to be there by ten, and it's a forty-minute drive." Nikki dreaded going. She'd been angry yesterday, but today her heart ached.

Blue moseyed into the room. Walking over to Snowball, he nudged her snout with his nose. She didn't budge.

Nikki leaned down and stroked the patch between Blue's ears. "I know you two are lonely now that most of the gang has been placed." She looked around at the unused toys scattered on the area rug and the Chihuahua's favorite chew rope peeking out from under the chair. "But we need to be glad that they have permanent homes. No more waiting for them."

Blue pulled away from her hand and circled the space at Nikki's feet twice before lying down with a humph. He yawned and nestled his head on his front paws.

The quiet of the house stretched to every crook and cranny. Nikki missed all the activity that the cats and dogs had provided. Shoot, she even missed the squawking of the birds.

But they were all placed one by one, either to new homes or reunited with their original owners. Her heart had soared when she handed over the Chihuahua to her original owner, who'd been looking for Petals all over Texas. Because of the lack of space and considerable number of displaced pets, many of the bigger cities had sent some of their rescued animals to other towns. It had taken the owner weeks to find Petals.

Nikki sighed. The animals had made her house a home. The only ones that remained in her care were Snowball, Blue, and Tinkerbelle. She rose from the couch, laying Snowball's head on the cushion. Walking into the kitchen with her cup of coffee, she checked the sticky note on the refrigerator. The wildlife ranger had called earlier, waking her from a sound sleep. He'd given her instructions for Tinkerbelle's release. She needed to be at the south entrance to the preserve at eight o'clock the next morning.

Glancing toward the laundry room, Nikki pondered how she'd manage to move the alligator along with the aquarium through the doorway and into the backseat of her compact Kia. She didn't relish the thought of taking Tinkerbelle to the preserve by herself. Mulling it over, she decided to ask Tabitha to go with her. Pulling her phone from her pocket, she sent a text.

What are you doing tomorrow morning? Tinkerbelle needs to be at the preserve by eight. Would you mind helping transport her?

She frowned at the screen not wanting to be an imposition. Why on earth had she bought a compact car when what she needed was a truck … like Dan's? She quashed that idea with a wave of her hand. Somehow, she'd figure something out before tomorrow.

Michael's truck sprang to mind, but she reconsidered. Not after their heart-to-heart. She sighed. Dan had been right about Michael thinking there was more to their friendship, and she didn't want to give him the wrong idea. She shook her head. Talk about naïve. Sipping her coffee, she searched her contacts on her phone.

The time appeared on her screen, nine o'clock. Gasping, she dashed to her bedroom and fished out a blue blouse with puffy, three-quarter sleeves from her closet. She had just enough time to dress and put on her makeup before hitting the road. Nikki stared at her reflection in the bathroom mirror as she applied her mascara. Between the blue shirt and the defining effect of the eyeliner, her blue eyes sparkled. Perfect. She wanted Dan to know she wasn't some naïve simpleton who could be fooled so easily by a handsome smile and a pair of pumped-up biceps.

Her phone dinged.

Sorry, I can't. I've already made plans for a morning hike with the hubby.

Rats. Nikki shoved her phone into her pocket. She'd have to figure out another plan later. All her contacts at the Cowboy Community Church would be busy with the work day scheduled, ending with the potluck dinner.

Nikki twisted the tube of lipstick and coated her lips with a light coral shade that complemented her complexion. Turning off the bathroom light, she scurried down the hall to the living room and grabbed her purse from the chair.

As she dug through her purse for her keys, Snowball lurched forward on the couch, making a noise that sounded like a cross between a cough and a hack.

Nikki glanced her way in time to see the dog spew water onto the area rug.

"Oh, sweetheart, what's wrong with you?" Nikki palmed her keys and tucked them into her front jean's pocket. If she didn't go now, she'd be late, but she couldn't leave a sick animal alone. Groaning, she tossed her purse aside and hurried to the kitchen. Removing the paper towels from the holder, she dug out the cleaning solution for pet stains from under the sink. Nikki dashed back to find Blue standing guard beside Snowball.

"It's okay, Blue. She's going to be all right." Nikki dropped to one knee and placed several paper towels over the puddle. Rising, she made another trip to the kitchen for dish gloves and the trash can. After poking her hands into the pink latex gloves, she hurried back to the living room. Should she go to Dan's or take Snowball to the vet?

Snowball lay on the couch with her head hanging over the edge, watching Nikki while Blue sat near the white dog.

"You don't look too good." Decision made, Nikki removed her gloves and called the town veterinarian.

"Dr. Hoffman's office, how can I help you?" his receptionist asked.

"Beth, this is Nikki Davis. I have a sick Maremma sheepdog that I'm fostering, and I was wondering if there is any way that Doc Hoffman could see her?"

"Can you hold for a moment?"

"Sure." Nikki rolled her eyes, glad that the woman on the other end couldn't see her.

A minute or two later, Beth returned, "He can see you if you can get here in the next hour. He's scheduled for surgery this afternoon, and a lunch date with his wife that he can't miss or she'll kill him." She snorted. "Those were his exact words."

"I'll be there." Nikki ended the call, stuffing her phone back into her pocket. Standing, she moved everything back to the kitchen and rinsed off the gloves. Once that was done, she headed into the laundry room and pulled out one of her collapsible kennels but decided against it. Instead, she snatched one of the leashes from the hook on the wall by the door.

Tinkerbelle hissed.

Nikki glanced at the aquarium to make sure the

clamps were still in place. She didn't need to hunt for a missing alligator when she returned. Alligators could be very territorial in their own environment. Luckily, Tinkerbelle had not adopted Nikki's home as her own and still seemed somewhat docile when she had to handle her. But she would be relieved once Tinkerbelle was back where she belonged, out in the wild and not living next to her washer.

Hoofing it to the living room, Nikki snapped the collar and the leash around Snowball's neck and tugged.

Snowball resisted, refusing to leave the couch.

"Come on. We've got to get you to the vet's to find out what's wrong."

Blue jumped on the couch with his tail wagging.

"No, Blue, this isn't a game." Nikki tugged harder.

Still Snowball remained glued to the cushion.

"Okay, you've left me no choice." Sprinting down the short hall to the kitchen, Nikki opened the refrigerator and took out a hotdog, Snowball's favorite. She picked up the leash and waved the hotdog under Snowball's nose.

Blue hopped off the couch and tried to catch the hotdog in his teeth.

"No, Blue." Nikki dangled the hotdog out of Snowball's reach while keeping Blue away with her hip.

Snowball leaped from the couch.

Walking backwards and keeping the hotdog out of

reach, Nikki coaxed the white dog through the front door and into the yard. Blue followed Snowball trying to get around her.

Once at the car, Nikki threw open the back door and tossed in the hotdog. Before she could stop him, Blue jumped into the backseat along with Snowball.

Nikki didn't have time to wrangle him back into the house. He'd have to go along for the ride. Hustling back into the living room, Nikki nabbed her purse and sent a silent prayer heavenward that Snowball would be all right.

She shoved her phone into her purse before pulling her keys from her front jean's pocket and sliding into the driver's seat. A glance in the rearview mirror showed Blue finishing off the wiener.

This is what she got for waiting to the last minute to get ready. If she hadn't dragged her feet, she'd already be at Silver Spur Ranch by now. But a wave of relief rolled over her that she wouldn't have to face Dan today.

Shoot, Dan. She needed to let him know she wasn't coming. Snowball groaned from the back seat. Calling Dan would have to wait.

Fifteen minutes later, she slowed down enough to make the turn into the vet's parking lot without fishtailing. She zipped her Kia into a space close to the door.

Blue barked at another dog exiting the building while Snowball remained quiet on the seat, not even stirring.

Leaning over the middle console, she reached for a leash she spotted on the floorboard. Since she worked at the rescue, Nikki always had spares in her car. She slipped the leash around Blue's neck and clipped it to itself, creating a makeshift collar. Sliding out of the driver's seat, she opened the back door, catching both leashes in her hand before either dog could bound from the vehicle. "Okay, you two. Let's go see if the doctor can tell us what's going on."

Beth showed them straight into the exam room, bypassing the waiting area.

The exam room was a large square space. In one corner stood a counter with a small sink. Three drawers ran down either side of it to the floor. On the countertop sat a computer and pushed against the wall stood varying sizes of cookie jars. Nikki figured they held treats. Extending from the wall to the center of the room stood a waist-high table that acted as the exam bed. Along the opposite wall ran a long, wide wooden bench, a place for patients and their owners to sit.

Once Beth got them settled, she left. Nikki couldn't help but worry. Something awful must be wrong with Snowball. She hadn't eaten for the last two days, and now she was vomiting. It couldn't be a good sign. Nikki hugged the dog that lay on the big wooden bench beside her. She'd grown to love this oversized fluff ball.

Tears sprang to her eyes. *I know better than to let*

myself get so attached when I'm fostering," She mumbled. It was the advice she'd given hundreds of times over the last two years to others who applied to foster pets. Why she'd thought she'd be immune from giving her heart away was beyond her. But she'd decided on the way to the vets if something was seriously wrong with Snowball, she was keeping her. She couldn't let her go, not knowing how someone else would care for her.

Blue barked and nudged her purse.

The dinging noise coming from her bag caught her attention. She grabbed her phone and discovered a text notification. Dan.

Where are you? Are you all right?

She'd forgotten about him. Glancing at the top of her phone, she realized it was well past ten, edging closer to eleven.

Emergency! *At vet's.*

Chapter Twenty-One

Dan burst through the glass doors of Doctor Hoffman's clinic and rushed to the circular desk where a woman in her thirties sat typing on a computer keyboard.

"Where is Nikki Davis?"

The receptionist kept her eyes glued to the screen in front of her and held up her pointer finger to indicate she needed a minute.

Dan tapped his fingers on the desk and shifted his weight. "She said there was an emergency." He frowned.

The woman shot him a disapproving glance and continued working.

Pulling to his full six feet two, Dan prepared to tell this woman what he thought of her dismissive attitude. But before he could, the receptionist moved from her screen.

"Yes, how can I help you?"

Dan scowled. "I'm looking for Nikki Davis. I

understand there's been an emergency with one of her animals."

"Are you related?"

"Are you kidding me, right now?" Dan yelled, not caring if he was rude. He'd had all he could stand. What he needed was answers. The whole way here, he'd imagined Blue whimpering in the middle of the road, hurt or worse. The dog couldn't stay out of trouble. The knots in his stomach tightened.

"Dan?"

Turning, he spotted Nikki in the doorway of one of the exam rooms.

"What are you doing here?" She asked.

He moved past the circular desk toward her.

"Sir, you can't go back there." The receptionist stood to catch him.

"It's okay, Beth. He's with me." When he came within reach, Nikki grabbed Dan's elbow and dragged him into the exam room shutting the door.

"Thanks." He nodded in the direction of the desk. "For saving me."

"No problem, Beth can be a real stickler for the rules." She crossed her arms. "Now, what are you doing here?"

Dan dropped to one knee, and Blue bounded toward him, licking his face. Running his hands along both sides of the hound's body, he let out a sigh of relief. "He's not hurt."

"No, Blue's not why we're here. It's Snowball."

"Well, you said you had an emergency. And you can't blame me for thinking it involved Blue." Dan rose and dusted off the knees of his jeans. Moving to the bench, he sat beside the docile dog and patted her head. "What's the matter?"

Snowball rolled her eyes to meet his gaze without lifting her head.

"Boy she's lethargic," Dan said.

"Yeah, she's been like this all morning, and she won't eat. And as I was about to leave, she vomited." Nikki's eyes filled with worry.

Dan stood and wrapped an arm around her shoulders pulling her to his side, wanting to make the worry go away. "It's going to be all right. I'm sure. Has the vet been in yet?"

"Yes, he drew some blood and said he wanted to run some tests to rule things out." She bit her lip.

"Did the vet seem anxious about her symptoms?"

Nikki frowned. "Now that you mention it, no, he didn't."

"See, if it'd been serious, he'd have been more concerned." Dan squeezed her shoulders.

As if he'd zapped her with electricity, she stepped out of his embrace. Not looking at him, Nikki sat on the bench next to Snowball. "I thought you had an interview this afternoon?"

"I did, but I rescheduled." Dan sat next to her, but she kept her attention on Snowball.

"I suppose it's not every day that a simple ranch

hand like yourself gets asked to do an interview for such a prestigious academic publication." She lifted her chin.

Dan could almost taste the coolness of her words. "No, I guess not."

"And I suppose you consider it an honor to be able to share your vast knowledge of the workings of a ranch. Since you're *so* experienced after managing the Silver Spur for all these years."

Something had changed. "All right, what's bothering you? I mean, besides the obvious." He gestured toward the dogs.

She shrugged one shoulder, never looking at him.

"You're going to have to give me a little more of a hint." He plopped back against the solid wood.

"Fine." She shifted in her seat to face him. "Marilyn came into the office yesterday."

Straightening, Dan's heart raced. "Marilyn came to see you. What for?" Had the woman let the proverbial cat out of the bag?

"Oh, well, let's see." Nikki stood, crossing her arms. "First, she informed me that you, Dan Harris Thibodeaux, are a liar and a fake, passing yourself off as a ranch hand when in fact, you're this super rich … person," Nikki huffed.

"Now, wait …" Dan sputtered.

"No," she said. "We've already established I don't wait." She pronounced each of the last three words, stabbing the air with her finger.

Dan groaned and stood. "Nikki, that's why I wanted you to come to the ranch today. I wanted to clear this up and explain why I didn't tell you about myself when I first arrived in Orange Blossom."

Blue rose and walked to Snowball. Nudging her snout, he tried to get her to respond. She moaned and rolled to her side on the bench.

"About that, it seems several people knew exactly who you were. Like Marilyn and all her friends, Pastor Connor, and even Purdy figured it out with a little help from a search engine."

Dan stood. "That's not fair, Nikki. I had no choice but to tell Marilyn so I could rent the house. And I've paid for it ever since. As far as Pastor Connor is concerned, he found out because my preacher called him before I arrived in town." A grin spread across his lips. "And Purdy, she's too smart for her own good."

"You think this is funny?" Nikki stomped her foot on the tile floor, tears moistening her lashes.

"No, but I wasn't trying to trick you. I just didn't want to have to deal with all the Marilyns in town. I wanted people to get to know me, not the hyped-up version of me that's in the press."

"Well, now the whole town thinks we're an item, and that I'm the biggest gold digger this side of the Mississippi."

Dan chuckled. "I'm sure you're exaggerating."

A red hue painted Nikki's face. "Remember Dawn, Marilyn's friend who spotted me leaving your house

Sunday morning carrying my duffel bag? Well, let's just say she doesn't think I slept on the couch."

Dan's heart dropped to his boots. "Oh." He hadn't even considered how the situation could've been misconstrued when he insisted that she stay at his house, so he could keep an eye on her. "It was a medical emergency. You needed supervision. Didn't you tell her that?"

"It's not like they came around to find out my side of the story before spreading rumors all over town about me."

"I think you mean us." His ire reflected in his words. "They are spreading rumors about us."

Nikki blinked. "I hadn't considered that your good reputation would be damaged too."

"Yeah, as a Christian, I don't go in for the billionaire-womanizer stereotype. And again, that's why I didn't want to advertise my family connections." Dan's lips pulled tight, and the muscle in his jaw tensed. "While I was married, I didn't have to worry about it as much. But now that I'm single again, it's a continuous battle. One I've grown to hate over the last three years."

Frustration stirred deep within him. He'd done everything he could to keep away from trouble, and even then, he'd brought it to Nikki's front door.

The veterinarian entered the room grinning from ear to ear. "I think I've solved the mystery of Snowball's illness."

Moving toward the bench, Nikki took a seat next to the large white dog and ran her hand down her coat.

Dan, confused by the doctor's body language, waited to see what he had to say.

"After running several tests, I've concluded that Snowball is expecting." He chuckled. "Congratulations, you're having puppies."

Chapter Twenty-Two

"Puppies?" Nikki echoed the doctor's words. "But how?"

The doctor's eyes widened with amusement. "Um, the usual way?"

"Who's the father?" Dan asked, eyeing Blue.

Nikki turned toward Dan. Her eyebrows knitted together. "Well, it must be Blue." She stared at the hound who sat at Dan's feet.

"Blue? Are you sure?" Dan shook his head. He couldn't imagine what the puppies would look like with a big hairy sheepdog and an indigo hound for parents.

"He's the only one it could be. Of the five dogs I fostered, three were female, and well, the other guy couldn't have puppies. If you know what I mean." Nikki squatted, patting her thighs.

Blue ambled over to her with his tongue lolling to one side. Dan could've sworn the dog wore a smile like a proud papa.

Nikki rubbed both sides of Blue's head before

placing a kiss on top. "So, you're going to be a family man now." She smiled, rising to her feet. "You'll have to start acting more responsible. Stop hogging all the toys and stay at home more often."

"Yeah, his running-around days are over." Dan chuckled.

Snowball moaned and lifted her head.

The vet moved to her and did a quick exam. "Seems she's two weeks along. Dogs tend to lose their appetite during this stage and vomit what they do eat. However, it only lasts for a short time."

"Oh, good. So, she'll start eating again?" Nikki said.

"Yes, in fact, you can expect her to gain some weight. She'll be eating for a litter." Doctor Hoffman nodded toward Blue. "She may also exhibit signs of irritability and tire easily. So, let her rest when she wants to, and you may have to keep Blue out of her way if she becomes aggressive toward him."

Dan was concerned how the dogs would do together in Nikki's small bungalow if Snowball wasn't going to be her usual low-key self.

"Is there anything else we need to do for her?" Nikki asked concerned.

"No." Doctor Hoffman scratched between Snowball's pointy ears. "From the look of her, I suspect you might have a few extra mouths to feed around Christmas, New Year's at the latest."

Nikki sat on the bench next to the vet. "I work at

the rescue, and I've seen dogs give birth, but I didn't realize how quick their pregnancies went. That's in two months."

Dan caught the hint of anxiety that laced Nikki's words.

"Yes, but you'll have time to prepare." Giving Snowball one last pat, he stood. "I'll have Beth start on your paperwork, and you'll be out of here in no time. But I have to run. I'm meeting my wife for lunch, and she threatened to toss out my favorite golf club if I'm late again." Doctor Hoffman nodded then headed out of the room.

Nikki sat stunned with her hand on her chest as if she were trying to keep her heart in place. "Well, that's that. I'm going to keep both Snowball and Blue." She looked like a deer caught in the headlights of an oncoming car.

Dan moved toward her. "Are you sure you want to do that? I mean, you could find them a nice home with a big yard and plenty of room for the pups." His own ranch popped into his mind. Once finished, it'd have ample room for all of Nikki's four-legged projects.

"The pups." Nikki's eyes filled with distress. "I'll have to place them when they get old enough." Nikki stood and clutched Snowball's leash. "I can't believe they're going to have puppies."

Dan grabbed the second leash from the bench to put on Blue. "How did you have this connected? He doesn't have a collar."

"I looped it around his neck and clipped it to itself." Nikki answered without looking at either him or Blue.

Dan worried that she'd feel obligated to keep all the puppies as well as the two older dogs. With the size of her house, there was no way she could manage. Of course, the woman had kept five dogs, two cats, two parrots, and an alligator for a couple of months, and nobody died.

He grinned. Nikki Davis was an exceptional woman. Her big heart made her hard not to love. Unsettled by that thought, Dan pulled the leash around Blue's neck, clipping it. "Are you ready to go?" he asked.

"Yeah, we'd better take the little mama home." Nikki tugged on Snowball's leash, and reluctantly, the dog hopped off the bench.

Dan followed Nikki back to her house, parking in his own driveway. He had no intention of feeding the Orange Blossom rumor mill any more crumbs. He slid out of the driver's seat, slamming the door, irritated that he had to be concerned about what others thought.

Nikki stood beside her Kia trying to urge Snowball out of the back seat.

A smile tugged at the corners of his lips. She was a spitfire. He admired her can-do attitude which she had about everything she tackled. The alligator in her laundry room testified to that fact.

The thought of anyone in town thinking she was a

gold digger made him want to come out swinging. But dealing with people in anger was futile. The incident with Michael still haunted him. He walked over to her car. "Can I help?"

"No, I don't need your help. I think you've done enough," Nikki answered struggling with the stubborn dog.

"I'm not the one spreading rumors." Dan widened his stance, crossing his arms over his chest. "Besides, I think it would be better to deal with this together. Show a united front against the false accusations."

Blue sat in the grass panting.

Nikki cut her eyes toward Dan as she pulled with all her might on Snowball's leash. The dog wiggled and rubbed her neck against the backseat, fighting against her.

"Here." He took the leash from her hand.

She stepped aside, placing her fists on her hips. "Fine. See how far you get."

Dan squatted, so he came to eye level with the dog. "Come on, girl. You'll be more comfortable in the house." He rubbed her head and scratched the side of her belly with his fingertips.

Snowball blew out a breath.

Dan stood. "Come." And with a slight tug of the leash, the dog jumped from the backseat onto the driveway.

Nikki frowned. "Show-off." She slammed the back car door and grabbed her purse from the passenger seat before reaching for the leash.

Dan moved his hand with the leash behind him. "That's okay. I'll walk her in. Besides, we need to talk."

Nikki pivoted and marched toward the front porch without answering. "Come on, Blue."

Dan waited as the hound rose and trotted toward Nikki. She held open the screen door and let the dog enter. Glancing back toward him, she said, "Okay, let's talk."

Dan hustled across the lawn and took the steps two at a time as he pulled Snowball behind him.

Nikki let them enter first before following them onto the porch. The screen door slapped shut behind her.

Blue and Snowball stood by the door waiting. Poking her key into the lock, she swung the front door open. The dogs bounded inside, dragging their leashes behind them. Nikki crossed the threshold and slung her purse onto the couch. "Make yourself comfortable. Do you want anything to drink?" She called the dogs to her. Dropping to one knee, she unclipped the leash from Snowball's collar and worked to unclip Blue.

"Yeah, but you're busy. I'll get it." Once in the kitchen, Dan opened the refrigerator and pulled out a bottle of peach tea. As he shut the refrigerator door, the bright lime green sticky note hanging on the front of the fridge caught his eye. He pulled the paper from its spot and read it.

The sound of claws scratching against glass came from the laundry room. How in the world would she get that creature to the preserve tomorrow in her tiny car?

"Did you find something to drink?" Nikki walked into the kitchen. She opened the door to the laundry room and peeked in.

"How is your green friend?" Dan took a sip from the plastic bottle.

Nikki closed the door. "Everything looks good in there."

"I see you've scheduled her release." He showed her the sticky note in his hand before replacing it on the refrigerator. "How are you transporting Tinkerbelle to the preserve?" Dan held up his hand in the universal sign for stop. "Never mind. Dumb question. Michael's helping you, right?"

"No." Nikki sauntered over to the refrigerator and grabbed a bottle of peace tea for herself. She removed the lid and took a sip. "Turns out you were right."

"Right about what?" Dan's brow furrowed.

Leaning with her back against the counter, she focused on him. "About Michael. He does have feelings for me."

Curiosity got the better of him. "How do you know that?"

"He called me the other night. Said he couldn't stop thinking about seeing us together at The Flying Pig. He claimed it was driving him crazy thinking that we might be serious." She shook her head, glancing down at the tile floor. "So, you were right. The only reason he helped me as often as he did was because he hoped we'd get back together. Michael wants to prove that he's different. That he's changed and could put down roots."

Dan held his breath, afraid to hear the outcome of their conversation. But he had to know. "So, what did you tell him about us?"

"Well, of course this was before Marilyn and her bombshell, but I told him that we were just starting to get to know one another." She glanced up and met his gaze. "And that I didn't know how serious it was because it was all so new. But—" She pressed her lips together and shrugged.

"But what, Nikki?" His voice was rigid with tension, his eyes searching hers.

"But that I thought it could be serious."

Chapter Twenty-Three

Nikki tried to swallow, but her mouth was dry. She wanted to look away, but she couldn't. Dan stood in front of her with his warm misty-green eyes focused on her. He looked so handsome with his gray tee-shirt tucked into his just-right fitting jeans. And those darn biceps.

She licked her lips remembering his sweet kisses from the night of their date. They'd tasted like caramel and chocolate and everything delicious in the world.

But he'd lied.

Conflicted, she pushed away from the counter, walked to the table, and pulled out a chair.

Dan turned watching as she settled in her seat.

"You thought we should talk. I think you're right." She gestured to the seat across from her, placing her bottle of tea on the table.

Dan slid into the chair she had indicated. "First, let me say that I kept my identity quiet for self-preservation, and none of this was personal. Nor did I intend to hurt you."

"You've had weeks to tell me, but you didn't." Nikki's heart ached. She'd thought Dan could be trusted, completely. She'd bet her life on it. "You let me think you were a simple ranch hand. A regular working joe like me."

Dan sighed. "It's not that simple." Flopping back in the chair, he released a long breath. "Women like Marilyn make it hard for me to trust people. Once they know who I am and what I've inherited, all they see is the money. And trust me, the things that some women have done thinking they could get to the money, I'd be too embarrassed to share with a decent woman like you."

"But I'm not Marilyn or those women," Nikki protested. "And after getting to know me, you should've realized I'd never act like them or expect anything from you other than your friendship." She leaned forward placing her forearms on the table. Fiddling with the lid to her tea bottle, she added, "Do you know how foolish I felt when Marilyn rolled in with all her accusations?"

Nikki bit her lip to keep the tears at bay. She didn't want his sympathy. What she wanted was for the last two days to evaporate, so things could go back to the way they were when she was filled with the hope of a new beginning with someone so different from Brian or Michael.

"I can't tell you how sorry I am. If I could go back

and do it differently, I would. But that's why I wanted you to come out to the ranch. I wanted to explain everything to you and show you the land where I grew up. Nikki, I do want you to know who I am. It's been years since anyone's cared about me because of the man I am, and not because of my wealth. And with you, I found that again."

The softness in his voice melted her resolve. She'd tossed and turned most of the night replaying Marilyn's hurtful words. Ready to wring Dan's neck for keeping her in the dark. But now, all she could see was the warmth in his eyes.

"Even as friends, you cared about me because of me. Why else would you drag me to the Senior Citizen's Center workday and that auction? You didn't want to see me all alone. In that way, you remind me of Lilly. She cared about people too."

She met his gaze. "You told me she was the one who understood you."

He pressed his lips together and nodded. "Since she's been gone, it's like I've lost my way home." His voice cracked.

Nikki's aching heart connected with the hurt carried in his words. The anger she'd been holding onto dissipated all together.

"I've wanted to tell you for weeks. I started to tell you several times, but something always got in the way." Dan reached out to take her hand, and she let him. "You have to believe me. I never intended to lie to you, or for that matter anyone else. That's not the kind of person I am."

"But you did. And now, I've been branded a gold digger with a smudge on my reputation." Squeezing his hand, she released it. "Sorry, on *our* reputations. So, how do we fix this? You mentioned a unified front. What does that look like?"

"Well, I have an idea." He rubbed the back of his neck. "But I'm not sure you're gonna like it." He cringed. "And I need to speak with Pastor Connor and see what he thinks."

"What is it?" She frowned.

Dan was right. She didn't like the sound of involving Pastor Connor. He'd seen enough of their drama at The Flying Pig.

"Look, I know I'm asking a lot, but can you trust me to talk with Pastor Connor? Once I do, I'll tell you my idea. I'd feel better having his input about it."

She rolled her eyes. "That's a big ask after everything that's happened."

"I know." Dan met her gaze. "But it's for the best."

"Do you promise not to *do* anything without telling me first?" Nikki wanted to trust him, but her willingness to see the good in people was the very trait that had gotten her into this mess.

"Yes, but I will need to talk with the pastor. Is that all right?"

Nikki buried her face in her hands and groaned, frustrated that she didn't know if she should trust him.

Her heart pulled in one direction and her head in another. Finally, she met his gaze. "I'm going to trust you because I don't think you intentionally lied to me. Now that you've explained, I can understand your need to protect yourself against a certain type of woman."

"Thank you." Dan grabbed her hands and lifted them to his lips.

But before he could kiss them, Nikki jerked them from his grasp. "Whoa there, cowboy. I might have forgiven you for misrepresenting yourself, but that doesn't mean you're out of the woods yet. I still have a couple of days' worth of mad to go before there's any handholding or anything like that. Besides, I'd like to get to know *this* Dan Thibodeaux." She scowled. "And we still have our little problem of Marilyn and her gossipy friends. Let's wait to see how our unified front goes before we talk about—" She hesitated, the word strange on her tongue. "Us."

"That's fair." Dan drained the rest of his tea. Pushing back his chair, he stood and walked to the trash can. He pointed at the sticky note on the refrigerator. "Do you want help getting Tinkerbelle to the preserve?"

Nikki sighed. She needed his help and his truck, but she didn't know if spending that much time with Dan would be good at this point. It had taken all her strength to pull her hand away from his. But the thought of pushing the aquarium into the backseat of her Kia worried her. What would happen if Tinkerbelle got loose while she was driving? With that image in her head, she nodded. "Yeah, I think that would be best."

~

Dan opened the console between the two captains' chairs of his truck and fished out the box of tissues he kept stashed in there for emergencies. He'd seen women cry over the strangest things, like the time Marge cried over a sunken soufflé, or the time Lilly cried because he gave her a bouquet of flowers, but he'd never thought he'd see a woman cry over an alligator.

He passed Nikki the square box. "I know you have a big heart where animals are concerned and you love them all, but remember, Tinkerbelle belongs in the wild where she can grow old, fat, and sassy." He chanced a peek in Nikki's direction. The tears and sniffles slowed. Now, she sat in the passenger seat dabbing at her cheek with a crumpled tissue.

"I know. I know. But I can't help it. I'm going to miss her."

"Really? Weren't you scared she'd hurt you or one of the other animals if she got loose? Like that Sunday when I helped you?" He kept his eyes on the road and hoped that shifting the conversation to the logistics of having a reptile would help dull the sting of releasing Tinkerbelle back into her natural habitat for Nikki.

Shrugging, she sighed. "Yes, if I'm honest. I did fear for the other smaller animals, but she never did become aggressive. Somehow, she understood that my home wasn't where she belonged. And alligators aren't aggressive outside of their own territory. She was such a good girl."

Dan fought the grin that wanted to emerge. Nikki found the good in everybody whether they had two feet or four. He looked out the window and checked his side mirror to keep her from seeing his struggle. "Think of it this way—Tinkerbelle is home now and isn't displaced anymore."

Nikki nodded and poked her tissue into her purse before setting it on the floorboard. "You're right. I might miss the birds and cats and Tinkerbelle, but they now are all somewhere they can call home." She swiped under her eyes with her hand one last time. Turning toward him, she gave him a weak smile. "It's nearly lunchtime. You want to stop and have lunch when we get closer to town?"

"Are you asking me out on a date?" He grinned, tilting his head her way.

Her eyebrows winged up. "I'm surprised that you'd even consider going out with me since my reputation has gone to the dogs." She winked at him.

Her smile grew and the mischievous glint he'd seen in her eyes many times over the months now appeared. He hoped her teasing meant he was forgiven, but he figured it was too soon, so he let the date comment drop. "Speaking of dogs, are you still set on keeping Snowball and Blue?"

"Yes." She set the tissue box in the seat beside her. "With the puppies on the way, Snowball and Blue need a good stable home. Somewhere they can be until the puppies are born. Once the pups are here, I'll have to work on finding each of them a good home." Her brows knit together, and she turned to him. "Why?"

"Well, I was thinking since Blue seems to like me, I might adopt him. That way he could still see Snowball because we'd be right next door."

"Only until the ranch house is finished. When is that?" Nikki ran her finger along the edge of the tissue box without looking up.

Dan's heart lurched, and he fidgeted in his seat. He didn't want to talk about the spring when he'd be moving back to Silver Spur Ranch. He wanted to enjoy what time he could with his kindhearted, beautiful neighbor who cried over alligators.

"They say it'll be done in April as long as everything goes according to schedule." Dan pulled the steering wheel and followed the curves of the narrow road leading out of the preserve. "Since the vet said that Snowball might be a little agitated, I figured I'd give Blue a safe haven at least for the duration of the pregnancy, if you're not comfortable with me keeping him permanently."

Nikki bit her lip. "Let me think about it, okay?"

"Sure. But I think Blue and I would make great roommates."

"Really? After he's rolled in your bed, dug up the new hedges around your porch, and stunk up your truck? You think he'd make a good roommate?" Nikki laughed and shook her head. "You certainly have a strange criterion for what constitutes a great roomie."

"True, but Blue and his present owner have grown on me." The temptation to take her hand ran through him, but he didn't want to do anything that might spoil the moment. "And I'm learning to let go of the past and a lot of my preconceived notions of how my future will be."

She gave him a half grin. "Strange, I'm growing fond of the billionaire cowboy next door, and I, too, am learning to let go of my preconceived notions."

Dan cocked an eyebrow. "What preconceived notions are we talking about?"

"Oh, those about cowboys, billionaires, and displaced neighbors."

"I'm not one of your projects, am I?" Dan stole a glance at her.

"Maybe a little at first. But now that I know you're having a home built, I regard you as being placed."

"Oh." Dan grew quiet.

The truck wound along the pavement until they reached the exit of the wildlife preserve. Pulling to the side of the road, he put the truck in park. He turned toward Nikki. "I'm not just a cowboy, and I'm not just a billionaire, and I'm not just a neighbor."

Nikki licked her lips and ran her hands down the front of her jeans. Uncertainty clouded her face.

Dan had said too much and had scared her. He should stop, not push it, but he couldn't help himself—

he needed her to know. "I don't think it's the rebuilding of the house that makes me feel like I've found home."

She reached out and placed her finger over his lips. "Don't say anything else. I need time to get to know you, all the sides of you. Not simply the parts of your life you've shared but those that I'm discovering." Dropping her hand, she sighed.

"Okay, then help me out. Next Saturday, Pastor Connor is conducting a service for Lilly. I never spread her ashes, and I almost lost the chance when the hurricane hit."

"How could I help? Wouldn't it be strange for me to be there?"

"Maybe, but I need help setting up a reception for the people coming. And since the service is at the ranch, I've rented a tent and asked one of the local restaurants to cater it. But I need someone I trust to oversee it while I'm ..." He couldn't find the words to describe his role. "I need help, Nikki. My pastor thinks it's time to let go and move on. And Pastor Connor agreed."

"Is this the idea you were talking about yesterday? A unified front?" Nikki asked.

Dan nodded. "Last night, I spoke with Pastor Connor and explained why I thought you should be there. I don't want the rumor mill to win. And if you come to support me Saturday, it'll show everyone that we care about each other, and that it's not some torrid affair, but a friendship based on love and respect."

"Hmm. I don't know."

Taking her hand, he intertwined their fingers. "When I first got here, I didn't think I was ready to let go of Lilly. But now, I need to do this. I need to see it through." He met her gaze, her blue eyes filled with uncertainty. "I need to say goodbye, and knowing you'll be there when I'm done would mean so much to me."

Nikki shook her head. "I'm not sure I should. What would everyone think? The gold digger at the service for your first wife? No, it's not a good idea."

"Nikki, I'm not worried about everyone else. I'm telling you what I need. The only three people who count here are me, you, and Lilly. And I think she'd want me to have someone I could count on there for support. She wouldn't want me to go through this alone."

"You won't be alone. The others will be there to help you get through it."

"But they're not you." He sighed. "We didn't do anything wrong, Nikki. There's no reason for you not to be there if I've invited you. Don't let Marilyn's careless words ruin our chance to find out what this could be."

Biting her lip, she knit her brows together. After a moment, she squeezed his hands. "I'll pray about it. Give me a little time to think this through."

"I can do that." Dan released her hands and straightened in his seat, his heart racing at the words he'd spoken. He'd asked her to be there for him. Now, he'd have to wait and see what God had planned.

Shifting into drive, Dan pulled the vehicle back onto the road, hoping his future would be as smooth as the freshly paved blacktop under the wheels of his truck, but he had his doubts.

Chapter Twenty-Four

Nikki sighed as she skimmed what she'd typed to find her place in the document. Her eyes strayed to the bulletin board beside her desk. The retro cat poster pinned there read, *Hang in there, baby.* She sympathized with the cat dangling from the branch. Just like the feline, she'd been precariously hanging on by a thread all week. Now it was Thursday, and she needed to give Dan an answer.

He'd been patient and hadn't pressed her even when they'd had dinner together Tuesday night at her house. But she didn't have an answer. She'd prayed, read her Bible, and searched for one all week. So far, the Lord had been silent.

She closed her eyes and under her breath said a prayer for wisdom and strength. As she finished, the front door swished open. "Amen." Nikki glanced up to see who had entered.

There in living color stood Marilyn Kemp with her styled blond hair, her meticulous makeup, and a tailored business suit, all perfectly in place.

Looking heavenward, Nikki mumbled, "Really, Lord?"

Marilyn swung her satchel onto the counter and smiled her *Miss-America, Queen of the World* smile.

Nikki half expected confetti to rain down on her and a marching band to appear.

"Is Purdy here? I need to get some information from her about that cute new family that joined the church Sunday. Cathy Finn over at the coffee shop told me that they're renting. Now, we can't have that, can we?"

Nikki steeled herself and stood. "Purdy isn't here right now. But she should be back any minute. She ran some packages over to FedEx." Not wanting to be unprofessional, she gestured toward the chairs that ran along the wall behind Marilyn. "You can wait if you'd like."

Turning, Marilyn surveyed the chairs as if she'd never seen them before in her life. She scrunched her nose and shook her head. "I think I'll stand."

"Okay." Nikki, not wanting to engage with the woman any more than necessary, sat and rolled her chair to where she could reach the keyboard comfortably. She laid her hands on the keys. Her fingers flew as she worked on the remainder of Pastor Connor's Sunday sermon.

Marilyn cleared her throat.

Nikki paused and met her gaze. "Yes, what can I

do for you now?"

"I don't suppose you could give me the information?" Marilyn looked at her wristwatch and tapped its face. "I do have another appointment, and it would mean so much to me."

"I'm not sure if we hand out that type of information. I think I should let Purdy make that decision. Now, if that's all." Nikki pointed to the computer screen. "I do need to finish this."

Marilyn held up her hands in surrender. "No, don't let me keep you from your work. I admire your ethic. Most people might be tempted to let things slide. But not you. You're keeping on top of everything even though you might only be the assistant church secretary for a few more months. That is, if you play your cards right with Dan." Her Miss-America smile reappeared.

Nikki gripped the edge of her desk to stay seated. It took every ounce of her restraint not to march over to the counter and give Marilyn a piece of her mind. Gritting her teeth, she turned back to her work.

"I mean, I don't blame you. He is handsome and so successful it's hard not to be tempted. And with the two of you right next door to one another—thick as thieves, so to speak—no one could lay any blame at your feet for trying to lasso that cowboy."

The spark of irritation Nikki had tried to ignore ignited into full-blown rage. "That's it." Popping out of her chair, Nikki charged to the counter, wagging her finger in Marilyn's face, the solid surface keeping them apart. "Let's get this straight once and for all. Dan and I are friends and neighbors. He's been nothing but kind to me. Shoot, he even saved my life. And to have you and your little gang of busybodies going around spreading rumors and out-and-out lies about him is wrong. You should be ashamed of yourself."

Marilyn laid her hand on her chest, her mouth gaping. "Well, I've never been so insulted," she huffed. "You're supposed to be a representative of the church. I have a good mind to report you to Pastor Connor about this. And see what you have to say then."

"Fine. Go right ahead. He's in his office. But I won't hesitate to tell him how you've used this congregation as your own personal network for your business on more than one occasion." Nikki jammed her fists onto her hips and squinted at the bottle-blond wannabe. "Plus, I bet he won't be too happy that you've been spreading rumors about members of his congregation."

"They aren't rumors when you have facts to back them up." Marilyn's eyes filled with fire as she lifted her chin. "Dawn saw you leaving Dan's house carrying a duffel bag. You can't tell me you didn't stay the night." She leaned across the counter. "Go ahead, deny it."

Nikki swallowed aware that she'd backed herself into a corner. "I can't deny it."

A sneer swept across Marilyn's lips. She crossed her arms, nodding. "I knew it."

"It's not what you think at all. The day of the auction while we were picnicking, one of the dogs I foster got stuck in the middle of the pond. We went after him, and I reached the dog first. As I pushed Blue toward the shore, I lost my footing and went under. If Dan hadn't been there, I would've drowned."

"Oh." Marilyn dropped her arms.

Nikki could see the fire in her eyes cool.

"But what does that have to do with what Dawn saw?" Marilyn asked. "It doesn't explain why you stayed the night at his place?"

Nikki leaned on the counter, her tone softer. "He insisted on taking me to the emergency room. The doctor told him I needed twenty-four-hour supervision to make sure nothing popped up. I slept on his couch, Marilyn." Nikki sighed. "That's all there is to it."

"That's it?" Marilyn blinked. "You needed help, and he was there for you?" She walked to the chairs and slid into one, deflating before Nikki's eyes.

Not sure what to do, Nikki lifted the partition and walked around the counter. Sitting in the chair beside Marilyn, Nikki struggled to find something to say. She had experience dealing with the self-confident, in-your-face Marilyn, but this rag doll had her stumped. As she searched for the right words, she determined to make amends. She'd let her anger get the better of her, and now she regretted it. "Look, Marilyn, I'm sorry I got so angry, but my reputation is important to me. I know we've never been close, but I don't want us to be enemies. We're both part of the family of God. Can't we figure something out? A way we could coexist without hurting each other?"

"I don't want to be enemies either." Marilyn's gaze rested on her hands in her lap. "If I was honest, I'd have to say I'm a little jealous of you, Nikki Davis."

"Of me?" Nikki chuckled. "Why me? The woman who works two jobs to make ends meet and spends half her earnings on pet food. Not much there to be jealous of."

Marilyn shook her head, keeping her eyes on her hands. "No, you have a lot going for you. People like you. You have friends because you have a good heart." Marilyn shrugged. "Plus, no one has ever put themselves in danger for me the way Dan did for you. If I were drowning, I don't think anyone would jump in to save me." She swiped a single tear from her cheek.

"Yes, they would," Nikki argued. "I'd jump in to save you."

She raised her eyes, her bottom lashes moist, and met Nikki's gaze. "See, that's what I mean. Even after all that I've done to you, you'd still help me. You do have a good heart." The corners of her lips lifted into a genuine smile. "But do you know what bugs me the most about you?"

Nikki cocked one eyebrow. "No, what?" She steeled herself for what Marilyn might say.

"You're young, and I know that my best days are behind me. And that can be so annoying." Marilyn sighed. "Especially since my ex-husband takes every opportunity to remind me of that fact. Being traded in stinks."

"Well, it's his loss. 'Cause God isn't done with you yet. Not by a long shot. And His plan is for your good." Nikki bumped her shoulder against Marilyn's. "True?"

"True." Marilyn shifted in her chair and faced her. "Forgive me for the trouble I've caused you. I'll be sure to tell Dawn what really happened and straighten this out. I should've known better, but it's hard to see younger women getting ahead."

"I wouldn't consider being Dan's friend getting ahead. He's a regular guy who wants to be treated like any other man," Nikki said.

"From what you've told me, he seems like the type of guy who will be there when you need him, no matter what. Unlike a few others I could name."

A spark ignited in Nikki's heart, and the answer to Dan's question shimmered in the light. "Yes, he was there for me, saved me. So, I'll be there for him."

Grabbing Marilyn, she pulled her into a bear-hug. "Thank you so much."

Marilyn wrapped her arms around Nikki. "No, thank you."

At that moment, Purdy walked into the receptionist area. She froze mid-stride. "What's going on here?"

Nikki released Marilyn.

The look on Purdy's face was so priceless no

billionaire could have afforded it——not even Dan Harris Thibodeaux. "Just a little God moment." Nikki beamed.

"Yeah, just a little God moment," Marilyn echoed.

Chapter Twenty-Five

Dan bowed his head, listening to the prayer that Pastor Connor offered heavenward. The words stirred both his thankfulness for his time with Lilly and the pain of losing her. He'd known today would be rough. That's why he'd asked Nikki to be here, waiting for him when it was done.

The light streamed in through the broken branches of the trees and danced around the ground near Pastor Connor's feet. His rumbling voice echoed through the still woods, and the quiet of the place fell on the group gathered to pay their respects. The clearing near the river had been the spot of many of their childhood adventures, and it was the very place he'd asked her to marry him. This was their spot, and he'd made a point to bring her home.

Dan swiped the tears from his cheek with his handkerchief and tucked the urn close to his side. He'd kept Lilly with him these last three years, trying hard not to forget the sound of her voice or the sweet smell of her hair just after she'd washed it. He thought if he kept her ashes that it would somehow keep them connected. But he was wrong.

It was unfair of him not to give her the last thing she wanted. Selfish, some would say. In her will, she'd made her wishes clear. Her ashes were to be spread here where their friendship had grown into love.

So, today, he'd fulfill her last request of him. He hugged the urn closer, fighting back the tears. But as long as he lived, Lilly would always be a part of him. His connection with her didn't depend on a promise or a picture or a box full of memories. He drew in a deep breath filling his lungs with the scent of oak and pine. It had taken him three years to reach this point. A place where a new love had room to grow in his heart. An image of Nikki on his porch drifted into his mind. He released the breath and focused on the words of Pastor Connor's prayer.

"Her life was brief by many standards, Lord. But we know she is with you in a far better place. Amen."

"Amen," The crowd echoed as Pastor Connor motioned to Lilly's older sister.

A gentle breeze blew off the river giving the crowd a brief respite from the heat.

June stepped forward and stood beside the pastor. She closed her eyes and hummed a note. Softly she began to sing the words of the hymn "It Is Well with My Soul." Her rich voice grew in intensity. The notes of the tune she sang a capella engulfed the people gathered in the clearing, filling the space with God's presence.

A wave of sorrow washed over Dan at the words of Lilly's favorite hymn. He gasped trying to catch his breath. His shoulders shook as his chest heaved. Tears coursed down his cheeks.

Rod moved to his side and wrapped an arm around his shoulders. Dan held the handkerchief over his eyes. The words of the song melted into his soul, ministering healing to his spirit. The others sniffled and moaned all around him. Rod prayed softly over him, never letting go.

Dan's younger brother, Wade, stood nearby. Though they hadn't been close in years, his presence today leant Dan the extra strength he'd needed.

When the song ended, Dolly, Rod's wife, moved to him. "It's time, Dan. We need to say our final goodbyes." Her voice cracked.

"I'm right here with you. And so is God." Rod released him.

Dan nodded. Wiping his eyes, he moved to the front of the gathering. Swallowing the tears that threatened to return, he glanced down at the urn. "I want to thank all of you for coming today. It must seem strange that I've waited so long to do this, but until now, I wasn't ready. So, thank you for coming to be here for Lilly."

Some nodded.

"She was a wonderful woman. Lilly proved it

every day by putting up with me." A half smile lifted a corner of Dan's lips.

A gentle laughter skittered across the group.

"She was smart, loving, beautiful, and most of all, kind. When the world lost Lillian Nora Thibodeaux, they lost a true treasure."

"Yes, we did," Lilly's Aunt Pam said. "A real treasure."

June nodded, wiping her cheeks with a tissue. Her husband, Todd, took her hand.

Not able to say more, Dan turned to face the river. Removing the lid from the urn, he offered his own prayer. "Lord, you gave, and I will be forever grateful. Then you took away. Now, she is with you. Blessed be your name. May your daughter be ever in your presence. In Jesus' name I ask this. Amen."

Tilting the urn, the ashes poured forth, and the light breeze from the river scattered them among the grasses growing on its banks.

~

Nikki used a piece of thin cardboard from a package she'd found near the coffee table to fan herself. The heat in the large tent was stifling even if it was November. The temperature on her phone display had read seventy-five when she arrived half an hour ago.

Now, her black Audrey Hepburn-style dress clung to her body like a second skin. She pulled at the boat neckline and lifted her hair as she moved the makeshift fan around her face trying to alleviate her discomfort.

The tent hummed with activity. Caterers in short-sleeved white shirts with black bow ties hustled around her, setting out platters of food on the long folding tables in the center of the tent. A florist and her assistant busied themselves adding water to the arrangements on each of the serving tables.

Nikki stood still. Touching her stomach, she cringed. The smell of the food along with the heat and her nerves caused it to roil. She'd gone over a thousand excuses as she dressed this morning, as to why she shouldn't come. But in the end, she couldn't leave Dan stranded. He'd asked her to be here, so she came. But she'd made up her mind before she ever left the house not to go with the others to spread Lilly's ashes. It wasn't right since she hadn't known her. Nikki shifted her weight, her high heels pinching her toes. Scanning the yard, she wondered how Dan was doing.

A few people emerged from the path at the side of the yard that led to the river and moved toward the tent.

The knot in her stomach tightened, too late to bail out now. She'd been surprised when Dan told her how many were attending. Lilly had died over three years ago, but it seemed she was loved and esteemed by many in the county. There were nearly seventy-five people at the gathering today. A wave of nervous jitters passed through her as she worried about how many of them would think she was a gold digger. Marilyn had made that assumption. What would stop others from jumping to the same conclusion? She groaned. Why had she agreed to come?

Her heart rang out the answer. She had a soft spot for Dan. He'd come to her rescue more than once, even though she'd been the one to get herself into trouble.

The first few people entered the tent trailed by a long line of others, talking together in groups of two or three.

One of the caterers met them at the entrance to the tent and directed them to the tables spread with hors d'oeuvres. Standing tables had been placed around the tent instead of the usual chairs and round tables at Dan's request.

Nikki wanted to be useful, but she wasn't sure what she should do.

A gray-haired man with a short military-style haircut approached her. He carried a plate with a few pigs in a blanket on it. Nikki prepared to direct him to the drink tables, but before she could get the words out, he greeted her.

"You must be Nikki. I've heard so much about you." He smiled. "I'm Rod Carson. Dan's ranch manager."

Nikki returned his smile. "Oh, it's so nice to meet you. Have you worked with Dan long?"

Rod barked a laugh. "I started working here when Dan was in diapers, and his Pops owned the place. His mother was a firecracker. Sure do miss her."

Reaching out, Nikki touched his forearm. "I know today must be hard for you if you've been with the family that long."

"Yeah, it never gets easier. First Dan's mother, then Pops, and now Lilly." Rod turned and looked towards the yard.

Nikki dropped her hand and followed his gaze. Dan and Pastor Connor were at the rear of the line, making their way toward the tent.

"He's been through a lot. For a while Dolly and I were worried about him. Dolly's my wife." He shook his head and turned his attention back to Nikki. "Lilly and his brothers had been there to help him grieve for his grandfather, but when she died so suddenly— drowning that way—I didn't know if he'd find his way back out of that black hole."

"I'm sure it helped to have you and Dolly around to look after him." Nikki clenched her hands together in front of her, not sure what to say. The man obviously cared a great deal for Dan.

"You know, if Dolly and I could've ever had kids, I'd want them to be like Dan."

"Yes, he's a good man." A smile lifted the corners of her lips as the image of him bandaging her burnt hand leaped into her mind. "He has a big heart."

"Funny, he says the same about you. That you have a big heart and a crazy love of animals." Rod chuckled. "Most people wouldn't take in a displaced alligator, injured or not."

"Well, I never told Dan this, but I was so thankful when Tinkerbelle's foot healed, and I could release her.

The day we found Tinkerbelle out of her aquarium was the day I decided it was time to find her a new home."

"I can only imagine." Rod's eyes widened.

"I'll never forget the sound of her hissing." Nikki scrunched her nose. "I hope it's the last time I have to play hostess to a reptile."

A woman walked up behind Rod and touched his shoulder. "Hey, hon, did you get something to drink?"

Rod stepped to one side, so the woman could join them. "Dolly, this is Nikki. The one I've been telling you about."

Nikki stifled the groan that rose in her. Great, they'd been discussing her and Dan. Did they think she was a gold digger on the prowl for her next victim?

"Oh, it is so nice to meet you." Dolly squealed and grabbed Nikki's hand giving it a squeeze. "Rod and Dan have had nothing but good things to say about you." Leaning in, Dolly lowered her voice. "We are thrilled, simply thrilled that Dan has grown so fond of you."

Nikki blinked, not sure what to say. "Dan's grown fond of me?"

"Well, he did ask you out on a date, right?" Dolly looked from Nikki to Rod.

"We shouldn't interfere." Rod slid his hand under his wife's elbow.

"No, it's fine. She's right. We are close. I'm just not sure what our relationship is right now."

"Oh." Dolly tilted her head, pursing her lips.

"Well, I think Dan is a catch. Of course, I'm a little biased." She grinned.

"Look, there's Cameron Beardsley. Didn't you want to ask him to donate a few giveaways for the Christmas Market this year?"

"Why yes, I did." Dolly glanced toward a table near the edge of the tent. "Let's see if we can join him at his table." Stopping, she addressed Nikki. "You've been good for him. And no matter what happens, I want to thank you for that. You were the push he needed to realize he still has a lot of life to live."

Rod gave Nikki a polite smile and directed Dolly by the elbow away from her. Looking over his shoulder, he said, "Nice to meet you."

The tent had filled with the guests and catering staff. The buzz of conversations around her made her head throb, and the intensity of the heat added to the knot in her stomach. She considered grabbing a plate of appetizers but decided against it. Weaving through the groupings of people, Nikki made her way to the drink table that held the ice bowl and tea urns. Something cool to drink sounded much better than food to her at this point.

She'd tried to locate Dan as she moved through the tent but hadn't been able to find him. It was probably for the best. He needed to be available for all the people who had come to pay their respects, and she'd only feel uncomfortable standing beside him as he reminisced with folks about Lilly. Not because she was jealous, but because it seemed so inappropriate. Even if they were friends.

Shaking her head to dispel the thoughts, she pulled a translucent plastic cup from a tower of cups and scooped in ice cubes from the glass bowl. The heat had melted half the ice into cold water, and she was tempted to splash a few droplets onto her face. Instead, she filled the ice-packed glass with tea and took a long drink.

Another woman who looked to be in her late thirties approached the drink table. "It's so hot in here. I think I'm going to melt like the ice." She chuckled.

Turning toward her, Nikki met her gaze. "Yes, it's almost unbearable, but that's southern Texas for you." Nikki stepped aside so the woman could have full access to the tea urns.

The woman grabbed a plastic cup. "How did you know Lilly?" She leaned over the ice bowl and grabbed the scoop.

"Oh, I didn't."

The woman looked up from scooping ice.

"I'm here for Dan. He is my neighbor. At least temporarily, and he asked me to be here today for support." Nikki took a sip of her tea. "Honestly, I feel a little odd being here," she confided to the stranger. Lifting her glass to her lips, she took another sip and scanned the area for Dan.

"Don't. If Dan needed support today, you did the right thing coming." The woman filled her cup with the dark brown tea before sticking out her hand toward

Nikki. "I'm June Collins. I'm Lilly's sister."

Nikki sputtered, spewing droplets of tea into the air. Coughing, she reached for a drink napkin on the table and wiped her mouth before dabbing at the damp spots on the front of her black dress. "I'm so sorry," she added as she reached for a second napkin to give June.

June took the napkin and dabbed the few spots on her blouse that were visible. "Are you okay?"

"I will be." Nikki placed her hand near her heart, trying to regain her composure. "It's nice to meet you."

June's lips wreathed into a smile. "It's nice to meet you, too. I didn't mean to upset you."

"No, no, it didn't dawn on me that I might meet members of Lilly's family today. It was a little shortsighted of me, to say the least. Obviously, I would. Or will." Nikki tensed. Her mouth kept moving, but her brain had frozen. She willed herself to stop talking.

June gave the damp spots one more swipe and tossed her napkin into the trash near the drink table.

Nikki followed suit, glad she hadn't caused any more damage to June's blouse than a few spots.

June's eyes twinkled. "Well, the fact that you came to support Dan speaks volumes. Like you said, it is an unusual situation. Anyone in your position would feel out of place, so to speak."

"Thank you for recognizing that." The tension in Nikki's stomach eased.

June had a peaceful manner. "Since you didn't know Lilly, it would be hard to be here. So, you must care for Dan very much to put yourself through an afternoon of celebrating someone you didn't even know."

"To be honest, Dan's told me enough about her. I feel like I know her a bit. I think we would've been friends."

"Yes, she was easy to like." June nodded.

"And he loved her deeply." Nikki's gaze fell to the ground.

"He did, but no one, including myself, expected Dan to stay single this long." June jiggled the melting ice in her tea. "He's the type of man who needs family. And he's lost so many people who were dear to him. I think his Uncle Charlie and Aunt Lana are the last relatives he has on his father's side. And of course, his mother was an only child. He and his brothers are the only ones left in the Harris line." June took a sip of her tea. Nodding toward the tables in the center of the tent, she said, "Yeah, he's not one to be alone. He needs family."

Nikki followed her gaze. There next to the platter of egg salad sandwiches stood Dan. His dark suit and cobalt blue tie looked out of place on him. She'd only seen the cowboy, the ranch hand. But today, Dan looked every inch the billionaire businessman.

Glancing at Nikki, June smiled. "You can't find a nicer, sweeter guy than Dan Thibodeaux. He made my sister happy, and I hope one day, he finds someone who can make him as happy as he made her." June leaned close and pulled Nikki in for an awkward hug, their purses and drinks getting in the way. "Thanks for being here for Dan. I know Lilly would appreciate you looking after him."

Chapter Twenty-Six

Nikki held the clear plastic plate in one hand and the silverware wrapped in a napkin in the other. Tucked under her arm, she carried her clutch. After her conversation with June, her nerves had settled enough so she could eat. Maybe she'd made the right choice in coming after all. Standing in the buffet line, she shuffled along between a man in a black cowboy hat who smelled of tobacco and an older woman who had a string of pearls looped around her neck several times, adding to her bulk.

The woman with the pearls spoke to the tall lady behind her who had stopped to add some Swedish meatballs to her plate.

The man in front of Nikki stopped to fish out toothpicks from the holder next to the platters. At this rate, she'd perish before she even had a chance to taste the delicacies on her plate.

"Josie, you can't account for manners," The woman with the pearls said with a thick Texas drawl. "I don't think I'd ever come to a funeral of a man's first wife even if we were dating. No matter what the reason. It's downright tacky."

Nikki stiffened.

"Of course not. That's unheard of." The tall woman clucked her tongue against her teeth. "Imagine. And on sweet Lilly's day of remembrance. That takes nerve."

"I mean, clearly no one expected him to remain single all his life. He's too young for that, but for the woman he's dating to show up here? Unbelievable."

The muscles in Nikki's stomach tightened. She stepped to the right to glance around the man in front of her, so she could see down the line. How much longer would it take? The man with the cowboy hat had succeeded in getting out the toothpicks with his beefy fingers and stood contemplating the selection of sandwiches.

Nikki peered over her shoulder to see if she recognized the two women. She didn't. Thank goodness.

"Some people have no decorum," the woman named Josie replied, shaking her head.

"Manners are a lost art. In my day, we used to study the how-to's of interpersonal communications and how to handle certain situations in home ec. But these days, that's not even a thing anymore. Instead, everybody tweets or snaps whatever's on their mind without a second thought." The woman's voice rose a notch or two.

"You do have to admit, though, this is a little different. Dan did wait a long time to have this event." Josie moved closer to her friend who stepped closer to Nikki.

Nikki, who wanted nothing better than to run, couldn't move. She was hemmed in on all sides. Even the groupings of people standing around the tall tables made it impossible for her to escape. She touched her stomach as the knot grew larger.

"Well, Marilyn told me a few weeks ago all this woman wants is Dan's money." The woman wearing the pearls bumped Nikki's arm. "Oh, excuse me, dear," she offered before returning to her conversation.

The tall woman leaned over the table and nabbed the tongs to grab a few pigs in a blanket. "Yeah, I'd heard the same. Gold digger. It figures. I feel sorry for Dan. He has so much more to offer a woman, and to get stuck with some money-grubbing floozy who will never appreciate him—" She plopped three of the small wieners wrapped in bread onto her plate. "That's so sad to me."

Nikki gasped, her hand flying to her mouth. So, this is what people thought of her dating Dan. She stifled the sobs that rose in her throat.

The woman with the pearls asked, "Are you all right?" And reached out to pat Nikki's shoulder.

The tears threatened to flow, but she didn't want to cause a scene. For goodness' sakes, she was already the talk of the town. She didn't want to add to it. Tossing her plate onto the table, she shrugged away from the woman's hand and pushed her way past the two gentlemen standing to her right. She dodged as many people as she could, but the tears blurred her vision as she shoved past the waiter who was busy refilling the tea urns near the back of the tent.

"Hey," he called, but she didn't answer.

She needed to get out of here. No matter what Rod and June had told her, it had been a mistake for her to come. The name *gold digger* rang in her ears as she fumbled her way to the exit. The damage had been done, even though Marilyn had sworn to make it right. Once the fire of gossip burned, it was hard to put out. And where Dan was concerned, it burned statewide.

Nikki managed to make it to her car without having to explain to anyone why she was upset. Laying her forehead on her hands on the steering wheel, she let the tears course down her cheeks. She didn't know exactly why she was crying. Whether it was because of her ruined reputation, or because the man she deeply cared for could no longer be a part of her life. The only way to kill the rumor was to stop seeing him. Her chest heaved as she sobbed. She had no choice. It was the best thing for them both. And as he'd pointed out, it wasn't only her reputation at stake. How had she gotten herself into this mess? Seemed she'd been branded again.

A gold digger.

A floozy.

A fool.

Nikki straightened and pulled a tissue from her clutch. Staring into the rearview mirror, she wiped the mascara from under her eyes. Leaning back, she huffed. What was that old saying? Fool me once shame on you; fool me twice shame on me. *What happens when I'm the one who's always playing the fool*? She had no one to blame but herself.

Shaking her head, Nikki made her decision. She put the car into reverse and pulled out of the grass onto the long, gravel driveway. Glancing in the mirror, she spotted Dan standing a few feet behind the car in the middle of the drive, waving for her to stop. Hesitating, she watched him move toward her. It was time to do what was right, even if her heart cracked into a million pieces. This time Dan couldn't rescue her. She'd have to be the one to end it.

Chapter Twenty-Seven

Nikki swiveled in her office chair to face her computer, trying to tune out Sarah's chatter. For a fourteen-year-old, she sure had a lot to say.

Sarah and Purdy were working on a strategy for her to win the Silver Medallion grand prize this semester. She'd turned in all her service hours she'd earned so far, and it looked like she and one other girl were neck in neck for first place.

"Grams, if I work an extra day here and ask Nikki if I can work a couple of hours a week at the Animal Ark Rescue, I might have enough to beat Megan."

Nikki cut her eyes in Sarah's direction. "You'll need to talk to Tabitha about that. I'm not at liberty to hire and fire people."

"Well, you're not hiring me. I'm a volunteer." Sarah beamed. "Besides, who doesn't want extra help during the holidays?"

"But I thought you only wanted to work a couple of hours over the next two weeks until the contest finishes."

"Yeah." Sarah shrugged.

"Then you won't be around during the holidays. You'll be home eating Christmas cookies and watching warm, fuzzy Christmas movies with your mom."

"Ew. No, I won't. At least not the movies. I prefer playing video games. Those movies have too much hugging and kissing in them. Nobody does that much hugging in real life." Sarah scrunched her nose liked she smelled something rotten.

Purdy laughed. "Just wait. You'll find out for yourself how much hugging is involved when you're in love." She twisted on her stool to face Nikki. "Right?"

Shrugging, Nikki pulled a face and focused her attention back to the sermon on her screen. It had been over two weeks since she'd last seen Dan, the day of Lilly's celebration of life. Of course, he'd tried to talk with her. He came over every day for the first week. It took every fiber of her being not to open the door and run into his arms.

Then last week, he sent multiple texts throughout the day and even a few in the wee hours of the night.

Her heart ached each time she deleted one.

This week he'd tried a new strategy, flowers. Monday, he'd sent a potted plant with a note asking to see her. Tuesday, a beautiful red and green Christmas bouquet appeared. That day, the delivery guy had given her the message directly. No note to ignore.

Today, the florist hadn't made any deliveries yet.

Glancing at the time on her computer, she noticed it was close to four. The nearest florist closed at five. She half hoped he'd given up and would leave her alone. All his efforts only made it harder for her to do the right thing by staying out of his life.

Purdy had commented on the plant and the bouquet, raving about how beautiful they were and how thoughtful it was of Dan. To Nikki's relief, Purdy had made her own assumptions about the flowers and hadn't asked any questions that would require her to explain. She didn't relish the thought of telling her about the rumor. A knot formed in her stomach every time she thought about the woman in the pearls.

Jotting down the number of the Animal Ark Rescue, Nikki stood and handed it to Sarah. "Here, you can call Tabitha and see what she has to say."

Sarah squealed and walked to her backpack to dig out her cell. "Thank you."

While Sarah placed the call, the front glass door of the Community Cowboy Church swung open, and in walked a delivery person carrying a large spray of red roses shaped like a heart. The flowers fanned out so wide it covered the delivery man's upper body.

Nikki gasped when she saw the arrangement. The roses draped open in full bloom, and there had to be at least a hundred of them. It looked more like a Valentine's Day gift rather than a Christmas one.

"Oh Nikki, how beautiful." Purdy shook her head and slid from her stool. "You are one lucky woman."

The delivery man slid the arrangement onto the counter. When he stepped back, Nikki gasped. Dan.

"What are you doing here?" She dropped her arms and glanced at Purdy who stood in front of the flowers smelling one of the blossoms.

"I need to talk to you. And you've been difficult to pin down." He frowned.

Catching the tension in Dan's voice, Purdy glanced between them. "Do I need to leave?"

"No."

"Yes, please." Dan said.

Confused, Purdy motioned for Sarah to follow her, and they went into the copier room, shutting the door behind them.

"You tricked me," Nikki snapped in a whisper to keep Purdy from hearing their conversation.

"Tricked you?" Dan walked to the partition and lifted it, letting himself into her workspace. "I wouldn't have to resort to such methods if you'd simply answer your door, or your phone, or your text." His frustration colored his words. He leaned his backside against the counter facing Nikki and crossed his arms.

She leaned against her desk, trying to remain calm. It appeared Dan wasn't going anywhere until he got some answers. Fine, she'd give him what he wanted and send him on his way.

"What's happened, Nikki? Why are you avoiding me?"

"It's called ghosting." She lifted her chin. "I'm

ghosting you. Kind of like how you treated me those weeks a while back."

Dan rolled his eyes heavenward. "For Pete's sake, is that what all this is about? I ghosted you months ago, and now you're out for revenge?"

"No, of course not. Don't be ridiculous."

"Well, tell me what I'm missing because I don't get it."

She shook her head, as her gaze fell to the blue carpet. "I think it's better if we keep our relationship strictly neighbors."

Dan tilted his head. "Hmph, I see. Neighbors." He pushed off the counter and took two steps toward her. "Well, I don't think neighbors kiss quite the way we did."

A blush crept to her cheeks. "No, but that's what I'm talking about. It would be better for both of us if we go back to being friends. Friends that don't kiss." She bit her lip before adding, "I don't see any reason to start something we both know won't go anywhere."

Dan flinched. "What do you mean by that?"

"You'll be moving back to your home, Silver Spur Ranch, in the spring, and I'll be here."

"Nikki, it's not like I live across the country. It's a forty-minute drive. Besides, I'd hoped once we got to know each other a little better, we might remedy that issue." A smile curled the corners of his lips, making the crinkles around his green eyes appear.

Her heart dropped. He wasn't making this easy.

The space between them shrunk with each step he took toward her, causing her heart to flip flop. She stood and moved to her desk chair to put a little more distance between them, fighting the urge to meet him halfway.

"That's n…not the only reason," she stammered.

"Okay, I'm listening." He stopped beside her desk still wearing his warm smile.

She pushed her rolling chair back, licking her lips. "It's…it's." She hesitated; aware her words would sting. But she had no choice.

"Go on. I want to know."

"It's Lilly," she said.

The smile fell from his lips. "Lilly? I thought you understood."

"I did too, but being at the celebration of life gave me perspective."

"What do you mean, *perspective*? What could've happened to change your opinion of me so drastically that you don't even want to see me?"

The hurt Nikki read on his face seeped into his tone, and her heart shredded into tiny pieces because of it.

"Lilly will always be a part of me, but—"

"I know. And I will always be second fiddle." Her gaze rested on her hands in her lap. Nikki couldn't bring herself to look him in the eye. She'd said what she'd needed to say to make him leave and not want to come back.

"You know better than that." Dan's jaw tightened, and his words held a sharp edge.

"Do I?"

Nikki hated what she was doing. But it was for the best. He didn't need his reputation tarnished, and she didn't want to go through life as the tart who struck gold.

"Yes, you do." Dan blew out a breath. Shoving his hands into his pockets, he studied her. "But if this is what you want, I'll respect your decision. I won't bother you anymore."

It wasn't what she wanted, but the gossips had won. She would surrender before their reputations met with any more damage. Knowing full well, it was too late for her heart. "I think it's for the best."

Chapter Twenty-Eight

Sarah grabbed her backpack and slung it onto her shoulder. "Thanks for all the help today."

"No problem, sweetie." Purdy kissed her granddaughter on the cheek before she lifted the partition to let her pass through to the front area where her mother was waiting for her in the car.

"I'll see you guys tomorrow. And thanks for Tabitha's number, Nikki."

"You're welcome." Nikki forced a smile onto her lips.

Once the door swooshed closed behind the teenager, Purdy turned and nailed her with a glare. "So, what's going on?"

Nikki shrugged and feigned ignorance. She didn't want to have this conversation right now. "What do you mean?"

Purdy gestured to the large heart-shaped arrangement of flowers sprawled on the counter. "You know what I mean. With Dan."

"I don't want to discuss it."

"Too bad." Purdy pushed her desk chair over to Nikki's desk and plopped into the seat. "You've been in a horrible mood ever since you went to Lilly's celebration of life. Now, these flower arrangements keep appearing, and today the guy I thought you had a huge crush on comes bearing a heart-shaped monstrosity, and you practically bite his head off." She paused for a breath. "Something's going on, and we're not leaving until you spill the beans."

Nikki rolled her shoulders trying to remain calm. Every time she thought about those women and their gossip, her blood boiled. "Okay, if you must know, I don't want to see Dan anymore."

Purdy placed her elbows on the edge of Nikki's desk and clasped her hands together under her chin. "Why not?"

Nikki groaned. "Can't you just let it go?"

"No, your happiness is at stake," Purdy replied stone-faced. "And as one of your closest, and I might add, wisest friends, I feel I must look out for you."

"Okay. I'll tell you what I told him. Because of the way he feels about Lilly, I'll always be second fiddle." Devoid of emotion, her words sounded hollow even to her own ears.

Purdy shook her head. "Nope, not buying it. Try again."

"You are impossible." Nikki balled her hands and rapped them once on her desk, letting out a low growl of frustration.

"I got all night, but you have dogs at home that need tending." She smiled and lifted her eyebrows.

Nikki's shoulders sagged, knowing Purdy had the upper hand.

"Now, out with it."

She sighed. "Okay, I give. I thought once I'd straightened everything out with Marilyn that all the gold-digger talk would end." Nikki shrugged.

"But it didn't."

"No, I supposed I didn't realize how quickly and how far it had spread. I overheard some ladies at the celebration of life talking about it. They called me a ..."

"A what?" Purdy stiffened and straightened in her seat.

"A floozy. More precisely a gold-digging floozy."

Purdy fell back against her chair shaking her head. "It's crazy what people will repeat."

"So, you see why I have to break it off with Dan. I can't pull his good reputation through the mud this way. His family is so well-known and respected. I can't be the one to put a black mark on all they've built."

"Goodness, child. You act like you've never dealt with gossip before. You remember how the rumors flew when you and Brian split. It may take a while to die down, but it will die down. And you can't wreck your future happiness over what other people might say."

"I didn't know these ladies. This is bigger than a few people spreading it around Orange Blossom. The

Harrises are regarded throughout the state as one of its leading families."

"Yeah, but Dan deserves a shot at being happy. And you make him happy."

She blinked back the tears, trying to keep her emotions in check. "How can you be so sure?"

"For starters, I've seen how he looks at you. But if you need more proof, let me point you to the giant heart of red roses behind me." Purdy twisted in her seat and gestured toward the counter like Vanna White.

Nikki gazed at the oversized heart. Like Dan's, it was too big for his own good. How could she have given a man like that the heave-ho because of what the rumor mill churned out?

"The man is crazy about you. And as long as you two know the truth, it doesn't matter what others say." She leaned forward and took Nikki's hand into hers.

No longer able to swallow her emotions, the tears trickled down her cheeks. She used her other hand to swipe them away.

"There are always going to be jealous, vicious people who want to believe the worst about others. You can't make your decisions based on the gossip of the day." Purdy released her hand and pulled a tissue from the box on Nikki's desk.

Nikki pressed her lips together to hold back the sobs and took the tissue, dabbing under her eyes. "What do you think I should do? I've ruined everything."

"Not possible." Purdy leaned back in her chair.

"You didn't see the look on his face when he left. I might as well have stabbed him in the heart and twisted the knife." A new batch of tears coursed down her face.

"Do you care for him?"

"Yes." She sniffled.

"Did you mean it when you said you thought you played second fiddle to Lilly?" Purdy patted her shoulder.

"No." She answered fighting to push down the hurt. Reaching for more tissues, she wiped away the salty droplets.

"So, stop torturing him and tell him how you feel. Together, you two will do the right thing." Purdy pulled Nikki toward her for a hug despite the awkward angle of the desk.

Nikki leaned on her friend's shoulder and soaked in the comfort she offered. She sniffled again. "Thanks, Purdy. It's nice to have such a good friend."

"Ditto, kiddo." Purdy released her and stood. Placing her hands on the back of her chair, she gave it a push in the direction of her own desk. Stopping, she looked back at Nikki. "And I wouldn't wait too long. Men like Dan don't come along often, and women like Marilyn know it."

Nodding, Nikki gave her eyes one last dab. "I won't. I'll go over this evening." She huffed. "If he'll even talk to me."

"Don't underestimate Dan. I bet he didn't buy the Lilly excuse either." She rolled her chair back to her desk. Pulling open her bottom drawer, Purdy grabbed her purse. "I'd better head home. My daughter and her family are coming over for dinner, and if I'm late, they may disown me."

"Like that would ever happen." Nikki forced a smile. Tossing the tissues into her trash, she pulled open her own bottom drawer and withdrew her bag. "My dogs, however, are a different story. Snowball's been so agitated and moody, and she can't seem to get enough to eat."

"Aw, poor Blue. The last few weeks must've been tough on him, living with a pregnant pooch and a grumpy owner." Purdy lifted the partition and scooted through the opening, holding it up for Nikki.

Nikki stood. "What did you say?"

"Blue, he must be miserable."

A slow grin inched across her lips. "Yes, he is miserable. And I know the perfect solution for the problem."

~

Dan scanned the shelves of the refrigerator. He had three slices of cheese, a jar of mayo, and a half-eaten pizza still in the box. Nothing tempted him. It didn't matter that it was dinnertime. His stomach had been in a knot for over a week ever since he realized Nikki was serious about not seeing him. He'd thought delivering the flowers himself might yield him some answers, but instead, he'd left with a shattered heart and a bruised ego.

He grabbed a can of soda and shut the refrigerator a little harder than necessary. Wandering back into the living room, he plopped onto the couch and pulled off his boots. Leaning back, he plunked his feet onto the coffee table with a sigh. He took a long drink of his soda letting his mind replay the scene from that afternoon.

So, she feels like she plays second fiddle to Lilly, huh?

Yes, his first love would always hold a place in his heart, but he had plenty of room left to love someone else deeply and without reservation. And he'd thought he'd shown that to Nikki. How could he have misread the situation? He'd thought they'd grown closer over the last two months, ever since he'd rescued her from the pond, and that she'd understood about Lilly and her place in his life.

Swinging his feet off the table, he leaned forward and set the can on the marred surface. Apparently, he'd been wrong. But something gnawed at him. Until today, she'd never mentioned any issues with Lilly. Not once. She'd never shown any signs of jealousy or hurt when he'd spoken of her. At least not until she came to the celebration of life.

A knock sounded from the front door.

Rising, he went to answer the door in his stockinged feet, not in the mood for company.

He flipped on the porch light and pulled on the doorknob, but the door stuck. Grumbling under his breath, he jiggled the knob and jerked on it. The door swung wide.

To his surprise, there stood a tall, blond-haired woman holding a leash and plate wrapped in foil. A feeling of déjà vu swept over him. Blue sat at her feet, his tail swishing back and forth across the wooden planks of the porch.

A slow, lazy smile crept across Dan's lips. "Well, hello, neighbor. How can I help you?" He had no intentions of making this easy on her. After what she'd put him through the last two weeks, it would take more than a warm smile and a hot meal to make up for it. He wanted answers.

"I've reconsidered your offer."

He stared at her not sure he understood. "What offer?"

"You told me you were willing to foster Blue during Snowball's pregnancy. So, I'm taking you up on the offer." She held out Blue's leash.

Dan crossed his arms over his chest and studied her. "If I take him, you know we'll have to come over and check on Snowball. Blue will be worried about her and the pups."

"Oh yeah, I'm aware the two of you will need to make daily visits to see that she's doing, all right."

He tilted his head and narrowed his eyes, not believing what he heard. "Especially, with the birth only two or three weeks away. And of course, we'll want to be present for the birth." He waited to see her reaction to his request.

"Totally understandable." Her gaze fell to the worn wood beneath her feet. "But it could happen at any time. I've found from working at the rescue, puppies tend to come at the most inopportune times." She fiddled with the leash in her hand. "Like early morning or when you're in the middle of apologizing for acting like a crazy woman toward a man you adore."

She lifted her cornflower-blue eyes and met his gaze, sending his pulse racing. He fought the urge to scoop her into his arms and tell her all was forgiven. It took all he had not to act on the impulse, but he needed to know the truth. What had happened to make her doubt him? Instead of wrapping his arms around her, he leaned his shoulder against the doorjamb placing him a little closer to her and Blue.

"I'm so sorry for the way I've treated you the last few weeks. It's unforgivable. And the things I said today." Her voice cracked. "I'm just ... just so sor...sorry." She handed him the leash without his consent and pulled a tissue from her jean pocket to catch the tears that clung to her lashes. Hugging the covered plate close to her side, she dabbed at the trickle of tears.

He squeezed the leash in his hand to keep from wiping away the ones she had missed. Noticing she still held the plate, he reached for it with his other hand. "Here, let me take that for you."

Blue, unaware of the drama going on around him,

wandered into the house, pulling his leash taut.

With the sudden yank, Dan nearly dropped the plate in mid-transaction.

"Sit, Blue." Dan commanded, and the dog sat.

Nikki giggled through her tears. "How do you do that?"

"It's a gift." He gave her a half smile and placed the plate on the small table next to the door. Not sure what to do with this new development, he made a snap decision. "Let's sit and talk for a minute."

"Okay." Nikki sniffled. "That sounds like a good idea."

Pointing at Blue, Dan said, "Stay." Then he pulled the door shut.

Nikki walked to the steps and settled on the top one.

Dan joined her unsure how to broach the subject of Lilly in a way that wouldn't upset her. But before he could collect his thoughts, Nikki beat him to it.

"Dan, I know what I said earlier hurt you. And I want you to know it's not true. I know you'd never expect someone to play second fiddle to Lilly. You've demonstrated that to me over and over again."

"Then why on earth did you say it? You must've known it would cut me to the quick." Dan furrowed his brow, trying to understand what had caused Nikki to act so out of character.

"I wanted to keep you away, and I figured that would do the trick." She hung her head, dabbing her cheeks, the porch light bathing her in a yellow glow.

"Why would you want me to stay away? I thought we'd grown rather fond of each other." His hand itched to take a hold of hers, so he leaned his elbows on his knees and clasped his hands in front of him.

"We have." She gave him a half-hearted smile. "And that's the problem."

"Okay, once again, I'm lost."

Nikki blew out a breath. "A few weeks ago, Marilyn and I had a sort of breakthrough in our relationship. I took the chance to straighten out the rumor she had been spreading about us and what her friend Dawn had thought she'd seen."

"Yeah, I remember you telling me about it."

"Well, apparently that rumor, along with the opinion that I'm a gold digger, had spread much further than the city limits of Orange Blossom."

Dan straightened. "How do you know?"

"Because I overheard two ladies talking about it at the celebration of life for Lilly."

"So, that's what happened." Dan shook his head wishing he could give those two women a piece of his mind. "Nikki, we can't worry about what everyone else is saying."

"But it was so horrible, listening to them call me a gold-digging floozy." She bit her lip. "I couldn't bear it if your good name was dragged through the mud because of me."

Dan laughed. He'd forgotten that not everyone

lived like he did—in the spotlight. "Do you honestly think this is the first time I've been at the center of a piece of malicious gossip? I'm the one who should be apologizing to you for sullying your good name." He turned toward her and took her hands in his. "Nikki, it doesn't matter who I date or what I do, my life will always be open to ridicule, scandal, and gossip. You're the one who needs protecting, not me." He pulled her into his arms. "My life's a fishbowl. It always has been, and unfortunately, it always will be. It goes lock, stock, and barrel with the Harris name."

"I don't like it." Nikki hiccupped and sniffled back the few remaining tears. "It hurts." She laid her head on his shoulder.

"Yes, and not to be callous, now you know why I wanted to be 'just Dan' when I first arrived. Once people find out about the money, it changes how they treat you, both for good and bad." He kissed the top of her head.

"Your life is hard." Nikki nuzzled closer.

The warmth of her against his side and the scent of spring on her skin melted away the hurt and anger of the last few weeks. "So that's the reason you've been avoiding me and ignoring my calls. To protect me."

"Yeah."

"If that's the case, I wish I hadn't invited you to the celebration. I hate that I put you through that."

"Well, it wasn't all bad." Nikki lifted her head from his shoulder. "I did meet Rod and Lilly's sister,

June."

"You did?" Dan smiled.

"Yes, and they were very complimentary about you."

"Really?" Dan couldn't wait to hear what kind of stories they had told her.

"Yep, it seems that Dan Thibodeaux is a pretty good guy. Not only does he save dogs and people, but he lets dog-loving women drag him around to community projects, and he pays to have lunch with them for good causes." She smiled and laid the palm of her hand on his cheek. "And I hear he loves his friends and family. Very loyal."

"Um, that's interesting." Dan placed his hand over hers.

"They also said any woman who caught your eye would be a fool to let you go. And you know how I hate to be foolish."

He grinned, leaning forward and kissed her.

She broke the connection and sighed. "You won't make me a fool, will you?" Her blue eyes searched his.

"Never." Capturing her lips with his, he deepened the kiss before pulling away. "Only a fool for love." He wiggled his eyebrows, teasing her. But in his heart, he recognized the truth. He loved her already.

A loud clatter rang from behind the front door, catching their attention.

Nikki groaned. "I think Blue found his dinner."

"That's all right. There's a pizza in the fridge."

Chapter Twenty-Nine

The song "O Holy Night" rang throughout the dim sanctuary as the candles flickered, casting shadows around those seated near Nikki. Dan stood beside her dressed in a stylish navy-blue suit. His rich tenor intertwined with the voices around him, adding depth to the chorus.

She smiled, her heart full. If anyone had suggested four months ago when they first met that they'd be so good together, she would've laughed. Sure, she admired his biceps and his easy smile and those warm green eyes, but he was known throughout the state for his family's wealth, and she was a woman working two jobs to make ends meet.

They were so different and yet so similar.

The last notes of the song faded into the dimness of the room. Pastor Connor moved to the podium. "May the God of Peace be present in your home and hearts tonight and throughout the New Year. Amen."

"Amen," echoed the congregation.

"Have a wonderful Christmas Eve, everyone. You are dismissed."

The lights popped on, and everyone began to stir, blowing out their candles and gathering their belongings.

Dan smiled down at Nikki. "You ready?"

"Yes, but you know how crowded the parking lot was tonight. It might take a minute for us to get out of the church."

"I'm in no hurry. But I'm not sure how Snowball would feel about it." He reached over and took her hand leading her to the end of the row. An older lady stood blocking the path, but Dan waited until she had gathered her Bible and cane.

Leaving Snowball to attend service had been a tough decision. The puppies could come at any time, and Nikki worried that Snowball would be scared if she were alone.

Making it into the aisle, Dan pushed forward step by step.

Nikki held onto his hand following him. But they didn't make it very far before someone called her name. She stood on tiptoe, scanning the area.

Pointing in front of him, Dan leaned close, so she could hear him. "Purdy is trying to get your attention." He waved, and a moment later, Purdy emerged from the crowd with Sarah in tow.

"There you two are." She grinned, glancing from one to the other. "You guys sure make a handsome couple."

Nikki blushed, the heat coloring her cheeks. "Well, we aim to please."

"Tell them, Grams." Sarah pulled at her grandmother's sleeve, bouncing in place.

"Tell us what?" Dan asked.

"I won. I won the grand prize," Sarah squealed. "Isn't that exciting? I get my very own computer and one hundred dollars. And a silver medal for my community service."

"That's wonderful." Nikki beamed. "Looks like all that extra time at the Animal Ark Rescue paid off."

"Yeah, I appreciate you giving me Tabitha's number. She was great and let me work a few hours after closing, cleaning the pens."

"When did you find out?" Nikki asked.

"Oh, last week before the semester ended, but I swore Grams to secrecy. I wanted to be the one to tell you, so I could thank you for all your help." Sarah grinned from ear to ear.

"Well, you are very welcome. It was fun having you around the office." Nikki opened her arms, and Sarah stepped in for a hug. "It'll be odd not having you there." She squeezed the teen tight around the shoulders. Letting go, she smiled. "Plus, you helped me learn all the latest lingo."

Sarah shrugged. "It's the least I could do. You know, keep you current." Turning, she waved to someone behind her. "Grams, there's Kim. Can I go say

Merry Christmas?"

"Sure."

Sarah caught Purdy's hand, pulling her toward her friend. "This way."

Turning, Purdy waved to them over her shoulder with her free hand. "Merry Christmas," she said before following her granddaughter into the crowd.

"Merry Christmas," Nikki called after her.

~

"Here comes another one." Nikki caressed the tiny pup and placed it on the towel in Dan's hands.

Dan rubbed the pup. It wiggled beneath his touch. "That makes three in the last three hours. I think this one is ticklish."

The pup yelped, taking in air.

"It's another girl." Dan placed the pup alongside Snowball's belly to keep her warm.

Snowball lay panting in her whelping box that Nikki had prepared for her the week before when she caught her nesting. Well, it wasn't actually a box. Tabitha had loaned her an old plastic kid's pool from the rescue. Nikki had lined it with newspaper and old towels for easy cleanup after the big event. Plus, the plastic pool acted as a kennel, keeping the newborn pups corralled for the first several weeks of life.

The round, shallow pool sat in the middle of Nikki's laundry room. She knelt beside it as close to Snowball as she could get. Dan sat cross-legged on the other side, acting as her assistant.

They had gathered the scissors, the unwaxed dental floss, and the other items on the list Tabitha had given them to have on hand in case they needed it. So far, Snowball had done all the hard work while Blue lay in the doorway, his dark eyes focused on the pups in the pool.

Nikki gave Snowball a drink of water and tidied the area after the last birth. "The vet confirmed six heartbeats when he did the ultrasound. That means we should have three more, and they usually come about an hour apart."

Pulling his phone from his pocket, Dan checked the time. "Well, what do you know? It's midnight."

"It is. Merry Christmas!" Nikki reached out her hand, and Dan took it.

Rising to his knees, he leaned over the blue pool to claim a kiss. "Merry Christmas to you, Sweetheart."

She grinned at the endearment. "I think we have some time before the next one comes. Would you like to go open your gift? It's under the tree." She waggled her eyebrows. Nikki hadn't been sure what to give Dan for Christmas since he could buy whatever he wanted. But Purdy had given her a great idea, and now she couldn't wait to give him the surprise.

"Do you think she'll be all right?" He nodded toward the white ball of fluff.

Snowball lifted her head and licked one of the pups.

"They'll be fine." Nikki rose and dusted off the

knees of her jeans. Gathering the used papers and towels, she stuffed them into a trash bag to take out later.

Dan stood. "Okay, but let's take Blue with us to keep him out of trouble with the Mrs."

"Good thinking."

Dan headed down the hallway from the kitchen into the living room and called Blue to follow him.

Once the dog moved out of the doorway, Nikki pulled the door shut, giving the new mom and her pups a minute alone to rest before the next round of labor pains.

Blue sat next to Dan who had plopped onto the couch.

Nikki went straight to the Christmas tree decorated with colored lights and tinsel and pulled a brightly wrapped gift from under its green limbs. She grinned at Dan and hid the large package behind her back. "Close your eyes," she said in a singsong voice.

He obeyed, closing his eyes.

She sat on the edge of the coffee table in front of him. Placing the package between them, she said, "Okay, you can open them."

"Oh, a box," he teased and squished the wrapping, making it crinkle under his touch.

"No, stop. Open it." She giggled.

Dan tore off the paper and flung it onto the floor like a kid. He radiated excitement. Sliding his finger under the tape, he broke it, loosening the lid. Flipping it open, he laughed. Staring back at him was a portrait of Blue with his tongue lolled to one side and his leash dragging on the ground. "It's perfect. Whoever painted it captured his true essence."

Nikki chuckled. "Do you like it?"

"Yes, I do. I'm going to hang it over the mantel when the ranch house is finished." Dan set the portrait aside. A gleam danced in his green eyes. "Do you want to open a gift?"

"Of course, do I have any here?" She grinned wondering what he was up to.

"Maybe." He stood and pulled a blue velvet sack from his front pocket.

"Oh, I like it already," Nikki said.

"Close your eyes," he teased.

She closed one, then the other. "Okay."

Dan lifted her hand and when she opened her eyes, he slid a ring of diamonds and sapphires onto her left ring finger.

"Oh, Dan, it's beautiful. But it's too much."

"Not if it's an engagement ring." Dan slid from the couch cushion onto one knee. "Nikki Marie Davis, will you do me the great honor of being my wife?"

Nikki's eyes widened, and her hand shot to her chest. Her heart thundered. She opened her mouth to say something, but nothing came out.

Dan's brows furrowed. "What is it? Is there something wrong?"

"I have one condition." Nikki clasped his hands in

hers and looked deep into his eyes.

"What's that?" Concern swept over his features.

"We keep the puppies." Her smile spread so wide her cheeks hurt. "They'll need a good home, and the ranch is perfect. There's plenty of room for them to run, and I know Blue and Snowball will love it."

Dan stood and pulled her to him. "Then, it's settled. No more being displaced. Everyone gets a home for Christmas."

"Even the billionaire?"

"Especially the billionaire."

Rising on her tiptoes, she ran her arms around his neck. "Home is nice." She sighed with a full heart right before she kissed him.

The End

Sign up for Beyond the Page newsletter for giveaways, book recommendations and more.

Click to here or go to www.bonitaymccoy.com

Dear Reader,

I hope you enjoyed this story about Dan the displaced billionaire cowboy and the spirited girl next door. It was great fun creating the secondary characters and the small town of Orange Blossom, Texas.

As is with any project, there are several people I'd like to thank. First, my family who always shows grace when dinner is late, or the laundry is still piled on the bed because I was busy pounding out the scene rattling around in my head.

I'd also like to thank all those who pray for me and my stories, the Jesus girls at my church and my prayer partner who listens to all my concerns.

And my Beta readers who read early copies for me and point out any plot holes or misspelled words. Thank you all! The stories are strong because of what you've added. I'd also like to thank Sherri Stewart, my editor, and Cynthia Hickey, my publisher. You two have made my dream of writing a reality.

Then there is you, the reader. Thank you for your time. I know there are millions of books out there and the fact you picked mine to read thrills my heart. I hope it met all your expectations and left you considering your own relationship with God, the Father.

May you find God's blessings blooming in your life,

Bonita Y. McCoy

Bonita Y. McCoy - Author

Bonita Y. McCoy hails from the Great State of Alabama where she lives on a five-acre farm with three dogs, three cows, one cat, and one husband who she's had since circa 1989.

She is a mother to three grown sons and a beautiful daughter-in-law, who joined the family from Japan.

She loves God, and she loves to write. Her blogs, devotions, and novels are an expression of both these passions.

Her desire is that her writing reflects the hope and love that is found in Christ alone.

Her award nominated and winning books include her Amy Kate Mystery series, several sweet romances, and devotions in the Coffee with God series, Divine Moments Christmas Spirit, and Chicken Soup for the Soul Thanks Dad edition.

On any given day, you can find her playing with her dogs, reading a good book, or chilling with her hubby on the front porch swing.

She is an active member of both American Christian Fiction Writers and Word Weavers International as well as the Cowboy Church of Limestone County.

Drop her a line at Facebook @bonitaymccoyauthor or sign up for her newsletter at www.bonitaymccoy.com.

Other books by this author through Winged Publications

Cozy Mysteries

Twisted Plots